UNLIKELY IN LOVE

A PARKER LAKE NOVEL
BOOK ONE

OLIVIA SHERWOOD

LIMITLESS PUBLISHING LLC

Unlikely in Love

First Print Edition: June 2021

Limitless Publishing, LLC

Kailua, HI 96734

www.limitlesspublishing.com

Formatting: Limitless Publishing

ISBN-13: 978-1-954194-23-6

DEDICATION

To my two amazing, wonderful, beautiful children: my world was made infinitely better when you entered the picture. I couldn't imagine life without you. Continue to shine bright like the stars you are. The world is yours.

To everyone who has read, reviewed, and liked my books: from the bottom of my heart, thank you. Your words of encouragement and kindness were sometimes the push I needed to finish. I love you all and cherish what you've so thoughtfully written about me.

CHAPTER 1

*D*amn the stupid pantyhose.

Annabelle Cleaver knew sitting in a lawyer's office listening to her granny's last will and testament being read would be hard. Wearing pantyhose under the only skirt she owned while the sweltering Oklahoma summer sun beat down on the roof of the ancient building, making the temperature rise at least ten degrees inside, was even harder.

She tried to discreetly pull on the pantyhose that had already started to creep down her legs. Double damn. Why on earth did she have to get the thigh highs instead of a regular pair she could practically pull up to her eyebrows? It wasn't like she had anyone to see the sexier pantyhose, anyway. *Hell,* why did she have to wear pantyhose at all?

She felt a trail of sweat running down her back and underneath her bra. The box fan in the corner of the lawyer's office was doing nothing but circulating the stifling air. Harry Donovan sat at his desk, his bifocals perched on the end of his nose and ever present bowtie choking his neck. Annie wanted to pull on the collar of her gray sleeveless blouse in empathy. He looked like an English bulldog whose collar was two sizes too tight.

She rolled her eyes and refrained from sighing. Harry, who'd probably been around when Lincoln was alive, was having a hard time reading the words of the will. Even though he was the one who typed it.

Why in the hell was she stupid enough to wear pantyhose, she thought for the millionth time in the fifteen minutes she'd been in the office. Other than her, Harry was the only person in the room. She could've worn a pair of cutoffs and her Lake Parker tank top and it wouldn't have made a difference. To him, she was probably just the blur sitting in the chair across from his desk anyway. He could've been reading Granny's will to a llama for all he knew.

This time, Annie did let out an audible sigh. Harry wasn't the problem. The ridiculous heat wasn't the problem. Even the stupid pantyhose weren't the problem. The problem was her granny was gone. Annie would never again see her cuss out the rabbits that liked to steal carrots out of the garden. Granny would never get to haggle the price of Mr. Grant's nicest pumpkin from *his* garden down to two-fifty because Granny knew "his darkest secret." Why Mr. Grant gave in to her granny was anyone's guess. Everyone in town knew he liked to dress up in his wife's lingerie while she was out of town at realtor conventions.

Annie refused to let the tears spill down her cheeks. Her granny would be too disappointed in her. *Cleaver women do not cry,* she heard her granny's voice say. Besides, it was just the reading of the will, not the actual funeral. She hadn't even started thinking about that. Lord knew she didn't have the money for anything extravagant. She barely had enough for the upkeep of Granny's hundred year old farmhouse and ten acres of land perched on the outskirts of Parker, Oklahoma, a tiny town located on the southernmost tip of Parker Lake.

A man by the name of Hamilton Parker was one of the first men to stake his land during the Oklahoma Land Run in 1889. He named his parcel of land Parker because he was a narcissistic asshole who got his wife and two sons to claim the parcels next to his, thus ensuring he had more land than anyone else in the state. He even had the balls to name the lake on his parcel of land after himself. At least that's how the story went. Annie didn't know if it was true or not.

Since all the people who participated in the Run were long-dead, the only sources she could rely on were Burt Gallagher and Marty Samson, the two old codgers who played checkers in front of Sadie's Cafe every morning. The only thing Annie knew about her town for sure was the nearest Wal-Mart or Aldi were fifteen miles away, the small grocery store in town charged triple the price for anything in it, and the few places to get anything to eat without it coming from a person's kitchen closed at seven o'clock.

Even though Annie's last name was the same as Beaver's, the iconic television character from the fifties, Annie didn't have Ward and June as parents. Instead, she had a drunk for a father who, after spending an entire evening at Griff's Bar, accidentally drove his truck off a bridge. Soon after, her mother left for God knows where, claiming she couldn't be a mother to a kid who looked just like her dead husband that used to knock her around when he was "drunk off his ass."

So Annie had moved from her family's single-wide, run down trailer on the wrong side of the tracks to her granny Sophie's farm at the ripe old age of ten. She had never even officially met Sophie until the day the social worker dropped Annie off at the farm. Annie's mother and granny, who was Annie's dad's mom, had a falling out before Annie was even born. About what, Annie's mom would never say. All she would tell Annie was Sophie was crazy and they were better off not knowing her. One time when Annie was about seven, she heard her mom yelling at her dad that she didn't want some bat shit crazy woman with voodoo eyes putting a curse on her. Her dad, being in a drunken stupor most of the time, didn't argue. *He* didn't talk to his mom…why would he care if his kid didn't?

Annie was paralyzed with fear when her mom walked out on her. She was afraid they would ship her to a big town where she didn't know anyone and make her live with strangers. Instead, her quirky, seventy-five-year-old granny, who had just buried her husband two weeks prior to her son driving his truck off a bridge, had taken Annie under her wing, and shown her how to run the farm. Annie learned how to milk the Jersey cows, Bambi and Thumper. She gathered eggs from the Disney princess hens—Aurora, Snow White, Ariel, Belle, and Cinderella. She delivered Cruella the Pig's piglets and learned how to scare the coyotes away by shooting her dearly departed Grandad's ancient Remington rifle her granny named Pongo. She even became a true farm girl, learning to ride the sole horse on the property, a beautiful palomino named Maleficent. What could she say? Her granny was a sucker for old Disney movies. It was probably why everyone thought she was crazy. Name a pig after a Dalmatian-skinning villain and people tended to think you had a few screws loose. Annie had caught her granny singing "Cruella the Pig" instead of "Cruella Deville" more times than she could count.

Crazy or not, her granny had lived to be ninety-one. Granny was the only mother Annie knew. She had explained to Annie what a period was and given her the birds and the bees talk when Jimmy Newton asked Annie to play train. She had listened to Annie cry when the first boy—ironically, Jimmy Newton—broke her heart. She had watched Annie walk across the stage for her high school graduation and helped Annie fill out the scholarships for the small community college in Lakeview, the town forty minutes from Parker. Annie had hoped to settle down and have grandkids before her granny went to be with the Man upstairs. Instead, here she was, a twenty-seven-year-old college dropout with not a man or baby in sight.

"Of course, Sophie left you the house and ten acres, seeing as you are her only living relative," Harry said in a warbling voice before hacking a phlegmy cough. *Ew.* Annie shuddered. She just hoped he didn't hock a loogie in the trashcan. If he did, Annie would walk out of the office and not look back. To hell with the will.

Henry pulled at the collar of his shirt, sweat running down his temple. Annie had the urge to reach across the desk and yank the purple and yellow plaid bowtie out of his collar and toss it in the trash can. The good manners her granny taught her, however, whispered in Annie's head to behave herself. So instead of ripping the bowtie off the ancient lawyer, she placed her hands under her butt and prayed the reading of the will wouldn't last much longer.

"She also left you the mineral rights to some land just west of town," he continued.

"What mineral rights? What land?" Annie asked. This was news to her. She thought her granny only had the ten acres where Annie had grown up. "And what exactly are mineral rights?"

"Mineral rights give the landowner, in this case, your grandmother, the right to sell or profit from minerals or oil extracted from the ground. Many people allow oil companies to lease the mineral rights and extract the minerals or oil from the land in return for the royalty income of the revenue. That's what your grandmother did. She still owned the land; the oil company just leased the mineral rights. Does that make sense?"

"A little," Annie replied. "Do I have to do anything with them?"

"No. The company who drills will just send you a check whenever they drill for oil or minerals and make a profit. Your grandmother put the royalties she received in the bank in a savings account for you," he replied.

"Okay," Annie said. "So I'll just get random checks in the mail?"

"That's right. Your grandmother inherited the land from her father when he died. She's been putting that money back for years and has saved quite the hefty sum."

Annie shrugged her shoulders. "I'm not worried about the money."

"I know you aren't, dear. But you'll probably be surprised at the amount."

"I guess I'll need to know it sometime. Might as well be now," she said. With the oil market currently struggling, Annie didn't think the amount would be too much, even though her granny was a tightwad when it came to her money and she'd supposedly been saving this money for years. Annie used to find mason jars hidden in random places all over the house. Granny said she didn't trust banks not to take her money and run. When Annie was a teenager, she finally convinced her granny to deposit her granddad's retirement money from the tire plant in Lambert for years into an account at First National Bank of Parker.

"She managed to save around two million dollars, give or take," Harry said. "I'm not sure of the exact amount. You'll need to ask the bank."

Annie nearly swallowed her teeth. "Come again?" she squeaked. "Because I thought you just said two million dollars."

"That's because I did say two million dollars. Remember, she inherited the land from your grandfather, so it's been in your family for quite some time. Your grandmother has been saving this money since she was in her twenties. Throughout the years, when the oil booms hit, she was sometimes getting ten thousand dollars a month."

"Sweet baby Jesus," Annie muttered, fanning herself with her hands. That was a *lot* of money. The sweat started pouring in rivulets now. The heat of the day, partnered with the realization she might possibly be a *millionaire,* had her feeling like she might pass out.

"Here is the number for the account and a copy of the will saying you are the beneficiary. Congratulations, Annie. It looks like you've just become the richest person in town."

WYATT HOLLOWAY GROANED as he wheeled himself out from underneath his granddad's 1954 International pickup. Wyatt had been working on the truck for a few months and could finally see the finish line. He had painted the outside of the truck its original baby blue and painstakingly researched on the internet until he had all original, authentic parts for inside the cab. He had just finished installing the carburetor and was waiting for the vintage door handles he had purchased from the eBay shipper, OldInternationalLover54. Once those were installed, the old truck would be restored to its former glory.

"Lookin' good, son." Wyatt's dad, Kirk, came out of the house and walked toward the barn where his son was working. "Your grandad would sure be proud of the work you've done on Miss Cleo."

Wyatt chuckled. "I never understood why he named the damn truck that."

"He said the best dog he'd ever had was a scraggly mutt that wandered up to the farm while he was plowing the north forty. Almost ran her over, so the story goes. Even after he almost ran her over with the tractor, the dog wouldn't quit following him around. It had a worn tag with the name Cleo attached to the collar. Figuring she was someone's dog, your granddad looked high and low for her owner but no one claimed her. Finally, he just quit trying. *He* said it was because she probably got dumped on the farm because the owner wanted to get rid of her. *I* think it was because he fell in love with the thing. Even though it dug up your meemaw's garden every year. *And* resembled a Gremlin more than an actual dog."

"Why haven't I ever heard that story?" Wyatt asked.

His dad grinned and held a glass out toward Wyatt. "Because you've never asked. Here, drink some of your mom's sweet tea. She made me bring it out here to you and said I had to watch until you drank every last drop."

Wyatt looked back toward the farmhouse where he grew up. Sure enough, his mom was at the screen door, arms crossed over her chest and a warning look on her face. He grabbed the glass from his dad and took a long swig. The tea was ice cold and felt amazing sliding smoothly down his throat. He held the glass to his forehead, sighing in pleasure as the sweat from the glass ran down his temple.

Wyatt didn't care what anyone said, the Middle East couldn't hold a candle to Oklahoma's July summer sun. It beat down incessantly, the Oklahoma wind stirring the heat until Wyatt felt like he was baking in an oven. All his buddies in his platoon complained constantly about the sand and the heat when they were stationed overseas. Wyatt would just smile and tell them to visit his farm in Oklahoma in July and they'd understand heat.

Wyatt smiled sadly. Some of his platoon members would

never make that journey. Mentally shaking off the dark thoughts, he downed the rest of the tea and handed the glass to his dad. His therapist always told him thinking the *what ifs* did nothing but stalemate all the progress he'd made. If he could call the shell of a man he now was progress.

"Tell Momma I said thanks for the tea," Wyatt said. "But I gotta get back to work."

"The truck's almost finished, son. What are you going to do with yourself then? You think you're ready for a job yet?"

When Wyatt came back from his third tour in Afghanistan, he was broken. He'd seen and heard things he didn't think he'd ever forget. Things that haunted his dreams, no matter how many sleep medications his therapist prescribed him. The cries of homeless little kids and women in bombed cities reduced to piles of rubble. Wrapping a belt around one of his fellow soldier's thighs to keep him from bleeding out after the mine they drove over exploded and blasted off part of his leg. The dead who returned home in caskets. The scar running down the right side of his face, a constant reminder he was one of the lucky ones who returned home when so many others didn't.

Wyatt sighed. "My therapist says I'm not ready. She doesn't think the pressure of having a job is something I can handle right now."

"I'm not trying to say I know better than someone who went to school longer than your niece has been alive, but you're my son. I think I know you a little better than her. And I think you're ready. Not for something big, something stressful. But I think something that would keep you occupied might help."

"Well, that's a nice thought, Dad," Wyatt replied, trying to keep the sarcasm out of his voice. He knew his dad was just trying to help. "But where do you suppose I'll find this job in the hopping metropolis that is our town of three thousand people?"

His dad kicked at the clod of red dirt in the front of the barn door and shrugged his shoulders. "Your mom told me Annabelle Cleaver was looking for help running her granny's farm. She died recently, and rumor has it Annabelle needs lots of help with the upkeep. I think it's become too much for her to take on alone."

"Who's Annabelle Cleaver?" Wyatt asked. The name rang a bell but he couldn't put a name with the face.

"She was a couple years younger than you in school, I think. She's Crazy Sophie's granddaughter."

Wyatt sighed at the mention of Annabelle's granny's name. His dad was right. Sophie was a crazy old bat. She once accused Wyatt and his friends of smashing her mailbox with a baseball bat. Wyatt didn't do it but he couldn't get her to believe him. He didn't even know why she was so dead set on thinking it was him. Even so, one day in Swanson's Market she stopped him in the meat aisle and told him she was going to put a curse on him with her voodoo dolls. Said he wouldn't be able to throw a football for a month. A week later, he had broken his arm in practice and was sidelined for the season. After that, every time he'd see Sophie in town she'd smile and give him a finger wave. He didn't believe in voodoo, but it still gave him the chills thinking about it.

Wyatt couldn't believe he had forgotten Annabelle Cleaver. His dad was right. She was a couple years younger than him but definitely memorable. Guess that was what three tours in the Middle East got him—he was now forgetting pretty girls.

Wyatt didn't tell his dad, but he remembered Annabelle always smelling like fresh hay and sunshine. After summer break, she always came back to school with a glow to her skin and her hair highlighted with streaks of blonde that could only come from the sun. She had an affinity for wearing long, flowing floral skirts with flannel shirts and cowboy boots. Wyatt also remembered the time she came back from summer break with henna tattoos running up and down her arms in swoops and swirls. Principal Hammond made her go home and wash them off because it was against school policy. Her crazy granny marched herself up to the principal's office and told him she was going to put a curse on him that would shrink his *pecker* two sizes if he didn't let Annabelle express herself in an artistic manner. Principal Hammond never mentioned the tattoos again. He didn't even say anything to her when she dyed her hair mint green.

Even though she was strange, Annabelle was definitely a beauty. Legs that went on for miles and sleek, toned muscles that came from the manual labor of working on a farm. But what Wyatt remembered most were her eyes. Big, hazel, and filled with flecks of gold and amber with a dark olive outline, and lashes that curled and touched her eyebrows. Striking. Memorable. He couldn't believe he'd forgotten those eyes.

Wyatt's buddy, Clark, once tried to ask for her phone number and was shot down. The team had given him hell for weeks, joking he got turned down by the strange farm nerd with the green hair. Then they'd laugh because the only boy they'd ever seen Annabelle with had been the science geek, Jimmy Newton. He wore thick, black glasses and had their biology textbook practically memorized. The team had called him Jimmy Neutron in jest because his name was close to the nerdy cartoon character on Nickelodeon. He'd even looked like him. He and his buddies were pretty big douche bags.

Wyatt and Annabelle *definitely* didn't run in the same circle. Even in a school as small as Parker High, cliques were present. Wyatt was a jock. He was voted Best Athlete by his senior class and led the Parker Wildcats to the state championship in football two years in a row. The two gold footballs won each year were still housed in the trophy case of the high school gymnasium. Wyatt wondered if the school still had his picture kissing the first gold ball in the case.

He was offered a small scholarship to play football at the next level, but when the Army recruiter showed up at school and talked to all the boys about enlisting, Wyatt bought in hook, line, and sinker. He knew he wasn't good enough to go pro in football. He was a damn good high school player but that was it. He didn't want to be stuck in Podunk Parker, Oklahoma, for the rest of his life. He had wanted to see the world.

That day, he signed with the army and hurried home to tell his parents the good news. His momma had immediately started crying and said her baby boy was going to get shot and killed in a God-forsaken country before she could become a grandma. His dad told him how proud he was his son had decided to serve his country, even though Wyatt knew he was holding back tears as well. His baby sister had punched him in the arm and called him an idiot. Wyatt had gotten his wish; he had seen the world. He'd also seen how cruel, unfair, and heartbreaking it could be.

"I *do* remember her," he told his dad. "She was really smart but a little strange. Pretty much kept to herself except for a couple of girlfriends. I was in a couple classes with her. She always knew every answer the teachers asked. I think she might've even tutored some of the football players. I figured as smart as she was she would leave this town first chance she got and run off to be a doctor or some other profession really smart people get into."

Wyatt's dad shook his head no. "She did go to college but came home shortly after. Sophie caught pneumonia and was in the hospital for two weeks. Annabelle came home to take care of her granny and help run the farm."

"What about Neutron?"

"Who?" his dad asked, a puzzled look on his face.

"If she wasn't with her other two friends, that's the boy we'd see her with. A guy named Jimmy Newton. We called him Neutron behind his back because he looked like the cartoon character, Jimmy Neutron. *And* he was just as smart as Annabelle."

"Boy, y'all were punk asses, weren't you?"

Wyatt chuckled. "That we were."

His dad laughed. "Well, that *Neutron* kid went to medical school. Last I heard, he was working at John Hopkins, trying to find a cure for cancer. Maybe you should've been calling him *less* names and had him tutor you instead. Lord knows you needed it."

"You're probably right about that," Wyatt replied. "Good for him."

"So, whaddya think? Gonna give her a call?"

Wyatt had to admire a woman who put her family first. But he still wasn't interested. "I think I'll try to find something else, Dad. But thanks for the advice."

His dad clapped him on the back. "The only other thing I know of in town is a stock boy in Swanson's Market. Just something to think about."

Wyatt sighed. It would be nice to do something other than hang out with his mom and dad. Living with them was starting to make him crazy. He loved them dearly, but if his mom looked at him sadly and asked him if he was all right one more time he was going to shit a brick. The only reprieve he got was when his kid sister, Lucy, visited with his five-year-old niece, Hattie.

Lucy had married her high school sweetheart straight out of high school. Jacob was a plumber just like his dad and helped run the family business, Perry Plumbing. Shortly after they married, Lucy had gotten pregnant and was content being a stay-at-home mom for their daughter. Hattie had curly black hair, sky blue eyes, and the biggest dimples he'd ever seen on a kid. Even better than how adorable she was, the fact his mom became totally engrossed in whatever Hattie was doing when Hattie and Lucy came to visit gave him a much needed break.

"I guess I could give her a call," he told his dad. "Do you have her number?"

"I don't, and your mom told me Sadie said she doesn't get good reception at Sophie's, anyway."

It's probably because Sophie buried all the voodoo dolls she had before she died and ruined any cell reception there was, Wyatt thought.

"I'd just go out there and see what she says," his dad continued. "You know where their farm is, right?"

Wyatt nodded. He did know where it was, even though he most definitely *wasn't* the one who bashed in her mailbox all those years ago.

CHAPTER 2

*A*nnie blew her bangs out of her eyes and wiped her sweat-soaked brow with her forearm. Feeling restless after yesterday's revelation she was a millionaire, Annie had decided to blow off some steam by working in her granny's yard. The heat of July had killed most of the plants in the flower beds, leaving nothing but curled, brown leaves and persistent weeds that seemed to survive through any weather Oklahoma had to offer. She had been working for a couple of hours, hauling everything she dug up to the burn barrel behind the barn. She was covered in dirt and stray leaves and smelled like smoke from the fire. But the flower beds were purged and she didn't have to sit in a farmhouse that echoed with emptiness now that her granny wasn't filling it with her humming as she swept the old plank floors or rattling pots and pans as she cooked in the kitchen.

Yesterday, after Harry read the will, Annie had gone to the bank and spoken to the president. Sure enough, Harry hadn't been pulling her leg. Her granny had left her a hefty amount of money—two point two million dollars, to be exact. Why granny had never told Annie about the money was beyond her. Lord knows they could've used some of it to fix the ancient farmhouse Annie had grown up in or made repairs to the barn—a stiff Oklahoma wind could probably blow over in one fell swoop.

Looking back on it now, though, she could remember times where money seemed to appear out of nowhere. One time, Sophie started cooking okra in the kitchen and then gone outside to water her flowers, forgetting about the okra on the stove. Thirteen-year-old Annie had walked into the kitchen to see flames shooting to the ceiling. Half the kitchen had to be replaced. Annie remembered her granny telling her to go get the biggest money jar out of the hayloft in the barn. Annie did as she was told and a month later, they had a brand new kitchen. Granted, their *brand new kitchen* was filled with appliances and cabinets her granny found at discount stores or garage sales because she "wasn't goin' to one of those high-falutin' stores and payin' out the wazoo." That was what she said when Annie suggested they go to the Lowe's in Lakeview. But it was still a new kitchen—at least to them.

When Annie was a teenager, she needed a car. A car appeared. It wasn't big or fancy; in fact, it was a little bit of a clunker. But it ran, the air worked, and it came with a tape deck for Annie to play all of her granddad's Roger Miller, Merle Haggard, and Jim Croce cassette tapes. Even better, her granny let her paint a mural on the outside of the car. Annie had painted lilies and daisies of all shapes and colors. She had driven a literal work of art.

Even though Annie was far from spoiled, she never wanted for anything. If she needed it, her granny got it for her. Annie thought it was her granddad's retirement money her granny was using when in fact, it was probably some of the *millions of dollars* her granny had been saving. She was just glad she convinced her granny to quit hiding all her money in mason jars and actually deposit it in the bank. If not, Annie would likely be digging up mason jars until the day she died and not find them all. Lord knows it would take a crap-ton of mason jars to hold two point two million dollars.

Annie loved growing up where she did. A person had to drive ten miles outside of town and then half a mile down a gravel road before even seeing her granny's rambling farmhouse. Even after the house could be *seen* from the road, a person had to drive a half mile down a meandering dirt path to reach it. The path wound through tall loblolly pines and elms, crossing a wooden bridge over Lakewood Creek. The setting of her home was beautiful, but Annie loved the house most of all.

Built in 1910, the house was a two story, white clapboard home with a wrap-around front porch. Her granny and grandad's ancient rockers sat on the front porch and her granny, always one to make an impression, had painted the front door a hot pink, discount paint named Sexy Pink Elephant she had found at Nailed It, the hardware store in town. Yep. That was the actual name of the paint. Annie had never seen a pink elephant. Or a sexy one at that. It was probably why it was on clearance. No one wanted to paint their walls and think of a sexy elephant. But her granny had declared it cheap and fancy, so a hot pink door it was.

Wide planked, oak hardwood floors ran throughout the house and white shiplap, now all the rage on HGTV's *Fixer Upper* home design show, covered most of the walls. Apparently, Granny Sophie had hip design in her home long before Joanna Gains ever made it famous. The baseboards and crown molding were wide, dark wood, the door frames were large and decorative, and the kitchen had a saloon door, which was Annie's absolute favorite part of the entire house.

She remembered slinging her toy guns from the holsters her granny had gotten Annie for her eleventh birthday and yelling, "Stick 'em up, ya no good cowards!" to her stuffed animals on the ancient plaid couch in the living room that faced a massive rock fireplace.

Annie took her cowboy boots off on the front porch, a habit instilled in her by her granny, and headed toward the kitchen at the back of the house. She grabbed her granny's last will and testament off the back of the couch before heading into the kitchen. Opening the fridge, she grabbed a cold Corona and a wedge of lime and headed back to the front porch where she plopped down on the top stair and leaned against the railing. Squeezing the lime into her beer, she took a long swallow and let out a sigh.

Her granny's cat, Sebastian, walked up to Annie and rubbed his head on her legs. Sebastian continued to weave his way between her legs, his black tail swishing back and forth and body rumbling with loud purrs. Annie took another swig of her beer. "What are we gonna do without Granny, huh, Bass? Can you tell me that? Because I have no clue."

Annie pulled her granny's will out of the back of her shorts and read through it again. Leave it to Sophie Cleaver to go out with a bang. Her will stated Annie was not to have a funeral. Instead, Granny wanted to be cremated, her ashes scattered over the farm a scoopful at a time by anyone who attended her "life celebration." The attendees had to wear pink, her granny's favorite color, and share something about Sophie that made them smile. Annie also had to provide a shot of fireball whiskey for everyone who wore pink and spread a scoop of ashes.

The kicker, however, was that Annie had to make copies of the picture of Granny winning the Charleston Swing Dance Competition in Oklahoma City when she was twenty-one and distribute it to everyone who came to the celebration. Her granny was dressed as a flapper in the picture and was sitting on the shoulder of her dance partner, a hunky soldier named Harrison, holding their trophy up in the air. Annie also had to play *Witchy Woman* by the Eagles and *Pink* by Aerosmith on repeat the entire time. Not exactly what Annie would want for *her* funeral, but hey, it wasn't her celebration. It was also probably why everyone thought her granny was crazy.

"What do you think people are gonna think, Bass?" she asked the cat who was now curled up in her lap, his paws wrapped around her arm. "I think it will reaffirm the idea to everyone in this town she was a nut case, but you know what? I don't even care. She was my granny and I loved her. And I have no clue what to do next. I don't even have any more flower beds to clean. Maybe I'll start on all the crap in the attic. Or the barn. Lord knows it needs a serious case of renovation. It is almost falling down. Hell, maybe I need to just tear it down and start from scratch. Does that sound like a plan?"

Sebastian bit her on the arm. "Ow! Okay, okay. No attic or barn. At least not right now. But I have to do it eventually. You know that, right?" At her words about postponing the work, the cat began purring again and batted at Annie's hand, wanting her to rub his head.

When her granny got sick and Annie had to come back home after three semesters of college, all she focused on was getting her granny well and out of the hospital. Once her granny was home, Annie's concentration had shifted to getting her granny back on her feet and keeping the farm from falling apart. Now here she was, almost a decade later. Her granny was dead, she was a millionaire, and she had absolutely no clue what came next.

WYATT BOUNCED on the balls of his feet and shook out his hands. He felt like he was in a scene from *Rocky*, which was ridiculous. All he was doing was asking a woman who just lost the only person who had loved and raised her if she needed help at her farm. From a wounded vet who may or may not have a serious case of PTSD.

Wyatt had gotten the handles for the International that morning and had installed them as soon as he opened the package. He was now standing in front of his beautiful, fully restored truck, trying to convince himself to get in it and drive to the rambling farm on the outskirts of town and ask for a job from a woman who may or may not be as crazy as her grandma.

"Just grow some balls and get in the damn truck already," he said to himself. "Take this one step to getting back to normal."

Wyatt finally hopped in his truck and turned south toward the lake. He was pretty sure he knew where to go, but he had never actually been to Sophie's farm, no matter what she tried to convince the town he had done to her mailbox.

Fifteen minutes later, he turned right at the mailbox with the words, "This is new. Bash it again and I will curse you with my voodoo" painted in faded, hot pink letters. Wyatt shook his head. This was a seriously bad idea.

He pulled to a stop in front of a rambling, two story farmhouse with a front door that matched the paint on the mailbox. Guess Sophie had a thing for hot pink. Walking up the front porch, he knocked on the door. After a few minutes of standing there, trying not to peek in the long windows on either side of the door to see if anyone was home, he knocked again. Wyatt put his hands in his pockets and whistled a Roger Miller song his dad taught him when he was a kid. Finally, with a shrug, Wyatt stepped off the porch and headed back to his truck.

"Can I help you?"

Wyatt jumped. One thing he couldn't take anymore was someone walking up behind him. Willing his heartbeat to slow, Wyatt turned toward the female voice and his mouth gaped open. Annabelle was standing in front of him, her hair pulled up in a messy bun on the top of her head, her skin tanned a deep bronze. She must have changed her sense of fashion since high school because she wasn't wearing a long skirt and flannel top. Instead, she had on a pair of cutoff jean shorts that hit her mid-thigh, a bright yellow bikini top, and a pair of brown and turquoise cowgirl boots.

"Huh...huh...hi," Wyatt stuttered. "I didn't think you were home."

"You thought wrong. I was at the barn feeding the animals. Why are you here?" she asked, hands on her hips. "Are you lost?"

"No, I'm not lost," he said. Damn, she was hot. Even hotter than she was as a seventeen-year-old high school student. Taking off those crazy, mismatched clothes was *definitely* working in her favor. The dirt on her cheek just made her more attractive. Wyatt liked a woman who wasn't afraid of hard work. "I just wanted to see how you were doing. You know, since your grandma died and everything."

Wyatt mentally slapped himself on the forehead. What a dumb ass statement to make. Of course she wasn't doing well. Her grandma had just kicked the bucket. He resisted the urge to turn tail and run. He was making an ass out of himself.

Annabelle crossed her arms over her chest and leveled him with a glare, drawing Wyatt's focus to her perky breasts that looked like they were about to fall out of the tiny bikini top. "My granny just died. I'm not doing so hot. Anyway, I have no clue who you are. So again, why are you here?"

He quickly took his eyes off her chest and locked eyes with her. They were even prettier than he remembered. "I'm Wyatt. Wyatt Holloway. We went to school together."

Annie stared at him, saying nothing. He tried not to squirm. She kept up her silence, still leveling him with a glare.

"I thought you were in Afghanistan," she finally said.

"I came home."

"Hmmm," she said, uncrossing her arms and placing her hands on her hips. "Still doesn't explain why you're here. Maybe to apologize for bashing in my granny's mailbox when you were in high school?"

Wyatt held up his hand. "Now, hold on just a second. I'll tell you what I told your cra—"

He stopped himself before he called her grandma crazy. That probably wouldn't do him any favors. "Sophie never listened when I told her I wasn't the one who bashed in her mailbox, no matter how many times I told her it wasn't me."

"Then who was it?"

"I don't know. And I don't know why she was convinced I did it. But I didn't. Why would I need to lie about it now?"

Annabelle shrugged. "I guess you wouldn't. But you really don't know who did it?"

"Nope. But I noticed she warned the next possible culprit away with a scary 'I'll put a curse on you and kill your cat' mumbo jumbo on the mailbox. I also noticed it was written in the hot pink paint that matches the front door."

Annabelle smiled a full-watt smile that crinkled her eyes and showcased an adorable dimple in her right cheek. Wyatt couldn't believe he had forgotten who she was. She was the prettiest thing he had seen in a long time. And her smile made her look like the high school student Wyatt remembered more vividly the longer he stood in front of her.

"She loved animals," Annabelle replied with a grin. "She would never kill anyone's cat. Even the paint is named after an animal. A sexy pink elephant, in fact."

"What did you just say?"

"I told you the name of the pink paint. Sexy Pink Elephant. It was on clearance at Nailed It."

"I'm shocked it was on clearance."

Annie laughed. "Right? But she *would* go out from time to time and repaint the letters in Sexy Pink Elephant pink when they started to fade. She said it would keep other people from getting any bright ideas about messing with her. I think all her voodoo talk to you in town had everyone else scared to even step foot on our property."

Wyatt kicked the toe of his boot in the dirt and shrugged. "It probably worked. I know I was scared shitless of her from there on out."

Annabelle laughed. "That was her M.O."

"Did she really know voodoo?"

"Absolutely not. She was just great at scare tactics."

At that confession, Wyatt laughed. "Annabelle, my greatest fear was one day having to come out here for something and finding voodoo dolls of all shapes and sizes in my likeness."

She laughed, a tiny, tinkling sound that reminded Wyatt of a fairy. "I guess her scare tactic worked, then."

Wyatt chuckled. "I guess it did."

"Wyatt?"

"Yeah?"

"I go by Annie."

"Good to know, Annie. I still go by Wyatt."

Annie climbed the steps of the porch and climbed into

one of the rockers looking out over the yard. "You still haven't told me why you're here."

Wyatt walked over to the porch and put his hands on the railing. "I guess I haven't."

She raised one eyebrow at him. "So, you ever plan on doing that? You look like you just saw a ghost. Come sit down. I don't bite. I don't even know voodoo."

"Your granny would be so disappointed," he said, walking up the steps and sitting in the other rocker. Rocking gently, his gaze wandered to the front yard.

Her farm sure was a peaceful, pretty place. Tall elm trees shaded the entire yard and a bird bath stood between two large, hot pink crepe myrtles framing a large picture window Wyatt guess looked into the living or dining room. Pale pink stargazer lilies and deep pink rose bushes were planted in front of the porch, statues of various animals scattered throughout. He could even hear the quiet sound of a stream behind the house. Wyatt's favorite part of the yard, however, was the giant magnolia tree several yards in front of the old farmhouse. Its blossoms filled the humid Oklahoma air with their light floral fragrance.

"I can tell your granny's favorite color was probably pink," he said softly. "I like it here. It's peaceful."

"It was," Annie said with a soft laugh. "She always said the world would be a much nicer place if it had a little more pink in it. Whatever the hell *that* meant."

"I don't know what the hell that means, either." He chuckled. "But if having more pink meant places feeling like *this* place, I think I'm a believer, too. Were you working on the yard before I got here? You have a little dirt on your face."

Annie wiped her arm on her cheek, which only smeared more dirt with the sweat. "Yeah. I was trying to clean out the flower beds. There was a lot of dead, overgrown stuff in them. Trying to keep myself busy, ya know?"

Wyatt nodded. He knew all about keeping himself busy to keep the thoughts at bay. "You succeeded in getting more dirt on your face. Here, let me help."

Wyatt got off his rocker and walked over to where Annie was still sitting. He crouched in front of her, pulled the bottom of his t-shirt up and gently wiped her face. "There you go. All clean."

CHAPTER 3

*A*nnie froze at Wyatt's touch. She hadn't had a man touch her since the last horrific blind date her granny had set up. She had made Annie a fake profile on Tinder and told her Jimmy Newton was in town visiting his parents. Annie thought she was meeting him at the Texas Roadhouse in Lakeview, but when she got there, it wasn't Jimmy who was waiting for her. Instead, it was a guy named Bernard, a mortician who owned Morton's Funeral Services and Crematorium.

His pasty complexion hinted he liked to spend more time with dead people than he did with the living. The entire time they were at the restaurant, Bernard explained the process of embalming and how it dated back to the time of Egyptian mummies. Annie wound up drinking two and a half frozen margaritas so she could get through the meal. After he tried to grope her and planted a slobbery kiss to her lips in the parking lot, Annie called her friend, Colleen, to pick her drunk ass up and drive her home. She didn't speak to her granny for two days because of that little bit of dishonesty.

When Annie finally broke her vow of silence, her granny

explained Bernard was the best funeral director in Lakeview and if Annie dated him she would probably get a discount when Sophie kicked the bucket. Annie had reminded her she wanted to be cremated, so the only discount she could get would be a discount on an urn or setting the fire at higher temperature so her granny would burn faster.

Granny had finally promised to cancel Annie's membership to the dating website as long as Annie tried on her own to find a man who didn't care Annie was taking care of her ancient grandmother. Annie had agreed but *ironically*, a man just never seemed to fit the bill.

But at Wyatt's touch, her breath hitched and a multitude of butterflies started flapping in her stomach. If his hand just on her *face* caused this much commotion, Annie could only imagine what his hand roaming *other* parts of her body would do.

When she saw him in her yard, Annie knew exactly who had set foot on her property, even though she pretended not to recognize him. She wouldn't be a true member of their little town if she didn't know who he was. Wyatt Holloway, God's gift to Parker athletics, the former athlete whose trophies, pictures, and signed balls of every shape and size filled the trophy case of the high school gymnasium. Big muscles and self-assurance seeping from his pores. Cheerleaders vying for a chance to be his date for the weekend. It was something Annie had secretly dreamed when she was a teenager. The nerdy recluse and popular jock falling in love, reminiscent of Freddy Prinze Jr. and Rachel Lee Cook in the nineties romance *She's All That.*

The army only made him better. His arm muscles bulged out of the sleeves of his olive gray army t-shirt and looked like they were sculpted from stone. What Annie could see of his abs when he raised the bottom of his shirt to wipe her face looked just as enticing. She had forgotten how green his eyes were, like a field of newly planted wheat just beginning to break through the earth. Mesmerizing. The only difference between high school Wyatt and grown man Wyatt was the jagged scar running down the right side of his face. She had a feeling there was a story behind that scar. Probably a sad one.

But he still hadn't answered the question of what he was doing on her farm. *And* why he thought it was okay to get all up in her personal bubble to wipe the dirt off her face. Annie pulled back from his hand and glared. "Why are you wiping my face with your shirt?"

Wyatt immediately dropped his hand, his shirt falling down and covering his abs. Dammit. She shouldn't have said anything. There went her view of the best male anatomy she had seen in a *long, long, long* time.

"I'm sorry. I wasn't thinking."

"You're damn right you weren't."

"I just wipe dirt off my niece's face with my shirt so much that I didn't really think about what I was doing."

"How old is your niece?"

"Five," he replied, his ears turning red on the tips.

"So you thought it was okay to rub your shirt all over my face because you do it for your *five-year-old* niece?"

"In hindsight, that probably wasn't my best idea."

"Ya think?" Annie said sarcastically before getting up and walking down the porch steps. She needed to put distance between herself and yummy army man Wyatt Holloway, because even if it wasn't his best idea, Wyatt wiping her face with his shirt and shoving his six-pack in Annie's face made her have some ideas of her own. Ideas consisting of him showcasing his army man muscles in nothing but his birthday suit. And that was something she didn't need added to her already full plate.

"I'm really sorry, Annabelle," Wyatt said, following her off the porch. "I didn't mean to piss you off."

Annie whirled around and leveled him with a glare. "I told you to call me Annie. Annabelle only reminds me of when my granny yelled at me when I was in trouble. She shouted my full name and it was awful."

Wyatt grinned and combed his hair off his forehead with his fingers. "I got *Wyatt James Holloway!* That's how I knew I was in *real* trouble."

Annie itched for *her* fingers to follow the trail of *his* fingers through his hair. The sun was high in the sky and blazing down on top of their heads, highlighting the soft copper colored strands running through his chestnut hair. *Gah!* She had to get her mind off of hottie Holloway.

"What was yours?"

Annie shook her head. "Come again?" she asked, willing herself not to stare at the wayward strand of hair that fell back over his forehead and into his eyes. He was too damn distracting for his own good.

"You don't want to be called Annabelle because it reminds you of when you got in trouble. What went with Annabelle?"

"I don't want to say."

"Why not?"

Annie put her hands over her face and peeked through the spaces of her fingers. "Because it's ridiculously embarrassing!"

Wyatt chuckled. "But I told you mine. It's only fair to share yours."

"Wyatt *James* Holloway is a perfectly normal, playground safe name. A name your parents could shout at you in the grocery store parking lot and not send you diving under the nearest car. Mine isn't."

"It can't be that bad."

"It is."

"Well, I can't make an honest judgment if you won't even tell me."

Annie sighed. She couldn't believe she was telling her deepest secret. "Annabelle Clara Diane Cleaver."

Wyatt raised his eyebrows. "That's long but not all that bad. Why does that make you embarrassed? I was expecting a Gertrude, Wilma, or Bertha. Something horrible."

"Because!" she shouted through her fingers still covering her face. "Haven't you put two and two together?"

He shrugged. "I guess not."

"Say my initials to yourself."

"What?"

"Just *do* it! Because you're obviously not getting it."

Wyatt scratched his head. "Okay. If you insist. A. C. D—"

He let out a bark of laughter when he realized what her initials meant put together. "Your parents named you that so your initials would be ACDC. That's pretty creative, if I do say so myself."

Annie removed her hands from her face. "My mom used to brag I was conceived at their concert while they sang *You Shook Me All Night Long*. I can't hear that song without shuddering. She used to yell out my initials when I didn't answer quickly enough. Bridgette Evans heard her one day in Swanson's Market and told my entire class. Second grade was awful because of it."

"How did a roomful of second graders know who an eighties rock band was?"

"Because Bridgette made a poster about them and brought it to school with her. Pictures, Lyrics. The works. Looking back on it now, I can see where she actually put a lot of effort into it. But as an eight year old already from the wrong side of the tracks, it was the final nail in my coffin."

Wyatt couldn't stop laughing. "Okay, you win." He

laughed. "Yours is pretty bad. I still don't want to call you Annie. Can I *please* call you ACDC?"

"Do it and I'll put a curse on you."

"I thought you said that was all made up."

"Maybe it is. Maybe it isn't. It's your choice to push your luck to find out."

"Whatever you say," he replied before softly saying, "ACDC."

Annie punched him in the shoulder. "You're playing with fire, Wyatt Holloway."

"What? ACDC is my favorite band."

"Really?"

"Scout's honor."

"Then name five of their songs."

"What?"

Annie crossed her arms over her chest. She was calling bullshit. She doubted if he could even name two.

"If you're such a *fan* and they're your *favorite*," she air-quoted, "You shouldn't have any trouble naming five of their hit songs. Any true groupie would be able to. I can name five Britney Spears songs in five seconds."

"Prove it."

"You Drive Me Crazy. Womanizer. Oops I Did It Again. Lucky. Hit Me Baby One More Time." She pretended to drop the mic. "Boom. Your turn. And you can't name *You Shook Me All Night Long.*"

"What? That's not fair."

"It's totally fair. You don't have to think on the fly with that one. Hell, I'll even double your time. You have ten seconds starting…now."

Wyatt started sputtering.

"You've already wasted a second," she said, staring at her watch.

"Highway to Hell…Thunderstruck…um…"

"Three, two—"

"Wait! I just need—"

"Time." Annie laughed and gave a Jersey Shore fist pump. "I knew it!"

"Knew what?"

"You were full of horse poo, that's what."

"Fine. I won't ever call you ACDC again."

"Thank you."

Annie rolled her eyes when Wyatt began softly whistling the chorus of *You Shook Me All Night Long*. She should've never opened her big, fat mouth.

WYATT DID NOT KNOW what he was thinking when he pulled up his shirt and wiped Annie's face. Hell, him *not* thinking was the problem. All decent thoughts had left his brain the minute she walked around the corner wearing those teeny, tiny shorts and scrap of material she called a bathing suit top. She smelled a little like the smoke from the leaves she was burning, but he could also detect faint traces of peach wafting by his nose when the breeze fanned through her hair. Peaches, which happened to be his favorite fruit, a yellow bikini top, which happened to be his favorite color, and Daisy Dukes, which happened to be *every* man's favorite pair of shorts. A perfect trifecta. He was so screwed.

"You still haven't told me why you're here," Annabelle had walked back to the porch, taken a Gulf Shores, Alabama t-shirt sitting on the empty flowerpot on the stand by the front door, and slipped it over her head. Dammit. There went his view. At least she didn't put on a pair of pants, too.

"Well, that's because I was learning all about you and your *fantastic* initials, ACDC," he replied. He chuckled when she shot a glare his way.

"I *told* you not to call me that!"

"Well, I told *you* I don't want to call you Annie, so it's either Annabelle or ACDC. Take your pick."

"Why don't you want to call me Annie?"

"Because it makes me think of the little orphan girl from the movie, and then I start thinking of all the kids I saw overseas who were turned into orphans in front of my eyes, and then I get sad and shit." Wyatt blinked in surprise. Damn. He hadn't expected *that* bit of information to come out of his mouth. He hadn't even said anything about the orphans to his family or therapist. But here he was, blurting it out to the practical stranger standing in front of him. It was the damn Daisy Dukes' fault. Well, those and the pair of mile long legs that were wearing them.

Annabelle's face softened. "That must have been hard, huh? Being overseas?"

"You could say that," he muttered.

"Well, on behalf of everyone in Parker, I'd like to thank you for your service."

Wyatt smiled a sad smile. "You're welcome."

"But now, Wyatt Holloway, you better tell me why you're here or I'm kicking you off my property."

"I was just wondering if you needed any help around here. My dad heard you were struggling with the upkeep with nobody to help you, so I thought I would offer my services."

"Are you asking me for a *job*?"

"I'm asking you if you need help. You wouldn't have to pay me. I just need something to keep me busy. My ther—" Wyatt stopped talking before he said the word *therapist*. If he told her his therapist said he wasn't ready for a job, she'd probably kick him off her farm before he went balls to the wall crazy on her.

"My mom is driving me crazy, I've already restored by

granddad's International pickup truck, and my dad got pissed at me when he realized I had rearranged everything in his garage by alphabetical order," he said instead. "You'd *think* I would have gotten a thanks. That place was a pit before I started working in it."

Annabelle laughed. "Maybe he just doesn't like people touching his things."

"That became abundantly clear the minute he came in the garage to see me putting the last tool away. I thought he was going to pop the blood vessel in his forehead he was so mad."

"What did you have in mind? For working here? Anything strike your fancy?"

"I don't know. I guess whatever you needed done. I noticed the gutters on the front of the house need to be replaced. I could start there. Maybe do some work on the barn? It looks like it could use a fresh coat of paint and some structure work. Do you keep animals in there?"

She frowned. "Yes."

"So you probably don't want it to topple on top of them, right?"

"Duh."

"I can help with that. Because we do live in Oklahoma. You know about the whole winds sweeping down the plains, right?"

Annabelle nodded.

"We wouldn't want you to be forced to make ol' Jasper into bacon before his time. Or whatever your pig's name is."

"How do you know I have a pig?"

"Because I have a nose. *And* I showed pigs in every live-stock show held in the county barn from the time I was old enough to wear an FFA jacket."

"I didn't know you showed."

Wyatt shrugged. "Not a lot of people did. I was more in the spotlight for sports. My participation in the Future

Farmers of America wasn't as cool as how far I could throw a football, I guess. But I don't care how many years it has been. You don't forget the smell of pigs."

She chuckled. "That's a fair statement."

"I never saw you at the shows. I thought it was a law that every Oklahoma farm girl had to show an animal at least one time in her life."

"Granny didn't want me to show."

"Why not?"

"I have no clue. Maybe she was worried I would be made fun of for our animals' names. I was already the oddball outcast by the time I moved in with her and she was the crazy lady on the farm. I guess she was saving me the heartache."

"Don't tell me. Your pig is Aerosmith. I'm thinking Nirvana for your horse, and Journey…no, *Kansas* for your cow."

Annabelle rolled her eyes. "Not even close."

"Let me take it back a decade or so then…Fleetwood Mac? Johnny Cash? Elvis? There always seems to be a pig named Elvis somewhere."

Annabelle motioned with her hand for him to follow. "Just come on. I'll introduce you."

They walked around the side of the barn. Wyatt noticed a pen holding three pigs—two adults and a piglet. There was also a black and white paint horse, four Jersey cows, and three goats in a field to the west of the barn, and three chickens housed in a coop. Wyatt jumped when a pair of ducks waddled in front of him, a black cat and Great Pyrenees following close behind. "Holy cow! You really *do* have a farm!"

"I don't have all this land for nothing. What else would I do with it? If I don't have animals on here I might as well move to a subdivision in town."

"Subdivisions? In Parker? Yeah, right."

Annabelle laughed. "You're right. Anyway, I am most defi-nitely *not* a subdivision girl."

"So are you going to introduce me? I need to know all of their names so I'll quit guessing eighties hair bands."

Annabelle walked over to the pig pen. "This is Anna, Christoph, and Elsa."

Wyatt followed her to the fence that separated the field from the barn.

"The cows are Cinderella, Drizella, Anastasia, and Fairy Godmother. The horse is Perdita, and the three goats are Timon, Pumba, and Nala. The ducks who waddled in front of you are Lilo and Stitch, the cat is Sebastian, the dog is Nemo, and the chickens are Merida, Pocahontas, and Rapunzel."

Wyatt stared at her, a dumfounded look on his face. "Are you serious? You can't be serious."

"Dead serious. My granny had a thing for Disney movies. I think every animal at one time or another has been a Disney princess, so she had to branch out and start using other characters. I once asked if we could name some pigs we had Shrek, Fiona, and Donkey. I thought she was going to throw me out of the house."

Wyatt started laughing and couldn't stop. He bent over, his hands on his knees. "That is the craziest thing I've ever heard."

"You're telling me. Between that and the voodoo, it's no wonder the entire town thought she was nuts."

"That's great," he said, standing up and wiping his eyes. "That made my day."

"Well, glad I could be of service. Come back tomorrow. My granny stories never end."

"Well, if you decide to hire me, I'll be out here every day."

Annabelle put a hand up to her face, her pointer finger

resting on her cheek and her thumb under her chin. "I *guess* I could use some help around here. I was going to start on the barn first. Are you up for it?"

Wyatt stuck his hand out for her to shake. "When do I start, Boss?"

CHAPTER 4

*A*nnie let out a groan when her alarm went off. The sun hadn't even made its appearance yet. She itched to press the snooze button again, but if she was going to have everything ready to go for her granny's life celebration, she had to get her lazy ass out of bed. She sighed. Mornings sucked.

Groggily, she hopped out of bed and stuck her feet in the most recent hot pink booties her granny had crocheted for her. Walking to the bathroom directly across from her room, she grabbed her toothbrush and squeezed a long line of paste on its bristles. While she was brushing, she turned on the knobs of the claw-foot bathtub and willed the water to heat up quickly. Cold showers were the worst. She spit the toothpaste in the sink, threw her "I don't do mornings" t-shirt on the floor, and checked the water. Nice and steamy, just like she liked it. The water gods must be taking it easy on her this morning. Usually it took at least three minutes for the water to heat to tepid. Annie turned the middle knob in the tub to send the water to the showerhead and stepped in, sighing in pleasure as the water ran down her back. She wrapped the curtain around the shower enclosure overhead and smiled when the steam from the hot water surrounded her.

Part of the reason Annie loved the home she grew up in was because it was filled with so many original features. The tub in her bathroom was original to the house, as was the pedestal sink and stained glass window on the wall beside the tub. Annie had painted the wide-planked, wooden floors antique white and distressed them, part of the original oak peeking through the paint. The only thing not original in the bathroom were the toilet and the floor-to-ceiling cabinets Annie had installed on either side of the sink.

She stood directly under the stream, letting the water run down her face and shoulders. Today was the day. She would say it was the day she would lay her granny to rest, but *scooped* her granny to rest would probably be more appropriate. Either way, there was no getting around what her granny had listed in descriptive step-by-step instructions in her will. Per Granny's wishes, Annie had typed up a flyer detailing her life celebration and what an attendee had to do in order to participate. A week ago, she had hung them up in places all over town—Swanson's Market, Griff's Bar, Sadie's Café, Nailed It—the hardware store, Colleen's Curls and More Salon, Benji's—the dog grooming salon, and the gas station, Got Gas?. She'd placed an ad in the Parker Publisher, hung even more flyers in the six churches in town, and given a lot of copies to all the businesses to put beside the registers in the checkout lines in case someone wanted to take one and post it on their fridge as a reminder. Hopefully, people would actually show up. Annie had probably killed two small trees making all the copies.

Turning the water off, Annie stepped out of the shower and wrapped herself in a coral colored towel that matched the coral flowers on her soft mint green shower curtain. She headed to her bedroom where the hot pink dress she had bought was laid across the tufted mint green chair in the corner of her room. It wasn't something Annie would normally pick out for herself. The top of the dress had a small ruffle running from one spaghetti strap to the other, dipping down in the middle to show just a hint of cleavage without being trashy. A gold leather belt cinched the waist and the flowy skirt hit Annie right above the knee. Annie had even bought a pair of gold wedge sandals, gold bangle bracelets, and dangly gold earrings to match. It made her feel very feminine and pretty, which working on a farm rarely allowed. Besides, she wanted to look nice for her granny.

But Annie couldn't put the dress on just yet. She had to prepare her granny's favorite foods, the bacon cheddar quiches and mini cheesecake bites Annie had purchased from Sam's Club. She also had to bake chocolate chip cookies her granny requested to be dyed pink as well as make the pink slushy punch her granny always made for Annie's birthday parties. Right before the celebrators showed up, Annie was to place all the food, as well as mini bottles of fireball whiskey, on the table on the front porch. Annie had to pick up chairs she was borrowing from the First Baptist Church, the helium tank, and ninety one pink balloons she had ordered from Pick Anything But Your Nose, the flower shop in town. Her will had stated whatever her age was when she kicked the bucket was how many balloons Annie had to buy. No one could say Sophie wouldn't go out with a bang. This was a funeral people would never forget.

Annie heard the front door creak open. "Knock, knock! Anyone need help planning their crazy grandma's funeral?"

Annie walked around the corner and smiled when she saw one of her best friends, Colleen, loving on Nemo. The big oaf was wagging his tail full-throttle, knocking into the front door and the back of Colleen's knees. "I was afraid you would decide it was too early for you to wake up," she said.

"I wouldn't wake up for anyone else. But I couldn't leave you in a lurch. And I knew I would be getting some love from this guy," she said, leaning down and wrapping her arms around Nemo's neck. "Since lord knows I'm not getting any lovin' from any *other* man on the planet, I figure beggars can't be choosers."

Where Annie was lanky and tan, Colleen was all curve and alabaster skin. As a professional hairstylist and nail technician, CC might have pixie-short, red hair one day and black, curly locks to the middle of her back the next. Annie and Breckin hadn't seen their friend's natural, light brown locks since elementary school.

Colleen, Annie, and Breckin had met when Annie was in third grade. They were all smart, quiet, and the oddballs of Parker Elementary. Colleen and Breckin's families had moved to town the same year Annie's dad died and her mom abandoned her to Sophie. Annie was being raised by her crazy grandma, Colleen's parents were hippies and dressed her like she was a flower child from the seventies, and Breckin was raised by a single dad who dressed her in boy clothes when she was little and wanted her to try out for the football team when she was a teenager. After bonding over their families' mutual weirdness, the girls were inseparable.

The women remained close even after graduation. Breckin had moved to Norman after high school to get an education degree at the University of Oklahoma, while CC, which is what Breckin and Annie called Colleen, had gone to cosmetology school. They had all planned on leaving Parker after graduation and never looking back but fate had other plans. CC's dad hit his midlife crisis and ran off with the red-headed bartender at Griff's, who was fifteen years his junior. CC had come home after graduating cosmetology school to help her mom run her beauty salon. Breckin's husband, Brad, had accepted the football job at Parker High after they both graduated from college but, after a few years of being back home, had dumped Breckin. He said it was just a coincidence, but Annie found it very suspicious he wanted a divorce from her friend as soon as the most popular senior cheerleader had walked off the graduation stage. Men who had been in the three women's lives sucked just like mornings and cold showers. At least they had each other.

"Where's Breck? I thought she was coming, too."

"Girl, you know how much she *hates* getting up in the morning. I think she's worse than *you*, if that is even possible." CC threw her turquoise and purple paisley Vera Bradley bag on the couch, walked over to Annie, and pulled her in for a hug. "How are you doing?"

"I never thought I'd be planning a pink life celebration for my granny but I'm holding up okay."

"But just think how happy Sophie will be when she looks down from heaven and is able to show the big Guy upstairs her granddaughter loved her *so* much she pulled out all the stops for the craziest funeral ever."

Annie pulled back from her friend and wiped the tear that had trickled down her cheek. "It *is* pretty crazy."

"So what all needs to be done?"

Annie started ticking all the to-dos on her fingers. "Make the food, pick up the chairs from the church, the balloons and helium tank from the flower shop, and all the mini bottles of fireball whiskey from the liquor store. Make sure the CD player is working and the songs are downloaded to my phone. And last, but certainly not least, make sure all my granny's remains *remain* safe in her hot pink urn until it's time to spread her over our farm, one scoop at a time."

"Is that all?" CC grinned. "I could make all that happen in about five minutes."

Annie plopped down on the sofa and leaned her head back into its comfy cushions. "Just so you know, I plan on getting plastered with any leftover fireball whiskey once everyone leaves. If no one comes, I'll get even *more* plastered."

"Oh, honey. People are going to come," CC replied, sitting down on the couch beside Annie, absentmindedly swirling her fingers through a turquoise and black sequined mermaid pillow Granny had gotten Annie on her last birthday.

Annie tried to hold back more tears that threatened to spill over her lashes. "How do you know? Everyone in town thought she was crazy!"

"I'm sure all the pre-k parents will come. Didn't she volunteer as a class grandma for their classes for like, three years in a row?"

Annie wiped her eyes. "She did do that."

"And what about all the people who make the Christmas baskets every year for the foster kids? Didn't she crochet a pair of booties for *every child* on the list?"

"Yeah."

"And what about everyone at the feed store? She kept them in business for years just by supplying all the feed for the hundreds of animals you guys have had at the farm throughout the years."

"Okay, okay. I get it."

"As someone who spent the majority of my middle school high school years in this house, I'll admit she was a little quirky. But everyone who truly knew Sophie also knows she had a heart of gold and would do anything for anyone."

Annie smiled. "She was pretty great, wasn't she?"

"She was. I know she was on my top three list of people I'd call if I were ever in a jam."

"Who were the other two?"

"Duh. You and Breck."

"Not your mom?"

"Puh-leaze, girl! Have you *met* my mom? She would not be someone I wanted to call if I were in a bind. I love her and all, but first, she'd freak out, then cry, then yell. Then, for the rest of my *life*, anytime I needed help with something she'd say, "Remember the time when…" No thanks."

Annie laughed. "You're probably right."

"I *know* I'm right. My dad was an asshole for leaving but sometimes, I kinda understand why he did. I don't even live with the woman and I've contemplated turning my car on the highway and not looking back."

"You wouldn't! What would Breck and I do without you?"

"That's why I said *contemplated.* I could never leave my girls. If one of us has to be stuck in Podunk Parker, then *all* of us have to be. We're in this together."

Annie pulled her friend in for another hug. "Thanks, CC. I love you."

"Ditto, sister. Now, let's call Breckin. I'll have her borrow her brother's truck and grab the chairs, whiskey, helium tank and balloons. We can start on the cookies and decorating the tables. Hell, I'll even help you feed all the animals. This whole thing will come together before you know it."

"You're the best."

"I know it. I won't even tell Breck I'm really your favorite friend," CC said with a wink.

The duo walked to the mudroom at the back of the house, each putting on a pair of cowgirl boots before stepping off the back porch.

"You know you're a really good best friend whenever you not only keep a spare set of boots at your friend's house, but also willingly help feed the million animals on this farm," CC grumbled. "I do hair and nails for a living. I can't tell you how many times I've lost a nail mucking stalls in your damn barn."

Annie grinned. "You know you love leaving the life of glamour and getting down and dirty on the farm every now and then."

CC rolled her eyes but Annie could see she was trying to hide her smile. CC talked a big talk, but she loved it on the farm as much as Annie did. The two women worked together in companionable silence for most of the morning. All the animals were fed and watered, the cows were milked, the chicken coop was checked for eggs and the stalls in the barn were cleaned. The women had also picked the ripe okra, squash, zucchini, tomatoes, and cantaloupe from the garden.

Living on the farm was amazing, but it really was a lot of work. Apparently, some of that work was going to be distributed to her hand? Employee? She really had no clue what to call Wyatt Holloway. Or what to do with him, for that matter. Because of the money her granny left, she had the funds to pay him, but Annie didn't know if she wanted that responsibility. To pay someone would mean he would be at her farm. Every day. Working. Probably without a shirt, because what else would he do when it was one hundred and four degrees outside? Then Annie wouldn't be able to get *any* work done because…well…because…those *abs!* Wyatt being on the farm on a daily basis would *not* be a good idea. When he came back on Monday morning, Annie would just tell him thanks but no thanks. End of story.

"Are you okay, Annie? I think I lost you for a second."

"Huh?" Annie looked at her friend, who was kicking her boots, now covered in mud and muck, off her feet and onto the back porch.

"I've been asking where you wanted to start. The cookies or the balloons? I'm sure Breckin will be here any minute."

"Oh, I don't care. Whatever you think will be best."

"Are you thinking about a *man?*"

"What? No!" Annie sputtered. "Why would you ask such a ridiculous question?!"

"Because that's the look I get on my face whenever I bump into Brant Billings in Swanson's. That man is so *hot.*"

"I don't know how many times I've told you I think you should ask him out."

"And I keep telling you he's *way* out of my league. A doctor? Are you kidding me? I just do hair and nails."

"He's actually just a nurse practitioner, not a *doctor,*" Annie argued. "Not to say he's not very qualified. He's really good at what he does. Besides, I don't even know why him being in a medical profession even matters. You're a pretty girl. He's a dreamy guy. Now you should just make some handsome babies."

CC rolled her eyes. "You're so dumb. He's had like, *years* of college while I graduated from cosmetology school at Platt College. There's no chance he's interested."

"Well, you'll never know unless you ask," Annie said with a waggle of her eyebrows.

"I guess we'll never know then. End of story. Besides, why are we talking about *my* nonexistent love life when yours is just as sad? When are you going to leave your farm and venture out into the dating world?"

"Never," Annie muttered. "Men are too much trouble. I'll take my animals, thank you very much. You always know where you stand with them."

"Yeah, and it's usually in a mound of shit," CC said, her hands on her hips. "Animals don't keep you warm at night, girl."

"Sebastian keeps me quite warm, thank you very much. And Nemo. Nemo keeps me warm."

"Only because he weighs a million pounds and is a ball of fur!"

"True story. And he is kind of a pillow hog, aren't you, boy?" Annie reached down and rubbed between Nemo's ears.

He had been following the duo around all morning while they were working.

"Well, I can guarantee you he doesn't keep you as warm as a man as hot as, oh, I don't know, sexy Wyatt Holloway would."

"*What* did you say?" Annie glared at her friend.

"Wyatt Holloway. He's back in town. Been back for a little bit, in fact. I heard he had to come home because he went all crazy overseas and they had to discharge him because of PTSD or something like that."

"And your point is?"

"I know you had a thing for him in high school."

"Did not!"

"*Right,*" CC replied sarcastically. "Then explain to me why *you*—a girl who had no interest in sports whatsoever—made it to all the football games, home *and* away, when he was a senior? You even made me and Breckin tag along because you didn't want to go by yourself."

"Maybe I realized how thrilling a football game could really be."

"More like you realized how thrilling staring at Wyatt Holloway's ass in a pair of football pants could be."

Annie stuck her tongue out at her friend. "You're mean."

"Woof!" Nemo barked enthusiastically.

CC stuck her tongue out in response. "I'm right. Even your dog agrees with me. Now, can we agree to stop talking about hot men we are *not* going to ask out? We have to finish up the details of your granny's life celebration. We don't want her ghost thinking we messed something up and putting a voodoo curse on us or anything."

Annie laughed. "Deal," she replied. She was perfectly okay with that plan because there was no way in *hell* she was telling her friend Wyatt Holloway had asked her for a job.

WYATT STOOD in front of his dresser, looking at himself in the mirror. He ran his fingers through his hair again, making a note to himself to get it trimmed by CC next time he was in town. Once he was discharged from the military, he decided to grow it out since it wasn't an option while he was in the army. But it was getting out of hand. The natural waves in his hair fell to his collar and wouldn't be tamed no matter how much gel, pomade, style cream, or whatever in the hell else he used. He itched to put a hat on his head, but knew where he was going hats would probably not be appreciated.

He had no idea what in the hell he was doing. The day after he met with Annie at her farm, he had met his mom at Sadie's Café for lunch. When he went to the counter to pay, a pile of fliers detailing Sophie's life celebration was sitting by the cash register. He had taken a copy and then, as if the International had its own mind, had driven to TJ Maxx in Lakeview.

Now, here Wyatt was, staring at himself in a pale pink button down shirt with a hot pink and light pink striped tie. A hot pink that suspiciously resembled Annie's Sexy Pink Elephant colored door. Wyatt sighed. There was no way he was going to that funeral. It would be so awkward. He just began loosening the tie from around his neck when his mother walked in the room.

"Well, don't you look *nice*," she said with a smile.

"Mom, have you ever heard of knocking? What if I had been naked?"

"Nothing I haven't seen before, honey," she said, sitting a basket of laundry on his bed. "I've known you for your twenty-nine years of life. I even spent twenty-seven hours of labor with you before the doctors realized you were too big to push through my vagina and had to have an emergency c-section."

"*Mom*! Good god, what are you trying to do? Traumatize me for life? I don't need to hear *again* how you couldn't push me through your...uh...I can't even say it."

"Vagina, dear. All women have one. I'm sure you've been up close and personal with several in your life."

"Mom!" He had to get out of his parents' house before he went crazy. This was *not* okay. "I told you I could do my own laundry," he finally muttered.

His mom chuckled. "Fine, fine. No more talk of womanly parts. But I think it's nice you're going to Sophie's funeral. I guess that means you got the job with Annie?"

"Yeah, I did."

"What are you going to do?"

"Start on the barn first. It looks like it could blow over any second. Hey, Mom, did you know Sophie named all of her animals after Disney cartoon characters?"

"I didn't know that but it doesn't surprise me. She was a character, that Sophie Cleaver."

"That's putting it mildly," he muttered.

"But her granddaughter...she's one of a kind. She is a great catch, if I do say so myself."

"Mom, I'm not going to this celebration or working for her to charm her into being my girlfriend. Besides, I'm sure me looking for a job was your idea. You just had Dad mention it so I wouldn't say you were nagging me."

"I have no clue what you're talking about," she replied.

"Whatever you say, Mom."

"I *might* have put a bug in his ear about a job, but him telling you to talk to Annie? That was *all* him."

"Stop playing matchmaker. I don't want or need a woman in my life."

"Oh, Honey. Don't you know not all women are like Jersey?"

"I told you to *never* say that name to me again," Wyatt snapped.

"I'm sorry. I didn't mean to upset you. I just want you to be happy."

Wyatt sighed. He knew his mom was just trying to help. But that name always sent a flame of anger through his body. "I didn't mean to snap."

"I know you didn't," she replied, patting his cheek. "That woman was a self-righteous, snobby bitch. I could see it the first time you introduced her to your dad and me. Even as a teenager, a smirk of superiority was always plastered on her face. She was probably a mean girl, too."

Wyatt tried not to grimace. His mom was right. She *was* a mean girl. But she hadn't always been. Jersey Hanover and Wyatt started kindergarten together when she was just a shy tomboy who refused to wear anything but Batman rain boots, shorts, and a Superman t-shirt with a cape attached. Fast forward ten years and that shy tomboy had morphed into the head cheerleader with legs that went on for days and size double D breasts. With the change, however, came a mean streak directed at anyone of the same sex who might threaten Jersey's reign as the queen of Parker High. Unfortunately, girls like Annabelle Cleaver, the ones who didn't have a name to hide behind, received the brunt of Jersey's meanness. The boys at school, however, vied for the attention of the beautiful girl.

Wyatt and Jersey had known each other their entire lives. She was the popular cheerleader; he was the star athlete. It made sense for them to be together. And they were. For six years. She even waited for him to return from every tour overseas. But when he came back with baggage and a massive scar on his face, she hit the road. Wyatt heard she was now a trophy wife for some plastic surgeon in L.A. since she couldn't make it as an actress. That was Jersey—always playing a part.

"I don't know how you didn't see how she was. Put some big boobs in front of a teenage boy's face and that's all he can see."

"Well, I sure as hell saw it the minute she walked out the door when she realized the scar on my face was a permanent feature."

"I always said you were too good for her. At least you realized it, too, before that huge ring you bought her bound you for life."

Wyatt sighed. "No doubt."

His mom tightened his tie and smiled. "Well, you better hurry if you want to make that life celebration. Knowing Sophie, I'm sure it will be interesting."

"I don't even know if I should go."

"Sure you should. You have to make a good impression on that new boss of yours," she said with a wink.

Wyatt sighed. It looked like he would be attending Sophie's life celebration after all. He rolled the sleeves of his button down shirt to his elbows and grabbed a pair of Sperry's out of his closet to wear. At least Sophie's funeral didn't require a suit and tie.

The thought of seeing Annabelle again put a pep in his step, which should probably bother him. Ever since Jersey had left town the second he came back from Afghanistan with a jagged scar running down his face, he hadn't looked at another woman. Hadn't wanted to. He knew what women wanted and they did not want a man with a jacked up face and a case of PTSD that only allowed him to sleep three hours solid on a good night. He should just call Annabelle up, tell her he found something else to do, and walk away. It would be best. Too bad his feet didn't agree, because they continued to walk down the stairs and head to the front door.

"You must be headed to Sophie's funeral." Wyatt's dad was sitting in the worn recliner his mom had bought him as a surprise on his fortieth birthday, a beer in one hand, the television remote in the other.

"Maybe. Why?"

"This is the only time I've ever seen you wear pink. Other than the vest and cummerbund you had to wear to match your date's dress for the senior prom."

At least his *dad* remembered not to say her name. "I figured if I'm going to work on Sophie's farm for her granddaughter, I should at least pay my respects."

"I think that's a good idea," his dad said, taking a swig of his beer. "When do you start?"

"Monday."

"Last weekend as a free man then."

"Yep. It's nothing but hard labor from here on out."

"I would say have fun, but since it's a fun—"

"Life celebration." Wyatt's mom came out of the kitchen, wiping her hands on her apron, the smell of apple pie wafting into the living room.

"Huh?" his dad said.

"Life celebration. That's what Sophie wanted it called. *Not* funeral."

"Why aren't you going, Mom?" Wyatt asked. At least she could keep him company.

"I have to watch Hattie. Your sister and Jacob are going on a date. Since it's one of the rare few since Hattie was born, I couldn't tell them no. You give my respects to Annie, though."

"I will."

Wyatt's dad held his beer up. "For me, too."

"Will do, Dad." Wyatt turned his eyes to the television on

the entertainment center in the corner of the room. His dad's favorite baseball team, the Texas Rangers, were playing the Seattle Mariners. "Are they winning?"

"Hell, no. I don't know why I cheer for these lousy suckers. They always let me down. I'd be better off cheering for the Cubs or Red Sox."

"You'd never stoop so low."

His dad chuckled. "You're right. Your granddaddy would roll over in his grave if he thought I was cheering for anyone other than the boys in red, white, and blue."

Wyatt gave a two-finger salute to his parents.

"Don't worry! We won't wait up!" his mom called.

Wyatt rolled his eyes. He didn't even bother answering. He headed out the door but before he could make it to his truck, he was nearly run over by a head of silky black curls.

"Uncle Wy! Uncle Wy! Where ya goin'?"

Wyatt smiled, picked his niece up, and threw her in the air. "Why you wanna know, Hattie Mae? You wanna go with me?"

"Nah," she said, pinching his cheeks. "Grammy's makin' me apple *pie*. And it's my most favoritest pie in the *world*! I even get to spend the night."

His niece held her hands up to his ear and whispered a secret. "Poppy said I could stay up as late as I want." She giggled. Her breath tickled his ear and filled his heart with love. He knew he was biased, but his niece was the cutest little kid in the world. And the smartest. "But you're *wearin'* my most favoritest color. Why you dressed all fancy, Uncle Wy?"

"I'm going to see someone, Miss Nosy Rosy Hattie Mae."

"And you gotta dress all *fancy*?" Hattie wrinkled her nose. "Is it a girl?"

"What makes you say that?"

"Mommy and Daddy like to dress fancy when they go

somewhere together. Look at 'em now." Hattie waggled her eyebrows. "Mommy's got a fancy dress on and Daddy *shaved*!"

Wyatt's baby sister walked up on the front porch. She was wearing a pretty green dress summer dress, the wind blowing her curly hair, identical to her daughter's, around her face. "I bet he's going to Miss Sophie's house, Hattie," she said. "See? He's wearing her favorite color."

"Miss *Sophie?*" she shrieked. "I *love* Miss Sophie."

Wyatt raised his eyebrows over his niece's head. "You know Miss Sophie, Hat? How?"

"She was a helper at my school! She'd play with us and dance with us and help us with our art stuff. I made a bunny out of sugar for Easter and Miss Sophie told me it was the best in the whole school!"

"Sophie volunteered at the pre-k center as a foster grand-parent. She was the volunteer in Hattie's room all last year. Hattie adored her."

"I thought Miss Sophie went to heaven? That's what Mommy told me," Hattie said, playing with Wyatt's tie. The smile dropped off her face. "I'll miss her. She was a good one."

"She did go to heaven. But I'm going to say goodbye to her."

"She talked about her granddaughter a lot. Said she was the smartest, prettiest girl she knew. 'Cept for me, of course."

"Well, of course! No one is as smart and pretty as you."

Hattie wrapped her arms around his neck and Wyatt inhaled deeply, breathing in the smell of strawberry shampoo and baby powder. "I love you, Uncle Wy."

"I love you, too, Hattie Mae."

"You sure look pretty. Pink was Miss Sophie's favorite color. Did you know that?"

"I did. That's why I'm wearing it."

"Will you do somethin' for me?"

"Absolutely."

"Will you give her granddaughter a big hug for me? Just so she knows I loved Miss Sophie, too?"

"Yeah, Wyatt. Why don't you give Annabelle a big hug from Hattie? To show her how much she loves her."

Wyatt glared at the smirk on his sister's face. It looked like Lucy and their mother had been scheming. "I'll give her a respectful handshake. How about that?"

"I think you haven't given a woman a good hug since *you know who* dropped you the minute she realized you weren't going to be her meal ticket out of this place."

"Who's you know who, Uncle Wy? 'Cuz I don't know *who*...well, 'cept for the Whos in Whoville."

"And those are the best Whos of all, Hattie Mae. Now, I gotta go." Wyatt put his niece down and she immediately ran into the house, asking his mom if the pie was ready.

"Why do you think it's okay to mention the bitch from hell around my niece?" he grumbled to his sister.

"Why do *you* think it is okay to swear off all women since one *was* the bitch from hell?" his sister spouted back, air-quoting the bitch from hell. "We're not all bad, big brother."

Wyatt pulled his sister in and rubbed his knuckles over her head. She squealed and tried to bat away his hand.

"Stop it!" she screeched. "You're messing up my hair!"

Wyatt stopped and then pulled her in for a hug. "Stop worrying about me, little sister."

"I'll stop worrying when you have a good girl making you meals and keeping you warm at night. Because *then* you'll be happy. You'd be surprised what a good girl can do."

"I need a lot more than a good woman to fix what's wrong with me," he said, giving her a sad smile. "Now, I really gotta go."

"I'm not going to quit trying to fix you, Wyatt James Holloway! Someone has to!"

Wyatt just shook his head and walked to his truck. He gave his sister's husband, Jacob, a finger wave.

"She's right, you know," Jacob said, rolling down their SUV's window. "She won't stop until you're happy with a gaggle of kids and a pretty wife on your arm."

"Not all of us are cut out for that kind of life, Jake," Wyatt replied.

"Don't knock it until you try it, man. Just look at my baby girl and tell me the nagging's not worth it."

Wyatt smiled a sad smile. "Oh, I totally know it's worth it. That's why I want to live vicariously through you. I'll get to spoil her, let her eat as much sugar as she wants, buy her a puppy and then send her home."

"I'm okay with the sugar. Just don't tell your sister. But the puppy...man, do me a solid and don't go there. I don't need something eating my shoe and waking me up with slobber on my face. Let me keep some of my dignity."

Wyatt laughed. "Okay, okay. No puppy."

"Thanks."

"Have fun taking out my sister, Jake."

"I always do."

Wyatt got in his truck and headed out to Annabelle's farm. His eyes widened in shock when he drove up Annie's driveway and saw how many cars were parked haphazardly on the grass. It looked like the entire town was here. He just hoped they were actually here to celebrate Sophie's life rather than gawk at what Wyatt knew was going to be eccentric at best.

CHAPTER 5

*A*nnie smiled sadly. Her granny's life celebration was going much better than expected. The outdoor string lights were casting a soft glow around the yard, highlighting the people standing all around. People were mingling on the front porch, eating the quiches, mini cheesecakes, and pink cookies. Some were already sharing memories of her granny, even though the official sharing wasn't going to begin for another ten minutes. As usual, her granny was right. This was celebrating her life, not mourning the loss of an amazing lady.

"Did you know *Wyatt Holloway* is here?" Annie's other best friend, Breckin, jumped on the porch, walked up to Annie, and whispered behind her hand. "Why is *he* here? He's the one who bashed Sophie's mailbox in high school. He didn't even *know* her!"

Despite all her daddy's efforts to mold Breckin into the son he never had, the first time Breckin had walked into Victoria's Secret had been the last nail in her not-so-boyish coffin. Breckin had a weakness for any undergarment made with lace, shoes of the high-heeled variety, and probably owned stock in Ulta. There was a girly-girl and then there was Breckin's version of *girly*. Annie was convinced her friend was overcompensating for all the lost years her dad made her wear jerseys of whatever sport was in season.

CC and Annie always teased Breckin that if Disney were ever hiring, she could get the job as Tinkerbell without even applying. She was petite and had such a youthful appearance she still got carded at the rated R movies. Even though she was five two on a good day, Breckin had all the sass and personality of a woman standing six feet tall. It was probably why Breckin had a penchant for shoes that made her at least three inches taller. Which, in her line of work as a school counselor, was an asset.

"He didn't do it, Breck," Annie tried not to roll her eyes. "And why are you whispering behind your hand? It's not like he's within hearing range."

"Actually, I am," Wyatt walked up the porch steps and leaned against the railing. "And to answer your question, Breckin Rose Henderson, I came to pay my respects. And despite what Sophie thought, I did *not* bash in her mailbox. I'd never even been here before except for a few days ago."

Breckin turned to Annie. "He's been here before?"

"*And* I'm still here," he said with a grin.

Annie was trying her best not to glance his way. She did, in fact, know Wyatt was here. Had known he was here the moment he stepped out of his truck. The pull to him was like a magnet. She could have sworn she felt the hair stand up on her arms as soon as he walked across her lawn. The pink he wore only made the green of his eyes stand out even more and the rolled sleeves of his shirt emphasized his muscled forearms. *Gah!* How in the hell were *forearms* sexy? She *definitely* needed to send him on his way Monday morning because him working on her farm was *not* a good idea.

"He has," she said, not offering any more information. She

did not intend to add fuel to the already hot fire her friend was building. "Wanna ask him how he knew your middle name, Breck? Isn't that more important than whether or not he's been to my house? It's kinda a stalkerish thing to know, if you ask me."

Breckin turned back to Wyatt and leveled him with a glare. "How *did* you know my middle name, Wyatt Holloway? Hmmmm?"

"Anyone whose middle name is Rose after the great Pete Rose is a win in my book. I still think he needs to be in the Hall of Fame. Besides, I make it my job to know pretty girls' middle names. I learned yours when your dad hollered at you in Swanson's Market in fifth grade when he thought you were lost. I never forget middle names. It's kinda my thing. In fact, I happen to know Annabelle's middle name is Clara D—"

Annabelle refrained from covering his mouth with her hand. "My friend already knows my middle *names*, Wyatt *James*," she said. "Now, why are you here?"

"I came to pay my respects to my future boss."

Her friend whirled around to face her. "What does he mean, future boss?"

"Nothing," Annabelle muttered. "I need to go make sure none of the balloons have flown off. Sophie had strict instructions not to release the balloons until ten p.m. sharp."

With that, Annie turned and stomped down the porch steps. To her extreme annoyance, Wyatt followed her. "Why are you following me?"

"To help you check on your balloons, of course."

"I don't need your help checking the damn balloons."

"Well, what if one of them did get loose and caught in a tree? You're tall, but I'm taller. I can probably reach them without trying. Besides, I wouldn't want you to ruin your pretty dress."

At his words, Annie locked eyes with him and could feel her face turning red. He was looking at her with heat in his eyes. Like he wanted to get her *out* of her dress more than he liked seeing her in it. This was not good. "Fine," she huffed, turning and walking away. "You can help check the balloons."

Annie walked toward the magnolia tree in the middle of the yard, where the balloons were tied onto the lowest branch and looked up. To her relief none of the balloons had floated away.

"Guess I don't have to be a hero and climb the tree after all," he said, standing beside her.

Their arms touched and a tingle ran up Annie's. Damn him. He was doing it on purpose. Annie put a step of space between them. "Looks like it."

"Did I tell you how much I like the music you're playing? Can't go wrong with the Eagles and Aerosmith."

"Sophie put it in her will those were the songs that had to play on repeat the entire time," she muttered. "I don't think I'm ever going to listen to them again."

Wyatt chuckled. "You did a good job. Your granny would be proud."

"I don't think you should come Monday," she blurted. Good lord, she was pathetic. One look at his *forearms* and she couldn't think about anything but what his *other* muscles would look like. Completely naked.

"What? Why?"

"I just don't think it's a good idea. I really don't need that much help."

"Well, too bad."

"What?"

"We shook on it. And I never go back on my handshakes. What kind of man does something like that?"

"A man who was just told his help was not wanted."

"Sorry. Not listening."

Annie rolled her eyes and refrained from stomping her foot. "Fine. Have it your way. I'll work you so hard you won't be able to walk the next day, much less do manual labor."

"Challenge accepted. The questions is—doing what? Manual labor or something else? Because that sentence…well—"

"Well what?"

"It *kinda* had a sexual connotation. Have you been thinking about me, ACDC?"

Of all the nerve. "I told you not to call me that!"

"It's okay. Your secret is still safe. No one heard me."

"I'm going to start the memories now. I don't have time for your ignorant sentence that held no bit of truth in it."

Liar, her inner-self professed. If the majority of the entire town weren't here, she'd probably be popping the buttons off Wyatt's shirt to get another look at his delicious abs.

"Memories?"

"Granny wanted everyone to gather around the picture of her where she's young and just won a dance competition with hunky soldier."

"I saw that picture. You look like her."

"You think?"

"I do. She sure was pretty."

"Is that your way of paying me a compliment, Wyatt Holloway?"

"Maybe so, Annabelle Cleaver."

Annie walked off before he could see her smile. She did not need to be charmed by this man. Annie stepped onto the porch and hit pause on her phone, silencing the music playing from the speakers.

"Excuse me, everyone," she said. "Can I have your attention?"

At her words, the people mingling in her yard stopped what they were doing and looked at her. "If you'd all head

61

over to the picture of my granny when she was a looker, we can start sharing her memories, spreading her ashes, and shooting the whiskey. Those are her words, not mine."

Everyone laughed softly and did as she requested. Once everyone was seated in the chairs in the lawn, Annie stood by the picture she had blown up and printed on a two feet by six feet canvas, an actual life-sized picture of her granny and her partner. Taking a deep breath, she began speaking.

"One of my favorite memories of my granny was the day we first met. Not the days I would see her across the aisle at Swanson's Market or we'd accidentally run into each other walking down the street. It was the day my caseworker dropped me off at this very door when my mom decided she didn't want me anymore."

Annie paused and drew a deep breath, willing the tears not to come.

"The door wasn't pink then. In fact, I think it was some shade of putrid yellow-greenish. Granny walked out on that very porch where I was just standing, her hair in a long braid down her back, dressed in a hot pink and turquoise muumuu and hot pink cowgirl boots, hands on her hips. 'Well, girly,' she said to me, 'I guess I need to paint the front door a color that doesn't resemble baby poo green now that I have a kid living with me again.' When I began to cry, she looked down at me and said, 'Now, li'l bit. You're not with your crazy momma anymore, thank the heavens. You're with your crazy *granny* now, and we don't cry. We paint our doors hot pink instead.' Then she lifted me up in a bear hug, walked me to the kitchen, and made me a peanut butter and jelly sandwich. That was the day I knew I was going to be okay."

Annie wiped her eyes, knowing her granny wouldn't want her crying today. It was a life *celebration*, dammit. She refused to shed any tears. Taking another breath, Annie continued. "My granny, while eccentric, was the best lady

I've ever known. She'd give you the shirt off her back. She'd take in anyone who needed help. It didn't matter if it were a stray dog or human being who'd lost their way. She was good and kind and everything I hope to be when I'm ninety-one. I probably just won't threaten to curse someone with voodoo if I think they bashed in my mailbox."

Annie walked to the table beside the picture and scooped some of her granny's ashes out of her hot pink urn. "I'm going to spread these under the magnolia tree. It was her favorite tree because my granddad planted it for her on their fifth wedding anniversary. He told her the fifth year present had to be something made of wood and he couldn't think of anything better made of wood than an actual tree."

Annie spread her scoop of ashes around the trunk and then walked back to the table. Setting the scooper by the urn, she took a mini bottle of the fireball whiskey, popped its top, and shot its contents. The whiskey, her granny's favorite, slid down her throat, leaving a trail of cinnamon in its wake. She slammed the bottle on the table. "Now, who wants to go next?"

WYATT SAT in the back row of chairs, listening as Annie shared her memories of her granny. He knew he should be paying closer attention to the actual celebration, but he couldn't seem to tear his eyes away from his boss. She was a vision in hot pink, paying tribute by wearing a shade of her granny's favorite color. A shade that was almost identical to her front door. She had paired the dress with a pair of fancy gold shoes that made her legs look longer than what should be legal. Her hair was falling in soft waves down her back, the mint green tips brushing her shoulder blades. The rest of the gold accessories she wore to match her shoes only made the summer tan on her skin glow even more. She was breathtaking.

What surprised Wyatt was the amount of people who were at the celebration, sharing their memories of Sophie Cleaver. Jenny Everett, one of the pre-k teachers at Parker Elementary, was currently telling how amazing Sophie was with all the children in her class.

"I always told Sophie she should've been a teacher herself. I've never seen someone love children so much. She would play with them, sing with them. She'd even clean their scrapes with hydrogen peroxide and entertain them with such funny stories while she was doing it the children wouldn't even cry. She was one of a kind and will be greatly missed. But she's definitely going out with a bang."

"Sophie Cleaver kept me in business all by herself buying feed for all the animals of her own as well as the ones she took in," Baker Hughes, owner of Jesse's Feed and Grain, said. "People knew her house was the place to drop off unwanted animals because she would always take them. I've seen her nurse dogs back to health even a no kill shelter would think about putting down they were in such bad shape. When Aladdin was dropped off, his back legs were paralyzed. I don't even know how he got down her driveway to the house. But he did and Sophie made him his own little wheelchair of sorts so he could run around with the other dogs. I swear, that dog probably lived for twenty years. And I know it was because of the love that woman had for him."

Annabelle's friends, Breckin and Colleen, both shared memories about practically growing up in Sophie's house.

"One night, she caught us talking about a boy being mean to us," Breckin said with a laugh. "We were in eighth grade and heartbroken because he was the cutest boy in school. Sophie gave us a voodoo doll, had us take it to school, and hide it in his locker. She told us the next time something bad happened to him, sing the chant she made up for us and tell him to look in his locker for the source of his misfortune."

Colleen and Annabelle died laughing when Breckin began the story. "We did exactly what she said. When we saw him trip over a broom in the cafeteria during lunch," Breckin continued, "We walked over to his table, got in a circle around him, sang the chant, and told him to search his locker. He never bothered us again. I remember telling her what happened. 'Voodoo is nothing but making another person think you have a hold on them,' she said. 'But you're really not holding anything but all the cards because they're stupid enough to believe in that shit. I buy my dolls online.' That was Sophie. Eccentric, loving, and not afraid to put the fear of God into people if it meant protecting people she loved."

Person after person stood by the picture and shared a story about Sophie. She made them laugh and believe in themselves. She taught them about life and what it meant to be your own person in a world full of people trying to copy others. They talked about her quirkiness and how endearing it made her. They would then spread a scoop of her ashes, many of them following Annabelle's lead and spreading them under the magnolia tree Sophie loved. They'd take a shot of whiskey, some even pulling out the voodoo dolls Sophie had given them to ward off mean people. Some even said they were the recipients of the voodoo dolls and Sophie would then talk to them after she had scared them shitless.

"Sophie was strange. Sophie was quirky and unpredictable. But one thing you could never say about Sophie was she didn't live life to the fullest." Sadie, the owner of the café in town, said. "She was my friend and she will be missed."

Wyatt was speechless. The only dealings he had with Sophie was when she accused him of bashing in her mailbox all those years ago. But the descriptions of Sophie by everyone attending the celebration painted a picture of a kind, loving, independent woman who didn't take any shit off anybody and was comfortable in her own quirky skin. Wyatt would have loved to meet *that* woman.

"If that is everyone who wants to say something," Annabelle said, standing and talking one last time," I'll wrap it up by saying thank you to you all. My granny would be so happy all of you are here, celebrating the life of an amazing person."

"I'd like to say something." He felt the words spill out of his mouth. What the *hell?* He didn't do public speaking. But as all heads turned his way, he knew this was something he couldn't take back. Like it or not, he'd opened his big, fat mouth. Now he just had to think of something to say.

Wyatt rose from his chair and walked to the table where Sophie's urn still sat. Taking a deep breath, Wyatt turned and face the sea of faces staring right at him. "I don't know the Sophie all of you have been talking about," he started. "But I wish I had. She sounds like an amazing lady. I guess I was one of the ones to believe in the stupid voodoo shit, because I fell for it hook, line, and sinker."

The people listening to him laughed. "She had me scared for my life, but it's nice to know she bought her dolls online and there wasn't a bit of truth to what she said to me. I can rest easy now knowing Sophie and her voodoo doll in my likeness won't haunt me from the...well, I would say grave, but I guess a more appropriate term would be from the ashes."

Wyatt turned his face toward the sky. "Sophie, if you're listening, I just want to say for the last time I was *not* the person who bashed in your mailbox."

At his final words, Wyatt walked over to the table, took a scoop of her ashes, and headed to the pink crepe myrtles in front of the picture windows. "I'm spreading her ashes here because, as we all know, pink was her favorite color. I can't spread them by the Sexy Pink Elephant front door, so I figure this is the next best thing."

Wyatt poured the ashes on the ground and then took a mini bottle of whiskey. "Here's to you, Sophie Cleaver," he said, shooting the contents of the bottle. "May we all live up to your example."

CHAPTER 6

"*I* can't believe Wyatt actually stood up and spoke at your granny's funeral."

CC, Breckin, and Annie were sprawled across various couches and chairs in Annie's living room.

"Life celebration," Annie said to CC, who had uttered the words. "It wasn't a funeral."

"*Still,*" CC continued as Nemo walked over and plopped his head in her lap. She scratched the top of the big dog's head, eliciting a happy woof in response. "Why did he even *come?*"

"I'll tell you why he came!" Breckin jumped out of Granny's favorite bright purple microfiber recliner.

Granny bought the chair two years ago for twenty-five dollars from Trixie Hartwell at the city wide garage sale held every spring. It leaned to the right and had a burn hole on the left arm. Trixie had fallen asleep with a cigarette in her mouth and when she started to snore, the cigarette fell out and landed on the arm of the chair. Granny had haggled Trixie down from the original fifty dollar asking price, claiming no one in their right mind would buy a chair that smelled like the Marlboro man.

Her granny had proudly brought the recliner home and mixed up one of her home remedy concoctions. If she didn't know, Annie would have never guessed the chair came from a chain smoker's home. After her granny had finished with it, the only thing it smelled like was Gain laundry detergent. Granny had even crocheted a colorful doily to cover the arm with the cigarette burn. The only thing her granny couldn't do was fix the lean. Guess that's the price you paid when you bought a recliner from a woman who weighed three hundred pounds.

Breckin stood in front of the fireplace, hands on her hips and frown on her face. "She—" Breckin said, pointing to Annie, who was sprawled out on the straight-out-of-the-eighties black couch printed with lilac orchids, "*Hired* him!"

CC turned to face Annie. "You *hired* him? What does that even mean?"

"Why do I feel like I'm on trial?" Annie complained. "I feel like the prosecutor just raked me over the coals!"

"See how she's deflecting, Cees? She's totally avoiding the question."

Annie took a leftover quiche off the plate in front of her and threw it at her friend. Instead of hitting Breckin, however, it flew to her right and hit Sebastian on top of the head. Bass yowled before realizing it was food. He quickly picked the quiche off the ground and took off toward his cat tree in the dining room, Nemo following close behind.

"I'm not deflecting! I just feel like you're judging me," Annie huffed.

"Do we have a *reason* to judge you?" CC asked.

"No!" Annie said at the exact same time Breckin said, "Yes!"

"He came to the funeral—"

"Life Celebration!"

"Fine. He came to the *life celebration,* walked up those porch steps, wooed our friend, and then *helped—*" Breckin finger-quoted the word, "Annie make sure Sophie's balloons hadn't flown away. The balloons that were *tied* to a branch in the magnolia tree."

"I *knew* you had a thing for Wyatt Holloway!" CC said with a grin. "When did he come and ask you for the job?"

"I don't remember."

"Liar!"

"Fine! It was like…I don't know…five or so days ago," Annie muttered.

"Five days!" Breckin squealed. "Why didn't you tell us?"

"Oh, I don't know," Annie said sarcastically. "Maybe because I knew you'd both act like *this?*"

It was CC's turn to gripe at her. "This morning, when we were talking about Wyatt, you didn't tell me you offered him a *job!*"

"That's because you didn't ask."

"Because I didn't *know* to ask. How the hell should I know the topic of conversation should have been—'Hey, Annie? You know the guy you had the hots for in high school who is now a wounded vet? You should totally offer him a job.'"

Annie tried to change the subject. "What happened to his face? That scar was *definitely* not there when he walked off the graduation stage."

CC's eyes grew sad. "You know he enlisted his senior year, right?"

Annie nodded.

"Well, he did three tours in Afghanistan. The last tour, he and his platoon were given orders to a town where possible Al Qaeda members were holing up. Right before they got to the town, their truck ran over a land mine. The tip they had gotten was a set up. The mine exploded. Several members of his platoon were thrown out of the truck and killed instantly. Some had limbs ripped off their bodies. One guy was burned over seventy-five percent of his."

"That's so sad," Breckin said softly.

"Wyatt's mom told my mom some of the shrapnel from the truck sliced open his face to the bone but Wyatt still managed to tie off a tourniquet around one of his platoon member's legs, even with his face gushing blood. Everyone said he saved that guy's life. By the time the guys who were still alive got to safety, Wyatt's face had ripped apart so much there was no way he *couldn't* have a scar. They said it was a miracle he didn't lose his eyesight. I heard plastic surgeons have offered free surgeries to try and diminish the scar but Wyatt won't let them."

"I wonder why not?" Breckin asked.

"I heard he said it served as a reminder he got out when way too many guys didn't."

Annie took a deep breath. Because that story did nothing but weaken her resolve to send him packing when he knocked on her door Monday morning.

"I'll tell you one thing," CC said.

"What's that?"

"That scar has done nothing to diminish his looks. Because that man is still *fine*. In fact, I dare say, after knowing his story, it makes him *more* attractive. Wouldn't you agree?"

"I know *I* would," Breckin said.

Annie wasn't even going to walk into that trap.

"But you still haven't explained how you decided to offer him a job. And we're not going until you tell us."

Annie rolled her eyes and let out a sigh. Her friends were not going to let this one slide. "He came by one day and asked if I needed help around the farm. His dad told him I was trying to manage it on my own. I was going to say no, but…"

"But what?" Breckin asked.

"But he looked sad. And he made me laugh. And I saw his abs...and I said yes." Annie covered her face with her hands.

"You saw his abs?" Breckin asked.

"Yes."

CC walked over and pulled Annie's hands away from her face. "Well? How were they?"

Annie could feel her face turning red. "Totally lick worthy."

CC smiled slyly and nodded her head. "I knew you were always staring at his ass in those football pants. So you didn't tell us about the job. Now, you have to swear to tell us as soon as you guys have sex. Deal?"

"We're not going to have sex."

Breckin rolled her eyes. "Yeah, right."

"What? We're not!"

"Says the woman who just uttered his abs were lick worthy."

"Can we change the subject now? I'm tired of talking about Wyatt Holloway," Annie grumbled. Even though she totally wasn't tired of Wyatt Holloway himself. Talking about him with her friends? Probably. Thinking about those abs and forearms? Definitely not. "How do you think Granny's celebration went? Do you think she'll be dancing in heaven or flipping me the bird?"

Breckin flopped down on the couch next to Annie and gave her a hug. "She's totally dancing."

Annie smiled. "I think so, too."

"You gotta admit, Ann," CC said. "It was a pretty bad ass funeral your granny planned for herself."

"Life—" Annie started to correct but gave up. Screw it. "You're right. It was one bad ass funeral."

"So, what now?" Breckin was running her fingers through Annie's hair. Annie groaned in pleasure.

"I don't know."

"Well, you do know one thing," CC said.

"What?"

"You know Wyatt Holloway is going to come knocking on your door Monday morning. The question is—do you know what you're going to do with him?"

Annie closed her eyes and sighed. Because she had no freaking clue.

"I THINK I'VE GOT A BITE."

Wyatt and his friend, Griffin Stephens, were sitting in Griff's bass boat in their favorite little cove on Parker Lake. It was the fishing hole they'd been coming to since they were twelve years old. After Sophie's life celebration, Wyatt couldn't sleep. Every time he dozed off he'd start thinking of how Annabelle looked in the dress she had worn. The pink hue had complemented her tan skin and hazel eyes. She had left her hair down, letting it fall in soft waves to the middle of her back. He even noticed her favorite color, mint green, tinting the tips, a fact he hadn't noticed when it was pulled up on top of her head.

After tossing and turning for hours, he finally realized sleep was going to elude him yet again and decided to give up the fight. So Wyatt had snuck down the stairs like he had done more times than he could count during his high school years, hopped in his truck, and headed to Griff's Bar.

Griffin was named after his maternal grandpa, Griffin Vanderburg, who built and opened Griff's Bar in 1952. The bar had been the exact same ever since Wyatt was allowed to enter its doors when he turned ten years old and was going to Griff's home, an apartment over the bar, for a sleepover. Same wood-paneled walls by the booths. Same mirrored wall behind the bar.

It was probably even the exact same pool table in the back. The only thing not in its original state was the jukebox. Wyatt knew because he was the one who had drank a bit *too* much stolen birthday tequila when he turned sixteen and crashed into the first edition jukebox in a drunken stupor. Grandpa Griffin was so mad he made Wyatt bus tables in the bar until he had paid for a brand new jukebox, which was what now stood in the corner.

When his grandpa had passed away three years ago and Griffin's mom lost her leg to diabetes, Griffin had left the bar he was tending in Oklahoma City to come home and run Griff's. Wyatt thought Griff would have done something to update the interior but it still remained the exact same as it was when they were growing up.

When Wyatt pulled up to the bar, Griffin was locking up and getting on his Harley to ride home. But at the mention of fishing in the wee hours of the morning, Griff had easily agreed. That was Griff. He was always willing to offer a helping hand to a friend. And fishing at three o'clock in the morning was definitely considered a helping hand.

"Are you sure?" Wyatt asked. He and Griff had zilch in the way of bites since they'd dropped the boat in the water.

"I have to be sure. We've been out here for two hours and haven't had any luck. You'd think the fishing gods would have mercy on us suckers stupid enough to come fishing at three o'clock in the morning."

"Thanks for coming with me, Griff," Wyatt said.

"Trouble sleeping still?"

Griff was one of the few people who knew about Wyatt's night terrors. He was the guy Wyatt had shared his first beer with. The friend he had told the first time he had made out with Jersey under the football bleachers when they were in eighth grade. Griff was Wyatt's go-to guy. It made sense to tell him about the nightmares. He knew Griff would keep his secret safe. And weird as it sounded, it helped that someone other than his parents and therapist knew. It made him feel he wasn't all that crazy.

"Yeah. Only this time, it wasn't from any nightmare."

"Then what was it?"

"Annabelle Cleaver."

Griff laughed and let out a whistle. "That woman *would* keep a man up at night. Those legs…"

Wyatt frowned. He didn't like his friend talking about her. Then he rolled his eyes at the absurdity of his jealousy over a woman who would become his official employer in two days. He was such an ass.

"When did you see her?" Griff asked. "I didn't think you guys ran in the same circle. Or even had a full conversation with each other."

"We hadn't. Dad suggested I find a job to keep me busy and—"

"Man, you really pissed him off reorganizing his garage, didn't you?"

Wyatt chuckled. "I guess so. Actually, if you want to know the truth, I think it was my mom and sister trying to scheme to get me a date."

Griff laughed. "Why doesn't that surprise me?"

"Yeah. Apparently, I've become that pathetic."

"So, did you ask her out?"

"Nope. I asked her for a job instead."

"And what did Miss Annabelle Cleaver say to that?"

"Well, after I rubbed dirt off her face with my shirt like I do my five-year-old niece, she said hell no."

Griff snorted. "What the hell? You didn't."

Wyatt sighed. "No wonder we can't catch a fish. You and your damn laugh have probably scared them all up to Harper's Marina."

"Stop changing the subject. Why in the hell did you wipe her face *with your shirt* like she was a little kid?"

"I don't know! She had dirt on her face. And it was mingling with the sweat and I had just seen her in a skimpy yellow bikini top and Daisy Dukes. I wasn't thinking."

"Obviously. But I probably wouldn't have been, either, if I had seen those legs in a pair of Daisy Dukes."

"It was a sight for sore eyes, I'll tell you that much."

"So you were thinking with your pecker instead of your head."

"If I were thinking with my pecker I would have kissed her instead of wiping her damn face with my shirt."

Griff laughed. "I'm guessing she didn't give you the job."

"No, she did. It took some finagling on my part, but I'm supposed to start Monday morning. But she's already trying to change her mind."

"I'm surprised you haven't changed your mind after embarrassing yourself like you did."

Wyatt flipped his friend the bird. "Shut the hell up."

"So you finally got her to say yes, even after you acted like an idiot. Now she's saying she doesn't want you to come. Why? And when did you even get a chance to see her again?"

"She told me it wasn't a good idea last night when I went to Sophie's life celebration."

"Dear lord! Why did you go to *that* circus? She was the crazy old bat who thought we bashed in her mailbox!"

"Yep. I told Annabelle we didn't do it."

"Did she believe you?"

"I think that might have been why she hired me."

"How was the funeral?"

"Life celebration."

"Potato. Puh-tah-toe. Dead is dead, man."

"It was interesting."

"I bet."

"And actually kind of nice, if I do say so myself."

"Really?"

"Yeah. Sophie really did make it a celebration of her life. Everyone had a chance to tell their favorite memory of Sophie at the end before spreading a scoop of her ashes and drinking a shot of fireball whiskey."

"That's so weird."

"I even said something."

Griff about choked on the water he was drinking. "What did you say?"

"I can't really remember. Something about it being obvious she had a lot of people who loved her. *And* I looked up at heaven and told Sophie we didn't bash in her mailbox."

"You are such a dumb ass."

Wyatt ignored his friend's barb. "It felt good, talking about her nicely. Especially when I heard what everyone else was saying."

"When did she tell you she didn't want you to come on Monday?"

"I got her to talk to me on her porch. I had to follow her around like a creeper in order to finally get her to."

"Well, what changed her mind?"

"I have no clue. She avoided me like the plague, and when she finally did talk, all she did was get mad and said Monday wasn't a good idea."

Griff whistled. "Have you been so far out of the dating game you don't realize what that means?"

"I guess so. Because I have no clue why she turned a complete one-eighty and decided she didn't need help after all."

"She's got the hots for you, man."

Wyatt snorted. "She does not."

"Does too. Think about it. You wipe her face like an idiot,

she still says yes. Then, the next time she sees you, she tells you it isn't a good idea."

"And your point being?"

"She probably started thinking about all your chiseled army muscles and it got her all hot and bothered."

Wyatt rolled his eyes. "That's the dumbest thing I've ever heard."

"No, it isn't. She probably saw your sixteen pack under that shirt of yours when you wiped her face and it left her wanting more. Then she got to thinkin' about you working on her farm without a shirt on and started freaking out about not being able to control herself."

"Where do you come *up* with this shit?"

"I'm a bartender. People like to tell me their problems by default. You get a little too much alcohol in them and some people like to tell you *way* more than you want to hear. I've talked to a fair share of drunk, pining women more times than I'd like to count. Trust me, she wants a piece of army man Wyatt Holloway."

Wyatt didn't argue anymore. It was pointless to tell his friend that no woman would want a man with a scarred face who suffered from PTSD. As his therapist always liked to tell him, that kind of thinking was counterproductive to his progress.

All of a sudden, Wyatt felt a tug on his line. "I really do think I've got one," he told Griff.

"Well, what are you waiting for? Reel 'er in. If we stay out here after the sun comes up, we might have enough to have ourselves a fish fry tonight to celebrate your new employment. Sound like a plan?"

Wyatt grinned. "Sounds like a plan."

CHAPTER 7

"Well, here goes nothing." Wyatt was again standing in front of the mirror in his bedroom. Instead of a pink outfit for a life celebration, however, he was dressed for a day on the farm. A pair of Wranglers, a plaid, pearl snap, short-sleeved shirt, and his favorite pair of Ariat farm boots.

As always, Wyatt was up before the sun. Only this time he actually had a reason to be up early. He followed the smell of coffee downstairs to find his mother at the stove cooking bacon and eggs.

"Whatcha doin', Mom?" he asked as two slices of toast popped out of the toaster.

"Cooking you breakfast before your big day."

Wyatt rolled his eyes. "Mom, I'm not a kid. I'm a grown man."

His mom turned toward him, spatula in hand. "Tell me what you were going to eat for breakfast, Wyatt James. If you tell me you were going to make yourself a healthy breakfast, which *is* the most important meal of the day, then I'll eat this plate of eggs, bacon, and toast myself."

Wyatt couldn't say anything. His plan for breakfast was grabbing a bag of Cheetos out of the snack basket on the counter as he was heading out the door.

"That's what I thought," she said, a smug smile on her face. "Remember, moms always know best."

"I'll keep that in mind," he said, snagging a piece of toast and slathering it with butter from the tub sitting on the counter.

"So, what do you plan on doing at Sophie's farm, hon?"

"I don't really know. I guess whatever Annabelle wants me to do. Although she might kick me out before I even get to do anything."

"Why would she do that?"

"Because she's already told me she doesn't need my help."

His mom chuckled. "Maybe she's just playing hard to get."

"Or maybe she really doesn't want me out there."

"Well, you'll never know until you actually get in your truck and drive over there."

"Not before I get a healthy breakfast. A wise, old woman once told me it was the most important meal of the day."

"Smart ass."

Wyatt grinned. No matter how much he complained about living with his parents, they were pretty great. Wyatt never had the need to get his own place. When he graduated from high school, he was sent to boot camp and then immediately overseas. He'd come back between tours but never long enough to warrant finding his own place. It would've just sat empty while he was defending the land of the free. But now that he was back home for good, he needed to get a place of his own. Twenty-nine years old and still living with his parents wasn't cutting it anymore.

Wyatt swiped the last bit of egg yolk off his plate with his toast and stuffed it in his mouth. Moving out was inevitable, but he was going to miss the way his mom made a perfect sunny side up egg. Taking his coffee mug to the counter, he reached into the top cabinet and pulled out his Yeti coffee mug and dumped the remainder of his coffee into it, then topped it off with more coffee from the pot.

"I don't know how you drink it black like that," his mom said with a grimace. "You're probably killing the lining of your stomach one sip at a time."

Wyatt kissed his mom on the cheek. "I didn't have all that fancy shit overseas, Mom. I'm used to it black and bitter."

She rolled her eyes. "You better get moving. You don't want to be late on your first day."

"It's not a desk job. I didn't even tell her what time I was coming."

"Well, you better hurry anyway, just in case she changes her mind for good."

Wyatt saluted his mom and started to head outside. "Hey, Mom?" he called, grabbing his truck keys off the hook by the front door.

"Yeah?" she replied, sticking her head around the corner, spatula in hand.

"Does Aunt Nancy still own Parker Lake Realty?"

"Yes. Why?"

"It's time I got my own place."

"Wyatt *James*—"

"Beverly *Mae*," he mimicked and chuckled when his mom stuck her tongue out at him. "Seriously, Mom. I'm twenty-nine. I've never gotten a place of my own because I haven't needed one. I was never home long enough to warrant buying or renting. But now that I'm home for good, it's time I started looking."

"Son, you've only been home for—"

"Three months. I've been home for three months."

"Still, your therapist said it was good for you to—"

"Have people make sure I'm okay. I know, Mom. I've been to all my sessions, too."

Wyatt's therapist was in Lakeview and had even seen his parents a few times with Wyatt in a family session. Dr. Wilkerson had said it was so they could better understand a little of what Wyatt went through on a daily basis and how his parents could help him. It actually helped a lot, having a neutral third party able to help express what he couldn't do by himself. It had made them closer as a family, but it had also elevated his mother's mother hen status from new-to-the-block-and-clueless chicken to I've-hatched-a-million-eggs-and-know-what's-best chicken.

"Besides," he said, ignoring her pointed look, "I thought you wanted me to settle down and give you more grandbabies. How am I going to do that if I'm still living with you? I'm not bringing a girl *here*."

"Why not? It's not like I didn't know Jersey snuck in your window a time or two in high school. One time wearing a very memorable outfit, if I remember correctly."

Wyatt felt his face turning red. "What?" he sputtered. "I have no clue what you are talking about."

Wyatt was lying out his ass, because he remembered what his mom was talking about like it was yesterday. After watching *Varsity Blues* one weekend during their junior year, Jersey had gotten the idea to sneak into Wyatt's bedroom window in the middle of the night wearing nothing but her birthday suit. When she got in the window, she pulled a Darcy and made herself a whip cream bikini.

Wyatt was a hormonal teenage boy and his girlfriend had double D's and legs that looked really good in a cheerleading suit. Even so, he knew his limits, and having sex with his girlfriend while his parents slept in the room two doors away was not happening. But he didn't have the willpower to push her back out the window and send her on her merry way. He might have taken a taste…or two…or three…before throwing one of his t-shirts over her head and telling her he would see her the next day. Hell, as a teenage boy, that was being downright chivalrous. He just never realized his mom *knew*.

His mom slapped him gently on his cheek. "Don't lie to your mother, dear. I can detect a lie a mile away."

"Why didn't you say anything if you knew?"

"Because I knew you would do the right thing."

"I was a horny teenage boy. How the hell did you know *that*? Because looking back on it now, as a parent I sure wouldn't have trusted younger me."

His mom's eyes softened. "You were a good kid, Wy. You were never disrespectful toward me, your father, your sister, *or* your girlfriend. You had a good head on your shoulders. Still do. Besides, if I had said something, it would have only made things worse with the little hussy. She had her talons in you pretty deep."

Wyatt chuckled. "You really didn't like her at all, did you?"

"Nope. But if I had told you that it would have only made her try to manipulate you even more than she already was. You were a smart kid. I knew you would figure it out eventually."

"I don't know, Mom. If my jacked up face hadn't scared her away, I might have still married her."

His mom pulled him in for a hug. "Then I'm glad you have that scar, Wyatt James. Because without it, she'd still be part of your life. And you are so much better than she ever will be."

Wyatt kissed her on top of the head. "I love you, Mom."

"I love you too, kid."

"I'm still getting my own place."

"Fine," his mom huffed. "Just promise you'll have a nice girl crawl through your bedroom window this time."

Wyatt shook his head. "Not having that conversation with you, Mom. I'm late for work."

"Now *that's* a girl I'd be perfectly fine crawling through your window," she called to his retreating back.

"Bye, Mom!" he said, ignoring her innuendo. Hell, he didn't want Annabelle Cleaver to crawl through his window. He just wanted her to let him *through* her door.

ANNABELLE WAS SPRAWLED out on her stomach in the middle of the bed. She groaned when she felt what could only be the paws of her granny's cat walking his way up her right leg before making himself at home right in the middle of her back.

"Go ahead and make yourself at home, Bass," she muttered into her pillow. "It's not like I was sleeping or anything."

As if he understood exactly what she said, Sebastian spun in a circle like a dog before curling up right in the small of her back, his body rumbling with purrs.

"Seriously?" she said. "You are ridiculous."

Annie stuck her tongue out at the cat before rolling her eyes at the absurdity of it. She needed a life.

Now that her granny's ashes were successfully spread across the farm and Annie was officially alone, she needed to figure out what to do with herself. When she graduated from high school, it was her intention to go to the community college in Lakeview to get her basics out of the way before transferring to Oklahoma State University and majoring in Veterinary Medicine. She had no interest in animals before living with her granny. Her parents sure as hell didn't offer any animal as a pet, which actually made Annie happy because she knew how a pet in that home would have been treated. But when she moved to the farm, her granny instilled a love of all animals, both big and small, in Annie. The longer she lived there, the more it grew. Now Annie was afraid she was going to become not just the crazy cat lady, but crazy animal lady following in her crazy granny's foot-steps. Annie, however, drew the line at muumuus. That was something she would never wear.

When Granny got pneumonia, all of Annie's plans for the future were put on hold. Ten-year-old Annie needed her granny and Sophie stepped up and took on the role of both mom and dad. When Sophie was admitted to the hospital, twenty-year-old Annie had no qualms returning the favor. That's what family did. The day CC called her with the news, Annie withdrew from her classes and returned home. Her granny pitched a fit and called Annie all kinds of stupid, but Annie wouldn't budge. She told her granny once she got back on her feet, she would go back to school.

She had every intention of doing just that. Annie was three credits shy of receiving her associate's degree and knew her grades were good enough to get accepted into OSU's vet program. She had even gotten her letter of accep-tance. But then Maleficent broke her leg and Annie had to put her down. Parker Lake and the creek flooded one spring, leaving Annie to clean up the aftermath. It seemed like one thing after another after another happened and Annie just kept staying. She picked up a part-time job at Sadie's Café waiting tables and helped her granny on the farm. That was her life and she was content living it. Eventually, her granny quit griping at her to go back to school and was just happy to have Annie's company.

But now that her granny had passed and she was alone, Annie had no clue what to do with herself. She didn't need to wait tables anymore now that she was a millionaire. Even though she had the money, Annie didn't think she wanted to go back to school for several more years just so she could add doctor of veterinary medicine to her name. That ship had sailed. Until she figured things out, Annie was more than happy to be lazy for a bit, content with a cat sleeping on her back. She had earned it.

Annie had just dozed off again, lulled to sleep by the vibrations of Sebastian's purrs on her back, when she heard a loud knock at the door. Seriously, it sounded less like a knock and more like a gorilla was pounding on the door because Annie took his last banana and he was all kinds of pissed. With a groan, Annie threw on a pair of shorts lying in her floor, grabbed a tank top from a drawer to throw over the sports bra she slept in, and stomped down the stairs. If the Jehovah's Witness people were the ones knocking *again*, they were going to get an earful.

Annie seriously doubted it was them since last time they came knocking Granny asked them if they still believed only one hundred and forty-four thousand were getting into heaven. When they somewhat agreed and tried to further explain, Granny had interrupted them and said they were screwed because she was pretty sure heaven was already at the full one hundred forty-four thousand capacity. They had quickly left and not been back since. Still, Annie wouldn't put it past them. They were nothing if not tenacious.

Annie flung the door open with a glare at whomever was on the other side and growled, "What?"

Her mouth almost hit the floor when she came face-to-face with sexy Wyatt Holloway. Dammit. She had forgotten it was Monday.

CHAPTER 8

*W*yatt tried not to stare. Annabelle was standing in front of him in a super tight tank top with the words, No Talking Before Coffee, emblazoned on the front and a pair of tiny black shorts featuring none other than Cookie Monster himself. What the hell was *with* this woman and short shorts? Didn't she own a pair of respectable knee-length grandma shorts? Where the hell were her long, floral skirts she loved in high school? And how in God's name was he not turned off by the hundreds of tiny pictures of the friggin' cartoon character from his child-hood who only uttered, "Me want cookies!"?

"Why are you here?" she grumbled, blowing a mint-tinted strand of hair out of her face. She had an obvious case of bedhead, strands falling out of the bun on top of her head she probably put up the night before and was now in a disheveled mess. She even had on a pair of large, hot pink nerd glasses. Nerd glasses that screamed sexy librarian. Good lord. He had to get his mind out of the gutter before he started thinking about her in nothing but a Darcy whip cream bikini.

"I'm here to work," he replied, willing himself to focus on the reason he was here and not the incredibly sexy woman in front of him.

"I told you not to come."

"And I disagreed with you telling me not to come. So here I am. Ready to work. Should I get started on my own or are you going to tell me what to do?"

Annabelle rolled her eyes and stomped toward what Wyatt guessed was the kitchen. "I'm not doing jack crap before coffee."

Wyatt followed behind her slowly, taking a look around the space. The living room was huge. A wooden staircase to his right probably led to the bedrooms upstairs. A large stone fireplace took up most of the wall to his left, a small entertainment center in the corner by the window housing a flat screen television. A bright purple recliner was sitting at an angle near the fireplace facing the entertainment center. A floral eighties couch faced the fireplace, an old wooden coffee table in front of it covered in various magazines and books. A variety of dream catchers in every color and size hung from the mantle of the fireplace, a picture of dogs playing poker above it. Wyatt's favorite part, however, were the pictures of Annabelle covering all the remaining walls.

A young Annabelle hugging a chicken, a gap-tooth smile on her face. A teenage Annabelle in pigtails, cowboy boots, and shorts on top of a beautiful palomino horse. Annabelle in her cap and gown, shaking hands with their high school principal. Annabelle in a boat on the lake, her hair blowing behind her and a carefree smile on her face.

"Now that Granny's gone, the first thing I'm going to do is take down this shrine of pictures."

Annabelle walked into the living room holding a mug with the words 'Life isn't worth living without coffee' on the front. "One time a few years ago, I tried taking all the pictures down and hiding them in the attic under an old quilt. Granny not only found those, but several others that were even *more* embarrassing. She told me if I took them down again she was going to make copies of all of them and hang them everywhere around town. I never touched them again."

"I don't know, Minty," he said. "I kinda like 'em."

"What did you call me?"

"Minty. You won't let me call you ACDC, I don't want to call you Annie, and you have mint colored tips in your hair. It fits."

She rolled her eyes. "Whatever. It's too early to argue. Do you want coffee? I made extra."

"Sure," he said, even though he really didn't. He'd drank a cup at his parents' house before finishing off the rest he had put in his Yeti cup on the drive to the farm. But coffee seemed to be her lifeline in the morning, so he would take anything that might change her from the angry grump she was now to some semblance of a human being.

Annabelle stomped back in the kitchen and he followed, smiling as he stepped into the room. The kitchen was an eclectic mix of items just like the living room. An avocado green fridge was in the left corner at the end of a long, lemon yellow countertop stretching the length of the wall. White-washed cabinets were under the counter, and open, wood shelving held on the wall by iron rails, lined the wall above. A picture window above the sink had a great view of the field behind the house where an old tire swing attached by a rope on the branch of a huge oak tree swung gently in the breeze. On the wall opposite the one Wyatt was facing was a top-of-the-line stainless steel gas stove surrounded by more cabinets, a bright orange hood vent above it. To the right was a bay window housing an alcove bench and worn table accented with a vase filled with orange and yellow daisies.

"I know what you're thinking," Annie grumbled, taking another mug off one of the open shelves to the right of the stove.

"What am I thinking, Miss Annabelle Cleaver?" he asked, teasing in his voice.

Annabelle leveled him with a glare. If looks could kill, they would definitely be spreading his ashes on the farm along with Sophie's.

"You're thinking my house is a crazy, eclectic mix of things that don't make a bit of sense together."

It was exactly what Wyatt was thinking, but there was no way he was voicing his agreement. He wasn't poking that beast. "Maybe I was thinking it looks just like something your Granny Sophie would put together," he said instead. Hopefully that would make her happy. He'd never seen a person who hated mornings as much as she did. And he grew up with his sister, who considered getting up before double digits early.

"My granny was a cheapskate," she replied, sitting in the alcove at the table and taking a sip of her coffee. "She burned down our kitchen cooking okra when I was thirteen but refused to go to Lowe's and buy anything new. Instead, we got this," she said, motioning around the space with her hand.

"Everything is a mix of what Granny found at yard sales, thrift stores, and clearance at Nailed It. It's why we have a yellow countertop, orange hood vent, and avocado green fridge. No one else wanted them. Not even color blind Bob Schwartz. That's where we got most of this. He's a total hoarder and his weakness is anything you can find in a kitchen. Once his wife found out their garage out back was filled to the brim, she made him sell almost everything in it. I hear he's on medication now to help him cope."

Wyatt chuckled. That made the kitchen make much more

sense. "Poor guy. You should never come between a hoarder and his belongings. I guess it's better than having a penchant for magazines. Or cats."

Annabelle smiled for the first time of the morning. Wyatt felt a sense of accomplishment, knowing he was the one to put the smile on her face.

"The only thing she bought firsthand was the stove. Said she refused to cook on a stove that probably was used by a person who sucked ass at cooking."

"The more I learn about this granny of yours, the more I think I would have really liked her."

"She was as amazing as she was quirky," Annabelle said with a smile. "I loved her more than I think even she knew."

"I'm sure she knew," he said softly. "You came home from college to stay with her without hesitation when she got sick. That had to mean something."

Annabelle looked at him, eyes wide. "How did you know I came home from school?"

"My mom told me. That's a pretty awesome thing to do, ACDC."

"I told you I hate that nickname."

Wyatt smiled. "Would you prefer Minty? Cookie? How about Boss?"

"I'd prefer my damn name."

"All right then, Annabelle. Your wish is my command."

ANNIE REFRAINED from sticking her tongue out at Wyatt. Minty? Cookie? ACDC? He was so annoying. He was also very, *very* attractive. Wyatt was leaning against her kitchen counter, a smirk on his face. It was a crime to make a pair of jeans look so good. They hugged his muscular thighs in all the right places and Annie bet he looked just as good from behind. Add in the ratty maroon and gold Parker High base-ball cap and she was wide awake. Dammit. She had always been a sucker for a man in a baseball cap.

Annie couldn't believe she had forgotten today was Monday. This was the day Wyatt Holloway was supposed to *not* come to her house. He especially shouldn't have come to her house looking so yummy.

Annie looked down at herself and tried not to shudder. In her hurry to answer the door, she had thrown on her Cookie Monster pajama shorts. Cookie. Monster. Not only did they have Cookie Monster's face all over them, they were also short. Like, really short. Almost boy short underwear short. And her tank top was tight and short, too. It almost didn't cover her stomach. Note to self…buy less tight, longer sleep-wear. She wanted to groan. Here was Wyatt, looking like he could be on the cover of *Cowboy Today* or whatever magazine featured covers of gorgeous cowboys and she was looking… well, she was looking like a hot friggin' mess.

"I'm going to change," she said, trying not to cover herself with her hands. First he'd seen her in a bikini top and Daisy Dukes. Now, she was dressed in what could possibly be classified as Cookie Monster porn.

"Good idea," Wyatt said.

"What does that mean?"

"I doubt you can work well on the farm wearing *that.*"

"You're probably right," Annie muttered. "I'll be right back."

Annie darted past Wyatt and refrained from running up the stairs. When she got to her room, she threw open her closet doors and stared. What could she wear that would be practical but also cute? The minute the thought ran through her head, she wondered why she cared about looking cute in front of Wyatt Holloway. She rolled her eyes and sighed. She cared because her inner high schooler was trying to get the attention of the popular, star athlete of Parker High School.

"Just dress like you'd normally dress," she said to herself. "Like it was just you and Granny. Or CC and Breckin. You don't have to impress that big oaf."

Annie threw on a pair of worn jeans, a lime green t-shirt with a faded, loopy Okie Dokie script on the front, and a pair of her favorite cowgirl boots. She ran her toothbrush quickly across her teeth, swiped some deodorant under her arms, and pulled her hair into another, albeit somewhat tamer, bun. With a shrug of her shoulders, she headed back down the stairs. She was going to make Wyatt so tired he wouldn't *want* to come back tomorrow.

She walked into the kitchen and stared. Annie was shocked speechless. Wyatt was sitting on the chair Annie had vacated when she went to change clothes, but that wasn't the source of her surprise. In his lap sat Sebastian. Sebastian, who hated men. Who hid under the couch and bit the ankles of the man *before* the mortician her granny tried to hook her up with. Who hissed and growled every time Barry, the very nice Fed Ex man, delivered a package on their front porch. *That* Sebastian.

"Your cat sure is nice," Wyatt said, scratching Bass under the chin. And then, traitorous cat that he was, Sebastian looked at her as if he knew she was shocked, swished his tail and began *purring*.

"What did you do to him?" she said with a glare. "He hates men. *All* men. Even Barry."

"Barry the Fed Ex man?" Wyatt replied. "He's a cool dude."

"Yes. *That* Barry. So what did you do? Did you bring some catnip with you or something?"

"That's not something I usually carry in my back pocket," he said, "So…that would be a no."

"Well, what did you *do* to him to get him to like you and not bite your ankles?"

"What?"

"That's what he did to my last date. He hid under the couch and bit the poor guy's ankles until he high-tailed it out our front door. He didn't even eat a piece of Granny's award winning coconut cream pie."

Wyatt chuckled. "That's pretty funny."

Annie tried not to smile. Because it really *was* funny. The guy Granny had chosen *that* go round had been muscled, sexy, handsome, and totally full of himself. Annie gave Sebastian Whiskas for an entire month after saving her from that man. It was worth putting up with his poop that smelled like tuna.

"I just want to know what you did to him to get him to like you."

"I didn't do anything! Scout's honor. I was just sitting here, drinking my coffee and he started weaving in and out of my legs. Then, he just jumped up in my lap and made himself at home. What can I say? He just must be a good judge of character."

Annie rolled her eyes. "The verdict is still out on that. Well, are you going to just sit here with my cat all day or are you going to do some work?"

"I was just waiting here patiently for my boss to tell me what to do."

"Then let's go."

"Aren't you going to eat any food? Or are you just going to let the coffee running through your veins be your only sustenance?"

"I don't need anything but coffee to get me going."

"A wise woman once told me breakfast was the most important meal of the day."

"You sound like my granny," she grumped.

"Again, the more I learn about your granny, the more I know she would've loved me."

"If you could convince her you weren't the one who bashed in her mailbox."

"I still have no clue why she thought that. I didn't do it."

"I don't either. But once my granny was convinced of something, it took God himself to change her mind."

"I believe it."

"Well?"

"Well what?"

"Are we going to sit here talking all day or are we actually going to do some work?"

"I'm just waiting for you to give the orders. I may not be enlisted anymore, but I'm an army man through and through."

"Does that mean I can tell you anything and you'll do it?"

"Within reason. And only if you decide to don a sergeant's uniform. Then, I'd take a bullet for you."

"I'll keep that in mind."

CHAPTER 9

Wyatt grinned. Annabelle sure was cute when she was mad. And apparently, weird as it was, her cat sitting in his lap definitely got her all riled up. "What are we going to do first, Boss?"

"I told you not to call me that."

"No…you told me not to call you Minty, Cookie, or ACDC. You sure are picky about your nickname."

"Maybe I don't *want* a nickname. Maybe I just want you to call me Annie."

"I told you I didn't want to call you that. Too many memories."

Annabelle's voice softened. She had forgotten about that. She couldn't imagine the horrors he must have seen on a daily basis. "Fine, you can call me whatever you want. Just *not* ACDC."

"*Anything?*"

"Within reason."

Wyatt rubbed his hands together in anticipation. "This is going to be *fun!*"

"What's going to be fun?"

"Thinking of a nickname for you."

"I thought you already had a couple of choices."

"Those are things I thought of on the fly. Just wait until I use this big, creative brain of mine to come up with something else. You'll be impressed."

"We shall see." Annabelle headed to the barn. "We need to feed the animals first. Think you can handle that?"

"I grew up on a farm. I was a member of FFA. I think I can handle that."

Wyatt followed her into the barn. Even though the outside was dilapidated, the inside was set up well. Stalls for the big animals, like the cows and horse, lined the left wall, a small alcove at the front holding the tack for the horse and milk buckets for the cows. On the right wall were stacks of feed sacks, rectangular bales of hay, and smaller stalls tailored for the pigs, goats, and chickens.

"Granny didn't want the animals caught in the middle of a bad storm, so she had my grandad make these smaller stalls for all the little guys," she said. Annie pointed to the back of the barn. "She even has a place for the ducks in the back, complete with a kiddie pool."

Wyatt smiled. "I think your animals might possibly have it better than some people."

"Just wait until you see the building she built to house the strays that wound up in our yard. We don't have any right now. She got tired pretty easily right before she died, so we found homes for the ones we had and didn't take any more in. But she sure did have a lot of them a few years ago."

Annabelle walked into the alcove and put on a pair of leather work gloves before walking over to the hay and grabbing a bale by the wire holding together. "You can grab another one and follow me to the field," she said. "We usually feed the cows and horse first."

"Are you sure you can handle that?" Wyatt asked, nodding

his head toward the bale she was holding. "I can get it for you."

Annabelle leveled him with a glare. "Yes, please carry both bales using your big army muscles because of course I've never carried a bale in my life."

Wyatt wanted to slap himself on the forehead. Even if he didn't know she worked on the farm on a daily basis, her sleek, muscular arms should have clued him in.

"I apologize for my stupidity," he said with a grin. "Of course you have. Let me just grab the other one."

"There's an extra set of gloves in the alcove where I got mine," she said. "You can meet me outside."

Wyatt quickly grabbed the gloves and the hay bale, trotting to catch up to his boss. She sure wasn't going to make it easy on him. Annabelle was already opening the gate to the field before he caught up to her. Taking a pair of wire clippers out of her back pocket, Annabelle threw her bale of hay on the ground, clipped off the baling wire and threw it on his side of the fence.

Wyatt followed suit, throwing his bale on the ground, and motioning for Annabelle to give him the clippers.

Wyatt walked over to Annabelle and the animals, running his hand up the flank of the paint horse. She was a pretty thing. White with random black splotches, and a black mane and tail. "I forgot this beauty's name."

"That's Perdita."

"Is that from a Disney movie?"

"Yeah. You probably know her as Perdy, though."

Wyatt looked at her blankly. "Not ringing a bell."

"I wanted to name her Domino, but Granny said it didn't go with our Disney theme, so I looked up the name of the momma dog on *101 Dalmatians*. Perdita, or Perdy for short."

Wyatt grinned. "That's very fitting."

Annabelle smiled back. "I thought so."

"Do you ever ride her?"

"I used to all the time. But then Granny got sick and I got caught up helping her and waiting tables at Sadie's, so I didn't really have much time for riding."

"I have a palomino named George," he replied. "I should bring him over one day and we could go for a ride."

"You named your horse George?"

Wyatt shrugged. "George Costanza is my favorite character on *Seinfeld*. Shrinkage, Festivus, 'This was supposed to be the summer of George.' Classic."

"That was my granny's favorite show. She just liked Kramer the best."

"I could see that. Did you watch it with her?"

Annabelle rolled her eyes. "Duh. It was on every night at ten-thirty. I bet we've seen every episode at least twenty times."

"That's a lot of *Seinfeld*."

"It never gets old."

"Who was your favorite character? Kramer, like your granny?"

"Nope."

"Then who?"

Annabelle started doing the classic Elaine Bennett dance, kicking and punching erratically. If he didn't know better, he would think it was a blonde version of Elaine dancing in front of him. He laughed. "Pretty good."

"Maybe a dingo ate your baby," she replied, grinning as she continued to dance before twirling in a circle and waving jazz hands in front of his face. "Elaine was the best."

"No, your version of Elaine's dance was the best. I think that might have even been worse than hers!"

Annabelle picked up a handful of feed and threw it his way. "I'm the best dancer you know."

Wyatt chuckled. "That's just because no one in my family dances. We're Baptist."

"You do too dance."

"How would you know?"

"I saw you dance at prom your senior year. You were even crowned prom king."

Wyatt raised one eyebrow her way. "Stalk me much, Boss?"

Annabelle rolled her eyes but he could still see her cheeks bloom a rosy red. "I wasn't stalking. I was at prom like everyone else."

"That's *right!* You went with Neutron! I forgot about that."

Again, Wyatt didn't know how he forgot about Miss Annabelle Cleaver. When they were in school, floor-length satin, sleeveless gowns with sequin designs on the chest were what the girls preferred. He remembered. The one Jersey wore for football homecoming was pale pink with hot pink sequined flowers. When he crowned Tasha the basketball homecoming queen, hers was hunter green satin with matching colored sequins. Jersey's prom dress was dark purple with light purple sequins.

But of course, Annabelle didn't follow the high school norm. She walked into prom on Neutron's arm wearing a dress so short and so tight, Wyatt didn't even know if it could be *classified* as a dress. It was made out of bright peacock blue lace with a tan layer underneath the lace that came *very close* to looking like her actual skin. There also wasn't a ruffle or scrap of satin in sight. She paired the dress with stiletto heels that were patterned just like a peacock feather. Thinking about it now, Wyatt remembered her hair was pulled up in some sort of complicated braid, real peacock feathers woven throughout. She was stunning.

Jersey had sneered when Annabelle and Neutron had

walked into the gymnasium. "What a ridiculous dress. Her crazy granny must've gotten it at the Lakeview Goodwill," she had muttered. Looking back on it, Wyatt now knew the words were uttered in pure jealousy. Annabelle had turned the heads of every person in the gym that night.

"Jimmy *Newton*," she said.

"What?"

"His name was Jimmy *Newton.* Not Neutron."

"Oh, I know. It was what—"

"You and your jackass friends called him behind his back. He knew all about the nickname and it really bothered him. Not cool. Makes me wonder what you called me behind *my* back."

Wyatt's smile fell. Kids could be so cruel. It saddened him to think he made anyone's teenage years miserable in any way. "It was a pretty jackass thing to do," he said. "There's no excuse, really. We were little shits."

Annabelle threw another handful of feed at him. "You are so dumb."

"What?"

"He didn't give a rat's ass what you thought."

"I thought you said it bothered him."

"I was lying to see if you felt bad."

"Really? That makes me feel better."

"It shouldn't."

"Why not?"

"Because he said you and your buddies would still be stuck in Podunk Parker for the rest of your lives while he was going to make something of himself."

"Ouch."

"Sometimes the truth hurts."

Wyatt shot her a sad smile. "Sometimes it does. I didn't plan on coming back to Podunk Parker, that's for sure. I guess my brain and body had a different idea. It seems this was the only place I *could* come back to."

The scowl fell from her face. "I totally understand that. This was *not* how I expected my life to go, either."

"So whatever happened to Neutron? My dad said he was some fancy doctor up north."

"He's an oncologist at Johns Hopkins. So yeah, he's kind of a big deal."

Wyatt grinned. "Well, nice to know someone got out of here."

"He asked me to go with him," she said.

"Really? Why didn't you?"

"Because I had my granny here. I wanted to leave, but I wanted to be close enough to come back to see her on a regular basis. Besides, the jackass broke my heart before I could even say yes."

"*Neutron?*"

"Yes, Neutron. Dammit—Newton! Why is that so hard to believe?"

"Because he was such a dork and you were...you *are*...stunning."

Annabelle stilled. "*I* was a dork, too."

"But you were so pretty it made up for all that dorkiness. Besides, I couldn't ever get the thought of those henna tattoos out of my mind. I even tried to get Jersey to get some."

Annabelle snorted. "Funny...I never saw them on her."

"That's because she didn't get any."

"Didn't want to copy the nerdy girl."

"More like didn't want the nerdy girl to upstage her."

Annabelle's eyes went wide and he could see the pulse beating an erratic rhythm in her delicate neck. He wanted desperately to put his mouth on that exact spot.

"As *if*," she replied, trying to act like she wasn't as affected as he was. She wasn't very convincing.

"Okay, Clueless," he said with a grin. He needed to get his mind focused on the job before she kicked him off her land for good.

"That *was* a favorite movie of mine. That and *She's All That*. Classics."

"So you never told me why Newton broke your heart. In my opinion, he's all kinds of dumb for that move, no matter how many degrees he has."

"That's a story that's been vaulted, the memories never to return. I'm over it. Besides, I didn't think I'd ever move back permanently."

"Then why did you?"

"Granny needed me." She shrugged. "When I needed her, she was there. I figured I should return the favor."

"That's a pretty kickass thing to do, Boss."

"It's what anyone would do for someone they loved."

"I don't think so, but I'm glad you still believe the world and the people on it are good."

"You don't?"

"I've seen too much to believe it anymore."

He and Annabelle had moved closer to each other during the conversation. She was close enough to touch if he wanted and he *totally* wanted. But if he was going to be employed by her for any length of time, he knew he better keep his hands to himself. Color him surprised if *Annabelle* didn't put her hand on his back and pat it gently.

"There's still good people and beautiful places in the world," she said. "You just have to make sure you focus on that stuff instead of your nightmares."

Wyatt stilled at the touch of her hand. Normally, someone putting their hands on him without his permission was a recipe for disaster. Annabelle's hand on his back, however, was the total opposite. Her touch was like the soothing salve his mom used to put on him as a kid when he got a horrible sunburn. Instead of soothing his skin, Annabelle's touch seemed to be soothing his soul. God, war had turned him into such a pussy.

"So why are you staying?" he asked, trying to keep her from focusing on the fact she was touching him of her own volition. He had a feeling it was something she didn't think about before doing and once she realized *what* she was doing, her hand would jump off his back like she was touching a hot stove. "Sophie is gone," he said gently. "If you want to leave, you can leave."

"But now, I have no clue where I'd go."

"Sky's the limit for a girl who thinks the world is still good, Disney," he said with a smile.

"Disney?"

"It's your new nickname. I told you I'd think of something better once my creative juices started flowing."

Annabelle rolled her eyes. "I guess it's better than Minty. Or Cookie Monster."

"You forgot ACD—"

"You want to keep your job, you better not finish that sentence."

Wyatt pretended to zip his lips and throw away the key. Annabelle slapped him on the back and let out a laugh. And damn if that laugh didn't make him smile like a blushing teenage boy.

$\backsim$

"So you really hired him?"

Annie, CC, and Breckin were sitting in their favorite booth at Sadie's Café sharing their favorite—a three scoop banana split sundae. This dessert had solidified their friendship in elementary school. Annie loved the strawberry ice cream with the strawberry topping, CC's favorite was the chocolate ice cream with the marshmallow fluff, and Breckin chowed down on the vanilla ice cream with hot fudge. And Sadie, the best café owner ever, made sure there were not two, but *three* maraschino cherries on top of the whipped cream. It was a trio match made in ice cream heaven. They were currently sitting in their favorite corner booth in the café, having their weekly Wednesday afternoon sundae date.

It had been almost three weeks since Wyatt started working at the farm with her. Since then, he had cleaned out her gutters and fixed all the fencing that separated the field from her backyard. He had also scraped the wood siding of the farmhouse and repainted it. The house had gone from a chipped, dirty white to a clean, bright white. He had also re-stained the boards of the front porch. He suggested painting her front door mint green to match her hair, but Annie had turned that suggestion down. To repaint her front door was to admit her granny was truly gone. She didn't know if she was ready for that yet.

What started out as reluctant annoyance on her part at him being there had turned into something...*nice.* She had gotten used to Wyatt's company and the easy, natural way they got along. That morning, they had started replacing some of the rotten boards in the barn and Wyatt said once the framework was sturdier he could replace the roof. The metal currently up there had probably been put up by her grandad during the Carter administration.

Annie took a big bite of her part of the sundae, stared out the window, and tried not to sigh. She didn't want to get comfortable having Wyatt Holloway around. It was unsettling. Instead of thinking about army man Wyatt and all his sexy muscles, she focused on what was going on outside the café window.

Burt Gallagher and Marty Samson were playing their daily game of checkers, Burt's finger waving in Marty's red face. Annie didn't know why they continued to play together all these years. It seemed like they argued more than they actually played. Last year, the chief of police had to break up an argument between them when Burt took off his red and black checkered bowtie and tried to wrap it around Marty's neck, all because he tried to double hop Burt *illegally*.

And, if she were being honest with herself, Annie didn't understand how they were actually still *alive*. Annie felt like they were pushing a hundred when she was in middle school. Maybe their checker argument kept them young at heart and of a sound mind.

Note to self, she thought. *Learn how to play checkers*.

"Hell-o? Anyone there?"

Annie started at CC's spoon waving in front of her face.

"Huh?"

"I *asked* if you really hired Wyatt Holloway."

"She did," Breckin answered for Annie.

"How do *you* know?" Annie frowned and took another bite of ice cream. Maybe if she kept stuffing her face her friends would leave her alone. Maybe it'd even help her put on a few extra pounds so Wyatt would quit *staring* at her. She had caught him doing it more times that she was comfortable with. But *again*, if she were being honest with herself, she'd been caught staring a time or two as well.

"Because Barry, the Fed Ex man, was delivering a package to the school the other day while I was in the office. He asked me if Wyatt was working at your place. He was delivering a package to Mr. Grant and passed Wyatt on the road to your house."

Annie rolled her eyes. Sometimes it seriously sucked living in a small town where everyone knew everyone else's business. She didn't even think Barry *lived* in Parker. He might as well, though. He was the only Fed Ex man who delivered to their town.

"Is that true?" CC asked, frowning Annie's way.

"Fine. He *may* be helping me out with a thing or two at the farm. But it's *nothing* to get excited about."

CC giggled. "Please tell me he's worked with his shirt off. I can't imagine how scrumptious he looks with his army man muscles on full display."

Annie sighed. On Thursday, she had gone into the house to take a private phone call and had come back to see a shirtless Wyatt working on the reframing of the cow's stall. CC was right. Wyatt's muscles were most definitely scrumptious. His back muscles rippled and flexed as he worked, the army's insignia tattooed from shoulder to shoulder moving as he did. Annie was pretty sure a little bit of drool had formed in the corner of her mouth. It unfortunately was one of the times *she'd* been caught staring.

"He did on Thursday."

CC and Breckin squealed. "Is he as gorgeous shirtless as he is fully dressed?" Breckin asked.

"What is *with* you two?" Annie frowned, ignoring her friend's questions. "You're acting like a bunch of hormonal teenage girls."

"What? We have to live vicariously through you since our sex lives are nonexistent," CC replied.

"I'm *not* having sex with Wyatt Holloway!" Annie let out a squeal of her own.

"Why not, dear?" Annie groaned when she heard Sadie's voice. She must've walked up behind the trio as they were discussing Wyatt's lack of clothing while sweating in Annie's barn. If there was a definition of requisite café owner in the dictionary, Annie was pretty sure Sadie's name would appear by the picture. She wore her white apron daily, her hair in the same beehive she probably sported at her senior prom and had a penchant for wearing cat eye, bright purple glasses she stuck in her hair when she wasn't taking an order.

"I hear he's suffering from PTSD something awful," she added. "Maybe a little lovin' is just what he needs to fix him."

Annie's heart went out to Wyatt. God only knew what he saw in his time with the military. She had learned in the short time he had worked for her to make her presence known before she walked behind him. The first time she had surprised him on accident, he had turned, hammer held defensively in his hand and a wild, haunted look in his eyes. "I don't think sex is a cure for PTSD, Sadie. It's not even a medical cure at all."

"I don't know, dear. You'd be surprised at how much really good sex heals a man. I know my Clyde came back from Vietnam really scarred. Several good rolls in the hay with me and he never had another nightmare. Girl Scout's honor."

"See?" Breckin said, waving her spoon in Annie's face. "All you two need is a good roll in the hay. He'll be all better and you won't act like you have a stick up your ass."

"I don't act like I have a stick up my ass!" Annie grumped.

Her friends looked at each other, a knowing look in their eyes. Annie shot a glare their way. "I just spread my granny's ashes all over my farm. I have a right to be a little grumpy."

Her friends nodded in understanding. "We know," Breckin said sympathetically. "That's why fantastic sex with Wyatt Holloway is just what the doctor ordered. If it can heal PTSD, it for sure will cure your grumpiness."

"Sex won't fix PTSD!" Annie muttered. "Just thinking that is ridiculous."

"Speaking of the man, he's walking in the door right now," CC whispered behind her hand.

Annie tried not to turn around at the sound of the bell above the door jingling to announce another patron. Somehow, she just *knew* Wyatt would be able to tell he had been the subject of conversation of the three women sitting at the table. Well, four if Sadie *hovering* at the end of the table counted.

"He's walking this way," CC screeched quietly. "Quick. Put on your best smile and fix that crazy hair that's sticking out on the right side of your head."

Annie's eyes went wide as she ran her fingers through her hair. Dammit. She was being ridiculous. This was *not* high school and she was not the wall flower nerd standing in the corner. She was a grown ass woman who had her shit together. Well, somewhat.

"Hey, Disney," he said, walking over and leaning on her side of the booth, his arm placed behind her head. "You cut out early today. I didn't even know you had left until I saw your truck missing."

"Disney?" Breckin asked, a question in her voice.

"It's my nickname for her," Wyatt replied. "Because she names all her animals after Disney characters."

"My granny was the one who did that," Annie muttered. "Maybe I'll start naming them after Dreamwork characters instead."

"That's funny, Wyatt," CC said. Annie was pretty sure her friend was batting her eyelashes, too. Dear. Lord.

"I thought it was pretty creative myself."

"I come here every Wednesday to have a sundae with my friends," she said, holding her spoon of ice cream in her hand. "I don't have to tell you when I'm leaving. You're a big boy. I'm sure you can take care of yourself."

"Well, I'll make a note to myself then."

"And that note will say?"

"Be sure to drive your boss to her weekly ice cream date on Wednesday afternoons."

Annie heard Breckin and CC giggle. She refrained from

rolling her eyes. They were such idiots. "In case you didn't notice, I can drive myself places. I didn't walk all the way into town. See that truck across the street? It's mine."

Wyatt grinned, which crinkled the corners of his eyes and showcased his cute dimple on his left cheek. Even with the huge scar running down the right side of his face, he was one attractive man. Lord only knows what happened to cause a scar that big.

"I did see that truck, Disney," he replied, sitting on the edge of the booth, his denim-clad thigh brushing hers. She shivered and tried to convince herself it was because the air conditioning had just kicked on. "But you see that truck parked beside yours?"

"Yes. You drive it every day to my farm. I know it's yours. So what? Are you bragging because it's fancier than mine?"

"Nope. I'm showing you because no one else has ridden in it."

Annie's eyes widened. "Seriously?"

"Seriously. I restored it myself but sadly, I'm the only one who's ridden in it."

"Why does that matter to me?"

"Because I want to take you for a ride."

"Oh, my lord," CC said breathily.

"A *ride*," Breckin replied, waggling her eyebrows. Annie refrained from throwing the ice cream on her spoon at her friends.

"Why me?" she asked.

"Why not?"

"Because you have friends. Family. All people more qualified to ride in it than me."

"See, that's where you're wrong, Boss. Because my family and friends are used to my tinkering. They've heard me talk about restoring my grandad's truck more times than they can count. But you...you haven't heard any of it. So I'll be able to talk shop and impress you with my restoration prowess."

"Wowzers," Sadie added in a whisper. "Prowess."

CC and Breckin giggled. Again. Annie was so going to kill them when Wyatt left.

"So whaddya think, Boss? Wanna cruise?"

"I don't know."

"You have to go."

"Oh, really? And why is that?"

"Because it's named after a Disney character. You can't say no to a Disney character."

"What is it? Lightning McQueen? Mater?"

"Close."

"Then what?"

"Sally."

"Who's Sally?"

"Lightning's crush. The little Carrera who stole his heart. So whaddya say? Wanna go for a ride in Sally?"

Annie rolled her eyes. "Why not?"

Wyatt smiled and tapped his knuckles on the top of the booth.

"It's a date, then. Ladies," he said, nodding to her friends before walking away and sitting down at the counter by the register. Annie saw Clyde, Sadie's husband, hand Wyatt a menu and nod at their booth before chuckling at something Wyatt said. Great. The whole town would probably have them engaged by the end of the day. Annie turned back to her friends.

"You guys are dead to me," she said with a glare.

"Why?" CC replied. "You're the one getting a *ride* next week to our sundae date. In a truck a super sexy man named after a Disney character. Something tells me you were his muse for the name, too. You're in so much trouble."

"If that's the kind of trouble following you around, I need

to find some trouble of my own," Breckin said. "Because that trouble is pretty damn tempting."

Annie sighed. Her friends were right on both counts. Wyatt Holloway was definitely tempting and was trouble with a capital T. And Annie had no clue what to do about it.

CHAPTER 10

"*W*yatt! Hurry up! We're going to be late and you know how much your Aunt Nancy hates it when she has to wait on *anyone*, even if it is her beloved nephew!"

Wyatt rolled his eyes at his mother's voice calling from the hallway. He had come home from Annabelle's early in order to see a couple of places his aunt had lined up as potential places he could buy. His mother, unfortunately, insisted on going, too. It was probably going to be an ugly edition of HGTV's *House Hunters*. He wouldn't even put it past his mom to film it on her phone.

"Cool your jets, Mom," he said, coming out of his room. "We're not going to be late. Besides, even if we are, all I have to do is sweet-talk Aunt Nancy and she'll be eating out of the palm of my hand in no time."

"More like biting your hand *off*," his mom muttered. "That woman is a shark."

Wyatt chuckled. His mom and aunt were only fourteen months apart in age. Where his mom was a soft, sweet, chocolate chip cookie baking woman, his Aunt Nancy was a driven, focused, never-baked-a-cookie-in-her-life woman. Wyatt was actually surprised his aunt had never moved away from their small town. His mom once told him Aunt Nancy had big dreams to sell real estate in the Big Apple. Why she stayed in Parker was anyone's guess. Her actual agency was based in Lakeview, even though she had her own office in Parker. So he guessed she did get out of Parker…somewhat.

"I'm waitin' on you, Momma. Let's go. I wanna take you for a ride in my truck."

Wyatt took his mom's arm and walked her down the porch to the passenger's side of Sally. With a smile, he opened the door and said, "I'd like to introduce you to Sally."

"Sally?"

"It's what I named her," he said, shutting her door before walking around to the driver's side and hopping in.

"Why Sally?"

Wyatt shrugged his shoulders. "It's like Sally from *Cars*. You know? Lightning McQueen's girlfriend. I thought it fit, seeing as they're both baby blue and all."

His mom smiled at him knowingly. "I seem to remember you telling me a lot of animals on Sophie's farm being named after Disney characters. Might that be your inspiration for the name, son?"

Wyatt wanted to bang his head on the steering wheel. He should've kept his damn mouth shut. He had forgotten he told his mom about Sophie's Disney-themed farm.

"Nope. I have no clue what you're talking about," he replied.

Wyatt heard words come out of his mom's mouth that sounded suspiciously like "Bullshit."

"What was that, Mom?"

"Nothing, dear," she said with a grin. "Let's get a move on. You know how much your aunt hates waiting."

A few minutes later, Wyatt and his mom pulled in front of

a dilapidated white-frame house. All the windows were boarded-over, a dingy gray shutter hanging on for dear life by a single nail by one of the windows. The cement on the porch was crumbling and the flowerbeds were filled with so many weeds and overgrown shrubbery they almost covered the front windows. Shady was the word that immediately came to mind. While crime in their town was practically nonexistent, Wyatt could totally picture a drug deal going down in this house. Or, you know, maybe a chainsaw massacre.

"Now, I don't want to give you the wrong impression right away." His aunt was standing in the driveway wearing a black skirt, ruffly white blouse, and a pair of bright red stiletto heels. He didn't know how she wasn't breaking an ankle walking on the cracked pavement that constituted the driveway. "It could actually be quite nice if someone handy like you could give it a little TLC. And most importantly, it's in your budget."

Wyatt had given his aunt specific instructions about what he could and couldn't afford. He didn't want to be house-poor like so many other people his age who felt like they had to keep up with the Joneses. Besides, it was just him and would probably be *only* him for the long haul. Immediately following that thought, an image of Annabelle flashed through his mind. He shook his head to clear her from his thoughts. Annabelle wasn't a factor in the equation. No matter how attracted he was to her, she was his boss, not to mention the fact of how messed up he was in his head. He wouldn't wish that baggage on anyone.

"As long as it has bachelor pad potential, I'm willing to look at it," he said.

"Well, it also has some extra bedrooms, just in *case* you ever decide you want to settle down," his aunt replied. Seeing his frown, she immediately added, "Or you could make it a game room, a pool room, or hell, even a drink in your under-wear room."

"I'm holding out hope for a someday grandbaby's room," his mom said.

Wyatt sighed. Yep. It was going to be one of those days.

His aunt opened the front door with the key hanging on the ring in her hand and walked into the room, Wyatt and his mom following close behind. The room was spacious. It also looked like it hadn't been redecorated since the seventies. Olive green shag carpeting covered the floors and was complemented by bright orange and olive striped wallpaper. A lava rock fireplace sat on the wall facing the front door, bookshelves lined with dark paneling on either side. Wyatt caught a peek of the olive green linoleum through the doorway that Wyatt figured led to the kitchen.

"Oh, my lord! What is that *smell?*" Wyatt saw his mom standing right by the front door, her fingers pinching her nose. "It smells like someone *died* in here."

"It's been vacant for quite some time," his aunt replied. "The owner passed away and all his children lived in different places in the country. They have no interest in keeping it. They just want to sell it as quickly as possible to split the profit and be done with it."

Wyatt could believe it. The house had the musty smell of a home that had been sitting too long in the heat of an Okla-homa summer without the air conditioner being run. "Are you going to wait in the truck, Mom, or are you going to suck it up and follow us in?" he asked.

"I'm coming with you guys," his mom replied in a stuffy voice caused by still holding her nose. "Just make it quick, Nancy."

Wyatt and his mom followed his aunt through the rest of the house. Like Wyatt thought, the kitchen was behind the living room and exited into a hall where there was a bathroom and two small bedrooms. Like the living room, the bedrooms featured olive green shag carpeting and the bathroom's linoleum matched the olive green linoleum in the kitchen. At least it was consistent.

"Someone really liked the color olive green," Wyatt said with a smile. "At least they branched out in the kitchen and got an avocado-colored fridge."

"Wait until you see the backyard," his aunt said. "I think you'll like it the most."

Wyatt followed his aunt out the backdoor. The lot was big, a large deck taking up a lot of the space.

"I figured this would be a great place to put a grill, fire pit, and some seating," his aunt said. "You could even add a hot tub. The deck is in pretty good shape. All you'd need to do is fix the roof covering the deck. The tin on top has some holes in it because of it being so old."

Wyatt spun in a circle, taking it all in. He could see his family and friends there. In his mind, he added an outdoor television on the wall and an outdoor kitchen. It was by far the best feature of the property.

"It has potential," he said.

"Are you *kidding* me?" his mom said, taking her fingers off her pinched nose. "This place is *horrible!*"

"Mom, didn't you hear your sister? The price is low enough in my budget that I can not only buy it, but also afford to fix it up. It won't look like this when I get finished with it."

"Wyatt, your father and I *told* you we'd help you—"

"I've already told you, Mom. I'm not taking any money from you and Dad. I'm doing this on my own."

His mom rolled her eyes. "Fine. Have it your way," she huffed.

Wyatt turned to his aunt. "Is this the only one you've got?"

"Not sold yet?"

He grinned. "Not until I see my other options."

His aunt smiled back. "I have a few more that might work."

By the end of the day, Wyatt had seen a house with nosy neighbors, one with extremely loud children living next door, and a home that was by the town animal shelter. Even Wyatt drew the line at smelling dog shit and listening to dogs barking on a daily basis.

"I don't know, Aunt Nancy," he said. "I don't *love* any of them, but I guess the first one has the most potential."

"*Seriously?*" his mom muttered.

"Seriously."

"Well, I have one more I could show you, but it's outside your budget," his aunt said. "But I think you will absolutely love it."

"I don't think—" Wyatt said but before he could finish his sentence, his mom butted into the conversation.

"We want to see it," she said.

"Mom! I said—"

"Wyatt, hush. You might be able to haggle the price down to make it within your budget. Am I right, Nancy?"

His aunt shrugged. "There's always a chance."

Wyatt sighed. When the sisters teamed up, there was no chance. "Fine. Let's see it."

Wyatt followed his aunt down Main Street and past the majority of businesses in town. Annabelle's friend, CC, was outside her beauty shop sweeping the sidewalk, and Burt and Marty were playing their never-ending games of checkers outside Sadie's café.

"They must have an intense game going," his mom said, staring past him out the window. "Marty and Burt usually finish up by noon before it gets too hot."

Wyatt could totally understand that. Even with the air

conditioner blowing as high as it could go, Wyatt could still feel the trail of sweat running down his back from being outside in the heat. Oklahoma summers were no joke.

"Where are we *going*?" he asked his mom. They had gone through town and were now headed toward Lake Parker. The road they were on had turned to gravel and his aunt had the blinker of her Mercedes on, indicating she was turning right down a dirt road.

"I'm surprised she's taking her fancy car down a dirt road," his mom remarked. "She must *really* want you to see this place. It must be *nice!*"

"And probably way outside my budget, Mom. Don't get your hopes up."

"We'll see."

After a few more minutes, Wyatt's aunt pulled onto a circle drive made of gravel in front of an A-frame log cabin with logs stained a light honey. In the front yard sat two giant elm trees, which offered shade over the house's roof. The shingles were weathered cedar, and the large front windows were large and inviting, the flower beds underneath filled with day lilies and fountain grass. The front door wasn't square. Instead, it was rounded at the top and featured a beautiful stained glass window. It looked like something out of a fairy tale. Wyatt exited his truck and could hear lapping of water on a shore. The house must sit right on the lake. And if Wyatt wasn't mistaken, this house was a straight shot across the lake from Annie's farm. If he were Tom Brady and had a deflated football, he could probably throw it and hit her roof.

"Oh, Wyatt," his mom breathed. "It's perfect."

His aunt walked up beside him and grinned. "What do you think?"

"I think this is way more than just a little out of my price range."

"Before I even tell you the price, I want you to see the inside. It also sits on five acres and has an empty lot on either side. Seclusion at its finest."

Wyatt and his mom followed his aunt into the house. The house was an open concept kitchen, living, and dining area. The walls of the cabin were stained the same honey color as the outside and the room featured concrete floors stained a dark brown that matched the color of the large beams on the ceiling. A wood-burning stove was in one corner of the house and a curved, iron staircase led to an upstairs loft overlooking the room. Wyatt's favorite part, however, were the floor to ceiling windows on the back wall. Wyatt could see a pier leading out to the lake, a fishing boat tied on one of the posts floating in the water.

"Aunt Nancy, why did you show me this place?"

"Isn't it perfect?"

"It is, but you know I can't afford it."

"That might not be true. I know the owner. He's a retired vet, just like you. He built this place for his wife and himself, but right after they finished it, she was diagnosed with stage four lung cancer and died two weeks later. She had never even smoked a day in her life. Cleveland said he couldn't live here anymore because there were too many memories of his wife. He just wants to sell it and be done. Last I heard, he moved back to Louisiana to be closer to his kids."

"Cleveland Jones?" Wyatt asked. Surely it wasn't the same Cleveland Jones he knew. The Cleveland *he* knew was his drill sergeant and one of the meanest people Wyatt had ever met. But Cleveland wasn't a common name and he didn't think many people named Cleveland were from Louisiana.

"That's the one," his aunt said. "Why?"

"He was my drill sergeant in boot camp," Wyatt said. "I didn't even know he *lived* in Oklahoma."

"He didn't. He and his wife would vacation here because

her family was from Oklahoma. She always told him she wanted to eventually move back."

"What a small world," his mom said. "Maybe he'll drop the price for you since you know each other."

"I don't think so," Wyatt said. "He hated me."

"Isn't it a drill sergeant's job to make everyone hate them?"

"He had a special hatred for me, though."

When Wyatt enlisted, he was an eighteen year old punk who thought he was a bigger fish than he actually was. He was still basing his reputation on the star athlete he was at Park High. What he didn't realize, however, was no one in boot camp knew who Wyatt Holloway was or where Parker, Oklahoma was, nor did they care. He had to drop and give Cleveland twenty for his smart mouth more times than he could count. He was surprised they didn't kick him out.

"I doubt that, son. I can't see anyone hating you."

"That's because you're biased, Mom. You did give birth to me."

His mom reached up and patted him on the cheek. "You're probably right about that, kid."

Wyatt and his mom continued to follow his aunt through the house. The countertops in both the kitchen and bathrooms were also concrete that matched the color of the floors. The cabinets were painted cream and featured large copper handles that matched the sink fixtures. The bedrooms were large and also featured large windows to maximize the amazing view of the lake.

"Just wait until you go outside," his aunt said. "If it doesn't seal the deal, I don't know what will."

Wyatt walked through the French doors leading outside and was rendered speechless. The lake was literally the house's backyard. The lake met the shore at the end of the five acres, the waves lapping onto a small beach. A storage shed almost as big as the house stood in the corner of the fenceless yard. A deck even bigger than the one at the first house went from one end of the house to the other, a built-in fire pit and seating in the middle. A hammock was at the edge of the deck and faced a hot tub sitting under the awning of the roof. The outdoor kitchen was top of the line. All that was missing was an outdoor television.

"You just brought me here to show me what the deck of the first house could look like, didn't you, Aunt Nancy?"

"Nope. I brought you here so you could realize this place might be good for you. I know you've been struggling since you've been back. Maybe this place will help you heal. I know how much you love being in the outdoors."

Wyatt drew in a breath. His aunt was right. The minute he stepped onto the property, he felt a sense of peace he hadn't had since he returned home. There was only one problem. He had no idea how he was going to pay for that peace.

"How'd the house hunt with your aunt go?"

Annie and Wyatt were sitting on the front porch of her house drinking cold lemonade out of mason jars. After a couple weeks' worth of hard work, Wyatt had finally declared the inside structure of the barn sound enough to begin work on the outside without it caving in. It was his plan to start removing the tin from the barn's roof and reroof it with new tin the following week. Annie didn't know where all his stamina came from. He'd been working with her for two months and she barely recognized her farm. Wyatt was like the Energizer Bunny when it came to work. He never got tired. He kept going and going and going. Sometimes, Annie got tired just *watching* it.

If Annie were guessing, Wyatt worked hard to keep thoughts from running rampant in his head. That's what she did. When her thoughts turned sad thinking about her granny, she usually worked nonstop. The animals hated it, because her usual form of work was to give them all baths. Sebastian would see her get the Dawn soap from under the kitchen sink and would take off running. She'd dragged Nemo through the house, him howling the entire way to the bathroom, more times than she could count. Sometimes, she'd pretend she wanted to go for a walk by the stream and would *accidentally* bump him in when his guard was down. It was the best she could do since he now weighed as much as she did.

Nemo was one of the many animals that had been dumped at the farm. When he showed up on their doorstep, Nemo was a tiny, dirty, starving ball of limp white fur. Annie found him huddled under the porch swing, shaking from the rain that had been pouring from the sky in a storm only God himself could make. Instead of taking him to the building at the back of the property where Sophie had taken all the other strays, Annie had taken him in the house and hidden him in a basket in the mud room. Her granny hadn't said a word; she just acted like he had always been there. Annie had nursed him back to health and he had stayed in the house until at eighty-five pounds, he had knocked Annie's grandad's ashes off a table in the living room and had scattered him into a million tiny particles of ash throughout the house. When Granny had to sweep her husband of fifty-four years off the living room floor, she declared Nemo an outside dog and Annie hadn't argued. At that point, she didn't really mind because he was taking up more of her bed than she did.

"My mom went with us."

Annie's daydream was interrupted by Wyatt's reply to her question. "Is that a bad thing?"

"Let me put it to you this way. My mom and aunt are total opposites. My mom thinks her baby boy shouldn't live in the slums even though I've seen the worst slums in the world."

"We have slums in Parker? Trailer trash, yes. I was one. But a slum, not so much."

Wyatt frowned at her words. "You were far from trailer trash. But that was my point exactly. Parker doesn't even *have* slums."

"So what's the big deal? Your mom wants you to live in a nice place."

"Nice by *her* standards. Everything we looked at was wrong in my mom's eyes. Except for one. It was like a bad edition of *House Hunters.*"

"I wouldn't peg you as the *House Hunters* watching type."

Wyatt rolled his eyes. "I'm *not*. My mom is. Which is why she thinks she knows everything about finding a perfect house. It's also why I have to get out. If I have to watch one more episode of the damn show, I'm going to throw my shoe at the TV."

Annie giggled at the thought of Wyatt throwing his shoe. "So did you like the one your mom liked?"

Wyatt blew out a breath. "I did."

"Then problem solved. She approves of the house you chose and you like it. Easy peasy, lemon squeezy."

"I can't believe you chanted a phrase from elementary school."

Annie stuck out her tongue at him. "Judge me."

"Totally judging while also laughing on the inside at your maturity level."

"You didn't answer my question. Surely you aren't going to avoid buying a home just because your mom likes it. Who's knocking whose maturity level *now?*"

"I wouldn't do that. It's just the home is *way* out of my price range."

"Then why did your aunt show it to you?"

Wyatt didn't answer, opting instead to take a big drink of his lemonade. Annie sensed there was a story behind the pause. She just wanted to know if he would trust her enough to tell her. The more he worked at the farm, the more she enjoyed his company. Usually, Annie was hoping for a quick summer just because the heat was stifling. Now, she prayed it would last a *little* longer than usual, especially if it meant Wyatt would keep working with his shirt off. The more he did, the more his tan deepened and the more Annie drooled. Even his scar held more appeal the longer she saw it. It told a story; it had character. It was *so* adult Wyatt that she couldn't even remember what he looked like without it.

"She thought it would bring me some peace," he said softly.

"What does that mean?" Annie asked in a voice just as soft. She was afraid if she spoke in a normal voice it would spook him. She'd heard from CC what she *thought* happened but she wanted to hear it from him. She was hurting about the loss of her granny. He was hurting about the tragedy he saw during his time in the military. Maybe they could share their loss together.

"Ever since I came back, I've...struggled. With a lot of things. Things you probably wouldn't care about."

"You can't say that unless you told me what they are. Don't put words in my mouth and thoughts in my head, Wyatt James."

She was rewarded with a small smile. "You sound like my mother."

"I've always thought your mother was a smart woman. Well, at least what I've heard about her."

"I've seen things that haunt me. Things no one should see.

I have nightmares at night where I wake up covered in sweat, dreaming of bombs and death and scared little kids. I even started going to a therapist to see if it would help. So far, I'm still the same."

"So what makes this place special?"

"Whenever I was a kid, the lake was always the place I would go. To think. To calm myself when I got stressed with all the pressure of being the best kid I could be. One that wouldn't disappoint my parents. A leader. A sports star. A model student. I even got lucky a time or two after the bonfire died out and the party on the beach had ended."

Annie frowned. She didn't like the thought of Wyatt being with Jersey, his high school girlfriend. And it stung her pride a little to know she had never been invited to one of those parties meant for the cool kids.

"So what does that have to do with this house your mom wants for you?"

"It's right by the lake. It even had a boat dock in the back-yard. It has been renovated on the inside and feels like something out of a fairy tale it is so charming. As soon as I walked onto the property, it felt like a twenty pound weight lifted off my shoulders. It sounds stupid, but the voices, the sounds inside my head even stopped for the first time since I've been home."

"Sounds to me like it might be worth it to spend the money if it's that therapeutic."

"I don't know. I don't want to work to make a house payment."

"Maybe I should give you a raise." Annie sure as hell didn't need all the money her granny had left her. Might as well put it to good use. And if that house helped Wyatt heal, it was worth it because she wasn't going to suggest fantastic sex to heal him. Damn her stupid friends and their stupid ideas. The more he worked at her farm, the more she woke up in the night dreaming about what his hands roaming her body would feel like, how his muscles would feel as she ran her fingers down his skin. She even wanted to feel the jagged edges of his scar to show him it didn't define who he was.

"That's sweet of you, Disney, but you can't give me enough of a raise to help me afford that house. I'll find another way to heal. I gotta grow up sometime and stop being a pansy ass. Lots of men come home more scarred than me. It's time I stopped feeling sorry for myself."

Sometime during the conversation, Annie and Wyatt had forgotten about their jars of lemonade and had scooted closer to one another so much that their knees were touching. Annie turned to face him and gently placed her hand on his chest.

"You aren't a pansy. You have a right to grieve because of all you saw over there. Sure, you're scarred. But you're definitely not broken."

Annie's breath hitched when Wyatt took her hand from his chest and moved it to his face. The side of his face where the scar ran, a permanent reminder of all he had seen and heard, all he had lost.

"Who's gonna love me when I look like this?" he asked. "The person I thought I was going to spend the rest of my life with took one look at it and ran for the hills."

"I always thought she was a stupid, snobby girl who was more obsessed with you getting her out of this town than she was actually caring for you."

"Are you saying she's a Darcy from *Varsity Blues*?"

"Never seen it."

"Then next time I come over, I'll bring it with me. You have to hear Billy Bob yell—"It's a ten! A ten!' It'll make your day."

"I'll give it a shot," she replied, rubbing circles with her thumb over his scar. "You wanna know something, Wyatt?"

"I'm kinda dying to know now."

"I think this right here," she said, running her finger down his scar, "Makes you even sexier."

Wyatt grinned. "You think I'm sexy, Disney?"

"Totally."

"Then can I kiss you now? I've been wanting to feel your lips ever since I wiped your face with my shirt like a dumbass."

"We shouldn't. I *am* your boss, after all," she said breathlessly. She meant it, too. Annie shouldn't kiss Wyatt Holloway. It wasn't a good idea. He came with baggage; she came with baggage. It was probably a recipe for disaster. But at this moment, Annie didn't give a rat's ass. "But I guess I can put aside the boss-employee relationship for one kiss."

Wyatt grinned, his eyes crinkling at the corners like she loved. "Thank god."

Wyatt pulled her between his legs, placed one hand behind her head and laid his lips on hers. He placed his other hand on her cheek and ran his fingers softly down her face and neck. "I knew it."

"Knew what?" she asked, her breath mingling with his.

"That you would taste like mint and sugar and perfection. And your skin would be so soft that I'd never get tired of touching it."

With those words, Wyatt deepened the kiss, opening her mouth with his tongue, exploring its depths. Her tongue intertwined with his and her hand wrapped around his neck to pull him closer. He smelled like sweat and hay and the familiarity of home. His touch curled her toes and his kiss set her lips on fire. It was at that moment Annie realized she was screwed. Wyatt Holloway had worked his way so far under her skin that she had no idea how she'd ever get him out of her head.

"Annie," he whispered, his lips against hers. "What in the hell are you doing to me?"

Annie smiled against his lips.

"You think that's funny?"

"Nope."

"Then why are you smiling?"

"Because you just called me Annie. You said you didn't want to call me Annie because it brought up too many memories."

Wyatt pulled back and stared at her, a look of vulnerability on his face. "Well, damn, Disney. I guess I did. Huh."

"What's that huh mean?"

Wyatt grinned. "Maybe I don't need a fancy house to heal."

"What?"

"Maybe I just need to kiss you a little more."

Wyatt placed his lips against hers again and Annie let out a sigh. Kissing Wyatt sounded like a pretty good plan. Maybe her friend's idea about sex helping people heal wasn't so far-fetched. One kiss from Wyatt and she could feel the hole in her heart from her granny's death grow a little bit smaller.

CHAPTER 11

"*Y*ou are so screwed."

Annie rolled her eyes at her friend's words. She was sitting in Breckin's counselor's office at Parker High School, trying not to shudder. She had one too many memories of being called into this exact same office to discuss her *feelings*...about her dad dying and her mom leaving...her friends...her lot in life. Annie hoped Breckin was a better counselor than Mr. Marks. He smelled like menthol, wore high-water pants, and had a habit of staring a touch *too* long at the female students.

"Why do you say that? It was just a kiss."

Breckin leveled her with *the look* the best friends reserved for each other when one of them was lying out her ass. Annie forced herself to maintain eye contact. She didn't have a prayer of fooling her friend if she broke it.

"I'm around horny teenagers all day, every day. I know the signs."

"What signs?" Annie grumped, even though she knew exactly what *signs* her friend was seeing.

"Flushed cheeks, stupid grin, hop in your step. You've got it bad."

"I don't have it *bad*."

Again with the look.

"How do I have it *bad*? It was just a damn *kiss!*" Annie put her head in her hands and blew out a breath. "You're right. I'm totally screwed."

"No, you actually aren't, my friend. If you were *really* screwed, I'm pretty sure you'd be in bed right now, sleeping like a baby. Or maybe smoking a cigar. And you'd *definitely* be naked. With Wyatt Holloway. Having amazing second round sex. You, my dear, were just kissed so well you've been ruined for all other men. Now, are you going to tell me CC and I were right?"

"Right about what?"

"That mind-blowing sex with Wyatt Holloway is probably just what the doctor ordered. For you *and* him."

Annie was pretty sure the grin was splitting her face. "How is someone such a good *kisser*? I've never been kissed like Wyatt kissed me."

"That's because your only regular kissing experience came from playing tonsil hockey with Jimmy Neutron."

"That's not true!"

Another look from her friend. Annie was really getting tired of them. Hell, maybe she was just tired of Breckin being right.

"I've kissed other men," she grumped.

"But those other men haven't been Wyatt Holloway."

"What's that supposed to mean?"

"That you've had the hots for him since he was the high school all-star and you were the girl from the wrong side of the tracks being raised by her crazy grandmother."

"What am I going to do?"

"Do you even have to ask?"

"Apparently, I do, because I'm asking you."

"You're gonna *do* Wyatt Holloway. Way more than once. And you both are going to piece yourselves back together one raucous romp at a time."

Annie rolled her eyes. "You are so obnoxious."

"Girl, all I'm saying is if I had a man as beautiful as Wyatt Holloway kissing me so well he made my toes curl, jumping in his bed wouldn't even be a question."

"You're the school counselor and we're in your office. Should you be talking like this?"

"They don't have microphones in all the rooms of the building. Yet, anyway. Your sexual exploits with Wyatt are safe from virgin ears for now."

"I don't have any sexual *exploits!*"

"Let's see if you can say that by the end of the week."

Annie shook her head. "You are too much, Breck."

"If by too much, you mean too sex-starved that I have to live vicariously through you and your almost sexcapades, then yes. I totally agree."

"I'm sorry, Breck. How have things been since...you know."

"You mean since the man I married decided a year ago to run off with Cricket Wilson, Parker High's lead cheerleader, as soon as she walked off the graduation stage? Not all that well, believe it or not. At least the divorce was finalized last week."

"That's the *you know* I was referring to."

Breckin tossed the ACT prep booklet she was paging through on the table against the wall, let out a breath, and plopped down in the chair behind her desk. "I know. That *you know* is just hard to talk about, even with my best friends. I was the laughingstock of the entire town."

"You weren't."

"I was. What kind of woman doesn't know her husband had a thing for a high school cheerleader?"

"One who trusted a sleaze-ball, that's who. No one thinks you're at fault, Breck."

"Well, if they don't, they pity me. I don't know what's worse."

Annie pulled her friend in for a hug. "I love you, Breck. CC loves you. To hell with what everyone else thinks."

"I have the best friends in the world, you know that, right?"

"Damn straight you do."

"Ms. Henderson?" The school's secretary's, Joan, voice came over the intercom in Breckin's office.

"Yes, Joan?"

"Todd Johnson is ready to see you. He said you were going to talk to him about some college scholarships he could apply for."

"Yep. I'm just about finished. Tell him I'll come get him in just a minute."

"Will do, Ms. Henderson."

Breckin smiled and shrugged her shoulders. "A counselor's job is never done."

Annie pulled her friend in for another hug. "I wish I had a counselor as good as you in high school instead of creepy Mr. Marks. You're helping so many kids, Breck."

"Thanks, Annie."

"Keep your chin up, ya hear?"

"Loud and clear."

Annie saluted her friend and walked out of the office. Todd, the student waiting to see Breckin, was sitting in one of the chairs in the secretary's office. He reminded Annie of Jimmy Newton, even down to the same glasses. His momma was Jesse Lewis, the owner of the feed store in town. If Todd was anything like his momma, he was a hard worker and had his head on straight. He hoped Breckin could help him out. She knew Jesse didn't have the money to send Todd to school on her own. Good thing her friend was a whiz at helping kids find scholarships to help them achieve their dreams.

Heck, maybe that was something Annie could do with her million dollars. Set up a scholarship fund for kids who couldn't afford college. She'd just have to find a way to do it without her friends and people in town knowing about the millionaire she had become. Her town was filled with good people but, like any town, it had its people who would take advantage of others, especially if they knew you had something to offer. Maybe she'd ask Harry what she could do. Surely a lawyer would know something about giving anonymously.

With a wave to Joan, Annie walked out of the office. It was back to the grind, if Annie could even call it that. Work wasn't really work when she had Wyatt and all his army man muscles to stare at day in and day out.

WYATT WALKED INTO GRIFF'S, the familiar notes of a George Strait song playing on the jukebox Wyatt paid for by bussing tables so long ago. The bar was pretty much empty except for old man Campbell sitting in the corner booth at the back. Wyatt nodded his head at the old man, who saluted Wyatt with the beer in his hand before directing his eyes to the Rangers game on the television hanging on the wall. Wyatt hopped onto a stool and tapped a couple of times with his knuckles. Griff's head popped up from behind the order window, a towel thrown over his shoulder.

"What are you doing at a bar at two in the afternoon?" Griff asked him, coming around the corner. "Woman trouble?"

Wyatt laughed. "You can't really count it as coming to a bar when my friend owns it. It's just like visiting my friend's house. Did you give old man Campbell the fifth degree when he walked in?"

"He comes in every day at one-thirty sharp to eat an average cheeseburger and take advantage of our happy hour from one-thirty to two-thirty."

"Does that mean I'm in time for happy hour, too?"

Griff grabbed an icy mug out of the freezer and a bottle of Blue Moon and an orange slice from the mini-fridge behind the bar. "You haven't been away so long I've forgotten your favorite. I've been saving 'em for you."

"Thanks, man," Wyatt said, using the countertop's edge to pop the top off the beer and pouring it into the frosty mug. He took a big drink. "Man, that's some good stuff right there. It's a scorcher out today."

"You must've forgotten what September in Oklahoma is like," Griff replied. "It's a scorcher every day."

"Ain't that the truth?"

"No doubt," Griff said, walking around the bar and plopping down on the stool beside Wyatt. "Now, you wanna really tell me why you're here?"

Wyatt took another swig of his beer and ignored his friend.

"Come on, Wy," Griff said with a grin. "We've known each other our entire lives. We both made all-state our senior year because we were so in-tune with each other as quarterback and wide receiver. Even though you've only been home a handful of times since you enlisted, I still know when you have something you want to tell me. So spill."

Wyatt weighed the pros and cons of telling his friend. He knew Griff would give him hell, but he had to tell someone and it sure wasn't going to be anyone in his family. They'd be planning the wedding. He finally sighed and said, "I kissed Annie."

"No shit!" Griff slapped Wyatt on the back, the beer in Wyatt's hand spilling over the top of the mug. "That's a lot better than wiping her face with your shirt, man. It was the muscles, wasn't it? She just couldn't resist the army muscles. I knew I shoulda joined up with you!"

Wyatt rolled his eyes. "Your muscles are big enough without the army helping you, man."

Calling Griffin Stephens big was an understatement. In high school, he was tall, lanky, fast, and had great hands, making him perfect as a wide receiver on the football team and a post player on the basketball team. Since high school, however, Griff had grown in girth rather than height. He was still an impressive six-three, but had definitely grown into his lankiness. Griff was built like a brick wall now, giving Wyatt's *army muscles* a run for their money. His hair was cut in a buzz, his beard would make Napoli from the Rangers jealous, and his arms were covered in sleeves of tats from shoulders to wrists.

To people who didn't know him, Griffin was one scary-looking man. However, people who *did* know Griff knew inside the tough exterior was a teddy bear. He still ate lunch with his mom and meemaw every Tuesday at Sadie's Café. Wyatt's mom told him when Griff's meemaw lost her license last year for driving her car all the way down Main Street in the opposite lane, Griff had taken it upon himself to drive her to Swanson's each week to buy her groceries. He even took her to poker night with her friends every Thursday.

"So, how was it?" Griff asked. "I'm sure it was spectacular if the cheesy ass grin on your face is any indication. But I want to hear it straight from the horse's mouth."

"It was more than spectacular. She's…"

"She's what, man? Don't leave a guy hangin'.'"

"She's friggin' amazing." Wyatt grinned and took another drink of his beer. "I don't even know how to describe her."

Griff whistled. "Man, you've got it bad. So when did this happen?"

"Yesterday. We were taking a break from working and…it just happened. I was telling her about being overseas and—"

Griff held his hand up. "Hold up. You told her about being *overseas*? That's even something you were reluctant to tell *me*! You've been working with her for the summer and you spill the beans? That's a whole other level of having it bad."

Wyatt shrugged his shoulders. "I didn't mean to. It just came out. She…I don't know. I feel like she gets me. She sure as hell doesn't judge me. I'm just comfortable with her. It just…I don't know…I guess it just comes easy."

Griff shook his head. "Did the kissing come just as easy?"

"You could say that. I haven't been that turned on since I kissed Jersey under the bleachers for the first time when I was fourteen."

Griff whistled again. "Damn. That's some serious shit."

"No joke. I just don't want to spook her. She's like a scared, wild colt. One wrong move and she'll run off for good. I need this job with her. She calms me."

"Just keep things slow. Take it from a wise bartender. Slow and steady wins the race."

Wyatt finished off the rest of his beer. "I agree."

"So, I know you work with her on a daily basis, but when are you gonna take her out? As in a man who takes out the girl he's interested in, not a man taking out his boss."

"I'm supposed to be driving her to her ice cream date with her best friends next Wednesday. I'm taking her for a ride in Sally."

"Sally?"

"I finally named my International."

"Why Sally?"

"She's blue."

"And?"

"Annabelle and her granny named all their animals after Disney characters. Sally is the name of Lightning McQueen's crush in the movie, *Cars*. I figured it wouldn't hurt my chances if I took her cue and named my truck after a Disney character."

Griff chuckled. "Slick, man. Remind me to take pointers from you next time I need to up my dating game."

"How's that going, by the way? I know you haven't dated since Randi."

Griff's long-time girlfriend had moved with him to the city when Griff had gotten his gig at the bar there. A year after they left, Randi had gotten killed in a bad motorcycle accident. A guy had run a red light and plowed right into Randi on her bike. She had been killed instantly. Griff was different since that happened. He was still *Griff;* he just walked around like a piece of himself was missing.

"I don't think I'm ready."

"I'm not tellin' you what to do, but it's been four years. I don't think Randi would want to see you like this."

"I don't think I'll get better than Randi. She was it, ya know? I'm not celibate, a man's gotta do what a man's gotta do to stay sane. But no one will ever come close to her. I'll be attached to her till the day I die."

Wyatt clapped his friend on the back. "Maybe one day someone will come around. She won't be able to replace Randi, but she'll still make you happy."

"So how'd the house hunt with your mom and aunt go?" Griff asked, changing the subject. Every time they talked about Randi his friend shut down. "Find anything?"

"Yeah. I found something I liked. Unfortunately, it was totally out of my price range."

"Well, that sucks. Think you can get the buyer to come down?"

"I don't know. He was actually my drill sergeant in boot camp, believe it or not. And he wasn't a fan of my punk ass."

Griff laughed. "No joke?"

Wyatt shook his head. "Nope."

"Man, it's a small world. Maybe he's not one to hold a grudge. You should try to talk to him, just to see."

"Maybe." Wyatt downed the last of his beer and slammed the mug back on the counter. He pulled out his wallet and threw a couple of ones next to it.

Griff took the ones and stuffed them back in Wyatt's hand. "Your money is no good here, don't you know that by now?"

Wyatt shook his head. "One day you're going to let me pay."

"I can't do that. You gotta save money for that fancy house you're wanting to buy."

"I think I'll need a little more than the two dollars I saved on my beer."

"Well, you gotta start somewhere, right?"

Wyatt chuckled. "You're probably right."

CHAPTER 12

"Oh. My. Lord." Annie groaned and tried to peel a wayward strand of sweat-soaked hair off her face. She and Wyatt had been working on the roof for an entire week and Annie was exhausted. She used muscles she didn't even know were muscles and had probably sweat her weight every day as the September sun beat down on them. Even with the numerous trees on her property offering shade, it was still sweltering.

Anyone who lived in Oklahoma knew there was no happy medium between summer and winter. Oklahoma didn't really have a fall. The weather in the state could be one hundred degree sunny weather one day, and then snowy thirty-two degree weather the next. Oklahomans knew not to change out their summer clothes in their closet for their winter ones until at least November. Even then, it was a toss-up on what type of weather Mother Nature would supply. Annie remembered one Christmas where she wore shorts and a tank top the entire day and then woke up to a foot of snow the following morning.

When they removed the old roof, Wyatt had discovered

even more rotted wood than he found in the stalls, which all had to be replaced. He had purchased all the wood from Nailed It, the hardware store in town, but had gone to the Lowe's in Lakeview for the insulation, edging, flashing, and metal panels, hoping to find better pricing than their small town could offer. Instead, he had come home empty-handed and told Annie he was going to special order the supplies from Max, the owner of Nailed It, because the materials Lowe's had in stock were *subpar.*

"If I'm going to special order everything, I might as well support the economy of our town," he had said. "It's probably going to be more money, though."

She still hadn't told him how she had an endless supply of money at her disposal, nor did she know how to bring it up. It seemed like Wyatt was always worried about spending too much, had even offered to foot the bill for the special-ordered materials. He probably thought she was scraping the bottom of the barrel to buy everything because he had yet to accept a paycheck.

"I'm just fixing the roof, not building my dream house," Annie had told him and then laughed at the horrified look on his face.

One thing she'd discovered since she hired him was that Wyatt Holloway was a perfectionist. She didn't know if it was something the army had taught him or if he was like that when he was younger, but it bordered on obsessive.

"Are we finished? Please tell me we're finished!" she begged, taking a drink of the bottle of cold water sitting in the cooler at her feet. She didn't know if she could haul another sheet of metal up the ladder and onto the roof. The first day, they thought they would be proactive and haul all the metal to the roof so they wouldn't have to traipse up and down the ladder. What they didn't take into consideration was the fact that the metal baking in the hot Oklahoma sun would be too hot to touch, much less install. They quickly figured it out, ensuring another trip *down* the ladder with it all to place it under the magnolia tree Annie loved so much. Its large leaves protected the metal from the sun's rays, thus protecting their tender hands in the process.

Annie laughed internally at the idea of Wyatt's hands being tender. She had seen him hammer nails, tear out rotted wood from the walls of the barn, clean out gutters and haul hay bales like they weighed a couple of pounds rather than fifty. But her laughing ceased as she also remembered the way he caressed her face with the rough pads of his fingertips when he kissed her on her front porch, the gentle way he rubbed small circles on her thigh after the kiss ceased, silently telling her he didn't want to stop touching her.

She had woken up several times in the week since it happened with the feel of his chapped lips on hers and his callused fingers running down her face and neck. It didn't help that the more comfortable they became with one another, the less clothing Wyatt wore while working. Today, he had shed his t-shirt as soon as they started to work, leaving him in only a pair of bright blue Nike shorts and his sneakers. The sun had tanned the farmer's tan line off his arms and chest, leaving nothing but a smooth, muscled, sexy canvas of tanned, sweating skin. "We're finished," he said with a grin, taking a bottle of water out of the chest.

"Thank god!" she said with a grin. "I don't know if I could survive another day of your brutal slave-driving!"

"*You're* the boss! You're the one supposed to be *my* slave-driver, not the other way around."

Annie laughed. "Maybe so. But I've never seen someone work as hard as you. I have to *make* you take breaks!"

Wyatt laughed with her. "But just take a look at the finished product, Disney. How's that for a bad-ass roof?"

Annie shielded her eyes and gazed at the roof of the barn.

Wyatt had told her what materials he was ordering but let her pick out the color. She had chosen a green a couple shades darker than the mint shade coloring the ends of her hair. Wyatt had said it reminded him of mint chocolate chip ice cream, which brought a smile to her face. He had even brought her a pint of Blue Bell mint chocolate chip the next day when she admitted it was her favorite flavor if she couldn't have a sundae with her friends.

"What are you thinking in that head of yours?" Wyatt stood beside her, his eyes also gazing at the roof.

"I'm thinking that I love it. I'm grateful you decided to help me out. And I'm wondering if I am going to have to stuff dollar bills down your pants like a stripper to get you to take money from me. Why won't you cash the checks I keep giving you?"

"I don't want your money."

"I *hired* you! You're my employee! It kind of comes with the territory."

Wyatt shrugged his shoulders. "I don't need it."

"You told me you found your dream house but you can't afford it. So why exactly do you think you don't need my money? Are you too good for my money?"

"I'm not too good for your money. I just don't want to take your money, Disney."

"Why not? You sure as hell have been working hard enough for it."

Wyatt turned his eyes away from the roof and faced Annie. "You inherited this land and all of the animals and buildings that go with it. That upkeep isn't cheap. And your granny sure as hell wasn't rich. I wouldn't feel right taking what little money you have."

Annie tried not to laugh, but she couldn't hold it back. It exploded out of her in uncontrollable hiccups. She wiped the tears streaming out of her eyes, the sting of the salt from her sweat mingling with the tears of laughter.

"What's so funny?" Wyatt said, hands crossed over his chest and a frown on his face. "I was trying to be helpful."

Annie pulled up the edge of her tank top to wipe her eyes. "You are helpful. So incredibly helpful. What you don't realize, though, is I could be helpful to you, too."

"I have no clue what you mean."

Annie shrugged her shoulders. "I'm a millionaire."

"Come again?"

"My granny left me two million dollars and change. Well, if you consider two hundred thousand dollars change."

Wyatt stared at her in shock. "How in the name of everything holy did she do *that*? I thought you guys were barely making ends meet."

"Me, too! But then Harry calls me into his office to read me her will. Apparently, her grandfather left her oil and mineral rights to some land and Granny saved almost all of them."

Annie started laughing again. "She sewed my clothes or I bought them at Goodwill or other thrift stores. We never had anything new. She was the cheapest, most tightwad person I knew. And all that time, she had two million dollars in the bank!"

"Why didn't she tell you?"

"I have no clue."

"What are you going to do with all that money?"

"I have no clue about that, either. All I know is I would gladly give all of it away if it meant I could see my granny one more time in her favorite muumuu, or hear her gruff voice give me sage advice she read on a fortune cookie slip."

Annie's tears of laughter turned to tears of sorrow. She hadn't let herself cry for the loss of the only person she called family. Not since her granny was sick. Not since she followed her granny's wishes in her will. Not since she and her granny's friends spread her ashes on the land Granny had loved with her whole heart.

"I just miss her so much. She was my only family, the only person who *wanted* me. And now she's gone."

"Aw, Disney. Come here." Wyatt pulled her into his chest and wrapped his arms around her. Annie let him. Even though they were both sweaty and smelled like they had been working hard all day, which they had. Even though it wasn't smart to let him. Wyatt, in such a short amount of time, had become an important person in her life, much more than she wanted to admit even to herself. He represented comfort and security, something Annie had been severely lacking since her granny passed away. And that scared the shit out of her.

Annie felt hot tears running out of her eyes and down Wyatt's chest. Embarrassed, she tried to pull away but Wyatt just held her tighter. Finally, once she realized he wasn't letting her go, Annie wrapped her arms around his waist and took the comfort he was offering. They stood like that for several minutes, Annie crying and Wyatt simply holding her. When she felt she had gotten herself under control, Annie pulled away. This time, Wyatt let her.

"I got tears and snot all over your chest," she said sheepishly.

Wyatt kissed her on the forehead. "Disney, you can cry on me whenever you want. I don't mind the tears. I'm not gonna lie, though. The snot is kind of gross. Good thing I deal with my niece and her snotty nose on a regular basis."

Annie smiled sheepishly and punched him in the arm. "Not funny."

"It was sorta funny."

Annie rolled her eyes. "I guess it was. *Sorta.*"

Wyatt chuckled before placing his finger under her chin

and fixing his gaze on her face. "It's okay to cry. It's okay to miss her. But you're not alone. You have friends who consider you family and you have me. That should count for something."

"It does," she whispered.

"Good. Then I am going to do something I've been dying to do since the moment we kissed on your front porch."

Wyatt backed Annie up against the trunk of her favorite magnolia tree, his lips trailing kisses down her neck and along her collar bone, his hand reaching up her shirt to trace the outline of her breast in the sports bra she was wearing under her tank top. Annie let out a gasp. His kisses were everywhere. His *hands* were everywhere, leaving trails of fire along her skin. She didn't know where he ended and she began. All too soon, he ceased his kissing, touched her forehead with his, and took a deep breath.

"You taste just as good as I remember."

Annie put her hand on his face. "And you kiss just as good as *I* remember. Maybe even better."

"I'm here for you, Disney. Always."

Annie felt her heart swell with...well, she didn't really know. But just like the last time he kissed her, she felt the hole in her heart close even more. In fact, her heart was now probably equal parts Wyatt and her granny. "Well, if you're always here for me, does that mean you'll start taking my money? Now that you know I can afford it?"

Wyatt grinned and kissed her forehead. "Not a chance in hell."

WYATT LOVED the way Annie's cheeks were flushed and her lips were swollen with his kisses. *His.* That's what he thought when he looked at her. And then she threw the curve ball at him that she was a millionaire. What in the *hell?* Her granny pulled one over on her for sure. He just hoped she didn't tell anyone else, except maybe her friends. He had a feeling if some people in the town knew, they'd take advantage of Annie's giving nature.

"Hey, Disney? Will you do me a favor?"

"Depends on what it is."

"Don't tell a lot of people your granny left you all that money. You're so trusting and a sucker for people who are hurting. I don't want someone to take advantage of you."

"I hadn't planned on it. But why do you say I'm a sucker for people who are hurting?"

"Because you dated Neutron. You were nice to the chubby girl in school who always seemed to have her skirt stuck in her tights when she left the bathroom. You'd play chess with Harvey Peters in the morning outside Sadie's café when his wife died. You care about people."

Annie's eyes softened. "You noticed that?"

"I noticed everything about you. I was just too embarrassed to admit it."

She grinned, the smile lighting up her face. It was a smile he would be happy seeing every day for the rest of his life. "You're forgiven."

"For what?"

"For being too embarrassed to talk to me. If I were as popular as you, I wouldn't have talked to me, either. I was the strange girl with an even stranger granny. I totally would have ruined your popularity."

"Well, high school me was a dumbass. There's no other way to say it. I shouldn't have cared."

Annie put her hand on his face. The side with the scar. Every time she did that, it took his breath away. Jersey had just seen it as something that marred his once handsome face. She had never looked the same way at him when he got off the plane. Annie didn't see the scar. Well, she did *see* it. Physically. But he knew it didn't matter to her. "Wyatt. It's okay. Really."

Wyatt leaned her back against her favorite magnolia tree again and kissed her softly. "You're pretty amazing, Disney."

She winked at him. "That's what all the boys say."

Wyatt kissed her again, this time with more urgency. He didn't feel like talking anymore. All he wanted was the feel of his lips on hers.

CHAPTER 13

"*H*i, guys! Welcome to Sadie's. Just find a seat. I'll be right with ya in a minute."

Annie handed three menus to the family who walked into the café before heading back to the register to cash out the last customer's ticket. When Sadie had called Annie because January, one of Sadie's best waitresses, had called in sick, it had been a no-brainer. Sadie had given Annie a job in high school when she needed one and then let her come back when she was nothing but a college dropout taking care of her granny. She owed the café owner. Besides, Annie loved waiting tables at Sadie's. She had missed it.

Making the right change, Annie walked back to the table of the family who had just finished their meal and gave them their change. "Y'all have a nice night," she said with a smile.

"Hey, Annie! I can't believe you're still working at Sadie's." Annie heard one of the people she had just seated call out to her.

Annie walked over to the table. In her years working at the café, Annie probably knew everyone who came into the establishment. Everyone local, that is. She couldn't possibly know all the visitors of their town who just came to enjoy Parker Lake. She had no clue who the person who called out to her was, but apparently, he knew her. Might as well see who it was.

"Can I help you guys?" she asked, walking over to the table.

"You don't have any idea who I am, do you?"

Annie faced the man staring at her expectantly. Silver hair. Startling blue eyes. Tortoise shell glasses. "Um—"

Silver-hair laughed. "Nice to see I made such an impression."

Annie's eyes went wide. "I'm so sorry. I'm horrible with faces," she lied. That totally wasn't true. She was just as good at remembering faces as her granny, which made it incredibly awkward when the person Annie hugged had no clue who she was. Annie finally started refraining from hugging until she knew the other person recognized her. What could she say? She was a hugger by nature.

"It's okay. I honestly don't expect you to remember me. I've changed a little."

"*I'll* say, Dad!" A cute girl with blonde pigtails and a gap-toothed smile said. "You used to be *super* fat!"

"Hey, now!" he said, ruffling his daughter's hair. "That's not nice."

"You always tell me to be honest."

"That I do."

"I'm sorry, sir. I still don't know—"

Silver-hair shook his head. "Right, right. You still have no clue who I am. I'm Donald Rice. Your biology professor from Lakeview Community College. I figured you'd be an established vet by now."

"Dr. Rice! I can't believe I didn't recognize you!"

"Now you're just being polite. I weighed one hundred

twenty pounds more last time I saw you. I can't believe I *expected* you to recognize me."

A pretty lady with a blonde bob and friendly smile chuckled. "Don't mind my husband, Annie. He doesn't realize how much different he looks now. I swear, I need to buy him a better mirror."

Dr. Rice smiled at his wife and patted her hand. Annie smiled. They were an adorable family.

"What brings you to town, Dr. Rice?"

"I had lap-band surgery a few years ago and lost all the weight. Two years ago, I had the surgery to remove all of that excess fat flesh, as I like to call it. Now I can do more with my family than I could ever dream of doing before. I've run a half and a full marathon. I've even zip-lined! We just bought a boat and one of the first places I wanted to take it to was Parker Lake. You're right. It's a beautiful lake. I couldn't wait to try the food here, either. I remember you telling me how great the food was at Ms. Sadie's. We decided to give it a try."

"Trust me, sir. You won't be disappointed."

"What's good?" Dr. Rice's daughter asked.

"Everything. But be sure to save room for dessert. Ms. Sadie's chocolate pie is *amazing*," Annie whispered behind her order pad. She was rewarded with a giggle from the little girl. She really was cute.

"Please tell me you went to vet school, Annie. You would make a wonderful vet."

Annie's smile fell. How would she tell one of her favorite college professors she dropped out?

"I didn't go," she whispered.

"What?"

"I didn't go," she said. "My granny got sick the semester after I took your class and I had to come home. Sadie gave me my old job back so I could work and take care of my granny at the same time."

"That was very noble of you. I hope she got better."

"She did."

"That's great."

"But then she got sick again, so I just stayed. She died a couple of months ago."

Dr. Rice's wife's face fell. "Oh, honey. I am so sorry."

"I had no idea," Dr. Rice said. "I'm sorry to have mentioned it."

Annie smiled. "How could you know? Besides, she lived a long, happy life. She was ninety-one when she died. I was happy to help her out when she needed me."

"Well, I'm sorry for your loss. I bet your granny was thankful she had a granddaughter as good as you."

"Thanks, Dr. Rice. It was good seeing you. Have fun at the lake. You might not get many more chances to go. According to *Farmer's Almanac*, we're supposed to have a crazy winter."

"I hope it's wrong. I'm not a fan of the cold."

"Me, either."

Annie took the family's order and walked behind the counter to put the order in the window for Sam, the café's cook who had been working for Sadie for as long as Annie could remember.

"Order up, Sam!" she called.

"Thanks so much for helping me tonight, Annie," Sadie said, ringing up a ticket at the register before running a card through the reader. "I don't know what I would've done if you hadn't said yes."

"You know I'll always say yes to you, Sadie. Besides, it's not like I have a busy night life or anything. I'd probably just spend it with Sebastian and Nemo on the couch, watching reruns of *Seinfeld*."

"You let Nemo back in the house?"

"As soon as granny's ashes were spread."

"You know she's probably rolling over in her grave, right?"

"She willed me the house. I can do what I want."

"Touché."

Annie giggled. She had forgotten how much fun Sadie was.

"So when are you going to take Wyatt up on that ride he suggested?"

Annie felt her face turning red and rolled her eyes. So much for fun Sadie. Nosey Sadie was now rearing her head. "What ride?"

"You know what ride. The ride you were supposed to hitch with him a couple of weeks ago to your Wednesday sundae date with the girls. Don't think I haven't noticed. Sadie Wilson notices *everything*."

Annie rolled her eyes. "*Sadie*! Quit being nosey."

"Nosey is my middle name, girl. Now spill."

"It's not that I haven't *come* with him, per se. We've both just been busy. And we haven't even had our Wednesday date a couple of times because Breckin was busy getting stuff ready for the new school year. It wasn't my fault."

"This doesn't have anything to do with that smoldering kiss you two shared, does it?"

Annie was going to kill Breckin. "No. It doesn't."

"Liar."

Annie blew her bangs out of her face in frustration. "I shouldn't be kissing my employees, Sadie. It's unprofessional."

Sadie pished at her. *Pished*. "We both know Wyatt Holloway is your employee in name only. He has the hots for you. You have the hots for him. I say you just go at it and be done with it. Maybe the sex will be awful and you don't have to worry about it."

"We don't have the *hots* for each other!"

Sadie just looked at her. Annie groaned. "There's no way sex with Wyatt Holloway would be awful," she muttered, banging her head on the countertop. "Not if he…well, *does it* as well as he kisses."

Sadie clapped her hands in glee. "I'm so happy for you both! You're both hurting. Might as well help each other heal."

"I *told* you, Sadie. Having sex with someone won't heal *anything*! It will just complicate an already complicated situation even more."

"What will complicate an already complicated situation?" Annie wanted to stab herself in the foot with a fork when she heard Wyatt's voice. She lifted her head, praying she was mistaken. Nope. There he was, sitting at a stool by the register, the ever present Parker High baseball cap perched on his head. He was wearing another olive-colored army t-shirt, which only enhanced the green of his eyes. The only difference was his hair wasn't curling out from under the cap like it usually was. How she hadn't noticed him come in she had no clue. Sadie apparently had. She had apparently plopped a sweet tea in front of him as soon as he sat down.

"Did you get a haircut?" Annie asked, trying to change the subject.

"I did. From your best friend. Thanks for noticing. By the way, do you know her hair is now lilac purple with violet streaks in it?"

"Nope. Did not know that. But thanks for preparing me. I never know what hair color she's going to be sporting from one day to the next."

"I don't think I've seen her natural hair color since high school."

"Nor will you ever. She says it makes her look like a mouse."

Wyatt chuckled. "Fair enough. Now, what was this complicated situation you and Sadie were talking about?"

"Order up!" Annie was saved by the literal bell Sam had just rung, signaling an order was ready. Luckily, it was Dr. Rice's family's meal.

"I gotta take this to my table," she said.

"Don't worry about that, hon," Sadie said with a wink, stepping in front of Annie and grabbing the order. "I've got this covered. You just sit there and have a nice conversation with Wyatt. Maybe talk about that sundae date he's supposed to be driving you to."

Annie glared at the back of Sadie's head. See if she ever helped fill in at the café again.

"Yeah, about that date. You *still* haven't ridden in Sally. Her feelings are hurt."

"Your truck has feelings?"

"Absolutely. Yesterday, she was crying as I was changing her oil. She told me you wouldn't ride in her because you were afraid to sit next to me because you wouldn't be able to control yourself. She blames me."

Annie couldn't help it. She laughed. "Well, tell Sally I'm sorry."

"Why don't you tell her yourself when I take you to your sundae date with your friends?"

"We haven't had one in a couple of weeks. Breck has been really busy with school starting and CC's business at the shop has really picked up lately."

"Then instead of me taking you to *that* date, why don't you go on a date with *me*?"

Annie nearly swallowed her tongue. "A date? With you?" she squeaked. "That's not a good idea."

"Why not?"

"Because I'm your boss. It's not professional."

Wyatt leaned over the bar. He was so close Annie could

feel his breath tickle her neck as he whispered in her ear, "I think the boss/employee relationship ended the minute you kissed me. Twice now."

Annie pulled back from him, a frown on her face. "I definitely remember you *asking* if you could kiss me!"

"And you said yes. It was definitely crossing the line, Boss. Or should I call you my kissing buddy now? I think I speak for the both of us when I say both times were mind-blowing. If I need to resign, I'll do so, especially if it means I'll get to kiss you again."

Annie wanted to stomp her foot in frustration. The man was infuriating. Even so, just thinking about that kiss and the sex all her friends said she and Wyatt should be having sent a tingle down her spine. She let out a breath. This was so not good. "Where do you want to go?" she huffed.

"Why don't I let Sally decide?"

"What does that mean?"

"That means it's going to be a surprise." Wyatt tapped his knuckles on the countertop and stood. "I guess I better go have that talk with Sally now. She'll probably want to do some planning. How does tomorrow sound? Since you're no longer my boss we can blow off work for the day. I hear it's going to be a scorcher."

"It's a scorcher every day right now."

"I know. But *Farmer's Almanac* says winter is going to be a bitch. We better take advantage of the scorching weather while we can."

Annie watched Wyatt as he walked out the door, waving at the locals as he went.

"Well, would you look at that? It seems like you and Wyatt finally have a date." Sadie stood behind Annie and patted her on the back. "It's about time. It looks like you both are on your way to some—"

Sadie paused for dramatic effect before singing, "Sexual healing!"

Annie rolled her eyes and didn't bother answering. She knew as soon as she left for the night, Sadie would be texting her friends to tell them the news if she hadn't already. It would be best not to fuel that fire. In their minds, her friends would be walking her down the aisle in the near future. She just couldn't give in to their ridiculous idea. She was just Wyatt's boss, no matter what he tried to say and what he called a date was nothing but going over what came next at the farm. At least that's what she tried telling herself. It was too bad she didn't believe a word of what she was saying.

WYATT WOKE with a scream dying on his lips. He was covered in sweat and his body was wracked with shivers from the remnants of the nightmare that had plagued him since he returned home. It was the same every damn time. A little kid, no more than eight years old, with a bomb strapped to his chest. Wyatt sitting on the roof of a building with another sniper whose guns were trained on the child in the middle of the street. The rest of his platoon clearing a building with no clue of the child headed straight toward him. Wyatt and the other sniper, Tom from Alabama, trying to radio in to their commander, but not reaching him. To this day, Wyatt didn't know why. Tom had been whispering to Wyatt to take the shot because he had a better angle. But Wyatt couldn't do it. He froze.

Wyatt remembered a couple members of his platoon coming out of the building. He remembered the child running toward them, hearing the sound of a bullet exiting a rifle and seeing the child drop to the ground, inches from his platoon members. Tom had taken the shot.

Even after that, the army had kept him overseas. It wasn't until their platoon was attacked and Wyatt almost lost half his face and *did* lose over half his unit that they sent him home. The army told him three tours in Afghanistan was enough and he needed to focus on his health, both mental and physical. He had returned home with an honorable discharge but the nightmare remained.

"Is everything okay, son?" Wyatt's dad was standing in the doorway, his body casting a shadow in the hallway.

This wasn't the first time Wyatt had called out in his sleep. His dad was the one who came to check on him every time. Wyatt figured his mom didn't want to embarrass him. It was one reason he needed his own place. He didn't want to subject his parents to any more of his nightmares.

"Yeah, I'm okay," Wyatt replied, trying to calm his breathing. "I'm sorry I woke you. Is Mom still asleep?"

"Yeah," his dad lied. Wyatt knew his mom woke up every single time. Maybe the lie helped his dad feel better.

"I'm really sorry, Dad. I promise I'm trying to find my own place."

Wyatt's dad shook his head. "Don't you worry about it, son," his dad replied, his voice thick with emotion. "I can't imagine the things you saw. If you ever want to talk about it, just let me know. I don't have a degree like Dr. Wilkerson, but your old dad is a good listener."

"About that. I don't think I'm going to go anymore."

"Are you sure that's a good idea?"

"There's only so much I can rehash before I start repeating myself. It's time."

"Whatever you want to do, son. Your mom and I support you in whatever you choose. And you can stay with us however long you need."

"Thanks, Dad." Wyatt appreciated his dad's offer, but he had to get out of their house as soon as possible. Much like his decision to stop going to his therapist, it was time to quit living with his parents.

"I love you, son."

"I love you, too."

His dad closed Wyatt's bedroom door and Wyatt drew in a deep breath. Why he kept dreaming that particular dream was a mystery. God knew he saw lots of other horrific tragedies during his time overseas, him losing half his platoon and almost half his face being one of the main ones. But it was always the kid with the bomb. Wyatt stared up at the ceiling. He knew he wouldn't be able to sleep for the rest of the night. He never could. Hopefully, it wouldn't ruin his date with Annie the following day. He had taken a step in the right direction with her. He could feel her resolve weakening and it made Wyatt smile.

Since he had returned, Wyatt's family and friends had tried setting him up on dates with various women, but Wyatt had no desire to take them up on their offers. He tried to blame it on Jersey leaving but knew it was more than that. The more Wyatt went overseas, the more he and Jersey had grown apart. Even if she hadn't seen the scar that messed up his face, she probably would've left him anyway. The scar was just the nail in the coffin.

No, Wyatt knew why he didn't want to go out with a woman. He didn't want to subject them to his problems, to his nightmares that woke him in the middle of the night. He was broken and he didn't know if he could ever be fixed.

But then he met Annabelle Cleaver. Well, gotten to know the woman she had become. If he were honest with himself, he would admit he'd always had a thing for her. Even with her kooky grandma, crazy outfits, outlandish hair, and completely weird, free spirit vibe she exuded, right down to her flower painted car, he had found her fascinating. She was smart and opinionated and nice to everyone she met. She defended Marcy Dayton, the girl with the lisp and horrible overbite who was often the subject of Jersey's meanness. She went to prom with Garvin Heathcliff before she got with Neutron. Heathcliff, who constantly had food stuck in his braces and wore suspenders on a regular basis. She was just good.

But Wyatt never approached her. Never really even said more than two words to her in high school. And it was all because of what his friends would say. He was terrified they would make fun of him for talking to the weirdest girl in school, just because she represented everything the popular students didn't understand and everything they were afraid of because she didn't fit the mold of what they considered cool. She didn't go with the norm. In fact, she seemed to revel being the rebel who didn't fit in.

Now, she was a beautiful woman who was just as fascinating as she was in high school. Probably more so. And now Wyatt was changed. He didn't give two shits what anyone thought, not that he had to worry about that. It seemed that everyone in their small town loved her. He just had to get her to see him as more than a friend, more than someone who was helping her on her farm. He hoped what he planned tomorrow was going to be enough.

CHAPTER 14

*W*yatt whistled as he finished filling Sally's bed with the items he needed to take Annie out. He was right. After the nightmare woke him up, he never went back to sleep. He wasn't tired like he expected to be, though. Instead of letting his nightmare plague him, he used his sleeplessness to his advantage. When he went to bed the night before, he had a vague idea of what he wanted to do with Annie. This morning, he got out of bed with an even better plan.

"How are you this morning, son?" Wyatt's mom walked down the steps of their farmhouse porch and headed his way. She had on her gardening hat—a big straw hat with a red and white polka-dotted band. She must be checking to see if she could harvest any more of the cherry tomatoes his niece was so fond of. Hattie popped them in her mouth like most kids would eat a bag of M&Ms.

"I'm all right, Mom. Thanks for checking. But why are you out in your gardening hat? Do you realize how early it is?"

"Oh, *I* know. Unfortunately, little missy over there—" his

mom pointed her thumb behind her, "Doesn't. So there goes my sleeping in on Saturday."

"Uncle Wy! We're gonna go check for 'matoes! Wanna come?" Hattie ran down the porch behind Wyatt's mom, an identical straw hat on top of her head. She had also donned a pair of ladybug gardening gloves that went up to her elbows, his mom's old sunglasses that took up half her face, a ruffled pink bikini top, overall shorts, and her favorite pair of purple cowgirl boots. On her arm was a canvas bag so big she had to continually hoist it up her arm to keep it from dragging the ground.

Wyatt chuckled. It was obviously choose-your-own-outfit Saturday. "I can't today, Hattie Mae. I gotta go somewhere."

"Are you going somewhere with a *girl?*"

Wyatt shot a pointed look his mom's way. "What makes you say that?"

"I heard Grammy talkin' to my mommy when she dropped me off to pick the 'matoes. Grammy whispered something to Mommy and Mommy yelled, "No *way! Annie Cleaver?*"

Wyatt tried to hide his grin and failed. His niece did a perfect impersonation of his sister, right down to the hands thrown in the air, wide-eyed look and shrieking voice. "Oh, really? What did you think about that?"

"I think if it's Miss Sophie's Annie Cleaver, then that makes me happy! I met her the other day, ya know." Hattie ran over to Wyatt and motioned for him to lean down so she could whisper in his ear. "At Sadie's. She has the *best* choco-late chip pancakes! Just don't tell Momma. She doesn't like me to have too much sugar. But I went with Daddy and *he* loves Sadie's pancakes, too."

His niece pulled the oversized sunglasses off her face and tried to wink at him, succeeding only in crinkling both eyes and blinking them really fast. He winked back and then chuckled when she continued her story.

"She was helping Sadie take people food the other day when Sadie needed help at the café. I told Sadie *I* would help but she said my arms were too tiny so I just needed to enjoy my date with my daddy. But *that's* when I saw her. Annie. And you wanna know somethin'?"

"I absolutely want to know something, Hattie Mae."

"My favorite ice cream flavor is mint chocolate chip. And the very bottom of Annie Cleaver's hair *matched* my favorite ice cream flavor! It was the most beautifulest hair in the world. When I grow up, I wanna have that hair *exactly*! Or maybe red 'cuz I love red. It reminds me of red 'matoes, which are yummy to my tummy."

Hattie rubbed her belly and licked her lips. "I *would* go with you, just so Annie would know you're a nice one, but I gotta get some more 'matoes. Daddy ate the rest of mine, the stingy Benji."

"Well, I certainly understand that. Stingy Benji daddies are no fun. And your grammy grows the *best* tomatoes in Oklahoma."

"I *know!*" Hattie raised her little arms in the air. "That's what I've been tellin' everybody!"

"Did you know before you were born, she had a tomato grow to be three pounds? It broke the record for the entire state for the biggest tomato. She even got to take it to the state fair in Oklahoma City and it won a huge, blue ribbon."

Hattie's eyes went wide and the sunglasses she had placed on her head when she tried to wink at Wyatt fell to the ground. "No. Way!"

Wyatt nodded. "Yes, way. You need to have your grammy get in the attic and find the picture of her with the tomato. She might even still have the ribbon. It's pretty cool."

Hattie turned to Wyatt's mom, her hands on her hips. "Grammy? Is this true?"

Wyatt's mom nodded her head in agreement. "It's true."

Hattie picked up her sunglasses and placed them on her nose. "Why am I always the last one to know anything?" she muttered, stomping off toward the garden, the canvas bag dragging behind her.

Wyatt shook his head and laughed. "That little girl is something else."

"She definitely is." Wyatt's mom walked over to his truck and peeked inside the bed. "What is all this?"

"Don't play dumb, Mom. I know the minute Annie agreed to go on a date with me Sadie sent a text to you and every other woman in town interested in my love life saying Annie and I were planning our nuptials. Am I right?"

Wyatt's mom shrugged sheepishly. "You might be a *little* right."

"By little, I'm taking that to mean exactly."

"Well then, now that the charade's over, are you going to tell me where you're going to take Miss Annabelle Cleaver? She deserves someone who will treat her like the amazing person she is."

"I agree."

"Seriously, Wyatt. She's a good one."

"I *know.*"

"I'm just making sure you do. Despite what you think, I didn't tell your daddy to send you to Annie's farm with the intent of doing anything but look for work. But I don't know if it's her or her farm or something else, but I've seen a peace come over you that I haven't seen since you've been back. You smile more. You laugh. You look happy. And that's saying something, kid."

"Thanks, Mom," Wyatt said, pulling her to him and kissing her on the cheek.

"I'm just saying what I see. Whatever this is you have going with Annie…it's a good thing. Just keep that in mind."

"Totally keeping it in mind. Now, you better go supervise that 'mato picking in the garden. I have a feeling Hattie is eating more than she's putting in the bag."

His mom rolled her eyes. "You're probably right about that."

"Hey, at least she's not scarfing Hershey kisses like that."

"Oh, she does that, too. I caught her hiding behind the cabinet in the entryway with the bowl of candy I keep on the island. She was covered in chocolate. When she knew she had been caught red-handed, she held up a Hershey kiss in a chocolate-coated hand and said, 'I saved you one.'"

Wyatt laughed. "That sister of mine has her hands full."

"That she does. Now all I need is for you to give me some grandbabies and you *both* can start paying for your raising."

"*Mom!*"

"*Wyatt James!*" His mother just shook her head and walked toward her garden.

"You know you love me!" he called. "I'm your favorite son!"

His mom waved her hand behind her head. "You're my only son!"

"Then I'm your favorite kid!"

"Give me grandbabies and we can make a deal."

Wyatt laughed. He had an incredible family. With one last look in the back of his truck, he hopped in the cab and headed toward Sophie's farm. He had a girl he needed to impress.

ANNIE PACED BACK and forth in front of her closet. She had no idea what to wear. And she wasn't a girl who *ever* thought twice about what she threw over her head. But ever since Wyatt Holloway entered the picture, she'd found herself staring in her closet at her clothes more than she'd like to admit.

The problem was Wyatt didn't tell her *what* to wear. He could be taking her on a helicopter ride, to a swanky restaurant in the city, or a haunted house for all she knew. When she asked where they were going, all he would say was, "It's a surprise." When she told him she hated surprises, all he said was, "Well, then prepared at being surprised by how much you'll like *this* surprise." He was infuriating. *And* the reason Annie was standing in front of her closet wearing nothing but her infamous Cookie Monster shorts and a Sandlot t-shirt.

"Damn you, Wyatt Holloway," she muttered under her breath. She was just going to tell him she wasn't going to go. It was nothing but a disaster waiting to happen, anyway. The simpler they kept their relationship, the better. Wyatt Holloway stayed away from Podunk Parker for eleven years. As soon as he recovered from whatever trauma he faced overseas, he would probably leave again for parts unknown. And Annie was staying put in Parker.

"Hello? Where are you, Disney?"

Annie heard Wyatt call from downstairs and sighed. She was just going to tell him to forget it.

"Now, I know I told you it was a surprise, but your Cookie Monster shorts are not appropriate." Wyatt walked into her room clad in a Parker High baseball t-shirt and a pair of blue and turquoise plaid swim trunks riding low on his hips.

Annie nearly jumped out of her skin. "Damn you, Wyatt Holloway! Don't freakin' *do* that!"

"Do what?" he said with a grin, knowing exactly what she meant.

"You know I startle—"

"Ridiculously easy? Yes, I know. That's why it's fun to do."

Annie tried to level him with a glare but didn't figure it was very convincing since she was dressed like a seven-year-old child. Besides the fact Wyatt was looking...well, looking pretty delicious. "Well, *don't*."

"Why aren't you dressed, Disney? We're leaving..." Wyatt pretended to look at an imaginary watch on his arm, "Now."

"I *know* we're supposed to leave now. But you didn't give me any clue about where we're going!"

"That's why it's a surprise. Did you ever get surprised as a kid?"

Annie continued to glare his way. "I don't like surprises."

"You don't like surprises. You don't like people to scare you. Were you born a seventy-five-year-old woman?"

Annie stuck her tongue out at him and plopped down on her mint green chair in the corner of her room. "I'm not leaving this room until you tell me where we're going and what I need to wear."

Wyatt looked at her in shock. "Oh, shit, Disney! Your hair just got four inches shorter. What kind of demon chair is that?"

Annie stared at him blankly. "What the hell are you talking about?"

Wyatt shrugged. "I was trying to be funny."

"By telling me my chair is possessed by Satan?"

"No. But your chair is the exact shade as the tips of your hair. I was making a joke, buzzkill."

Annie could feel her lips turning up at the corners. She didn't want to smile at him when he was being annoying. "You're so dumb."

"And you think I'm so funny."

Annie couldn't help it. She laughed. "That was the worst joke ever."

"Come on, Disney! Cut me a little slack. That was pretty good."

Annie crossed her arms over her chest. "I'm not cutting any slack until you tell me what I need to wear."

Wyatt rolled his eyes. "Fine. I'll just grab some stuff for you!"

Wyatt walked over to her closet, grabbed an empty bag off the floor, and started tossing things in it. Her yellow bikini, a black and white striped maxi dress, a pair of jeans, a cashmere sweater.

"Really, Wyatt? A sweater? It's one hundred degrees outside!"

"Hey, I'm just preparing for *everything*! You're the one who said you weren't coming until I packed for you."

"I said I wouldn't go until you *told me* where we're going!"

"Puh-tay-to, puh-tah-to."

Annie jumped off her chair, walked over to Wyatt, and pulled the bag out of his hands. "Fine! We can go. I think we're sufficiently prepared for any weather Oklahoma can deal."

"There's only one problem, Disney."

Annie threw her hands in the air. "What?"

"Cookie Monster isn't invited."

At his Cookie Monster comment, Annie had grabbed the bag out of his hands before stomping to what Wyatt figured was her bathroom and slamming the door. While she was gone, Wyatt took a look around her bedroom.

If he couldn't tell it by her hair, one look at her room and Wyatt knew mint green was definitely Annie's favorite color. In addition to the mint green chair in the corner, her bedspread was white with small mint green flowers spread randomly across the surface. The headboard was an old, ornate door painted mint green. She had an antique oak dresser on the wall across from the bed, mint green knobs on every drawer and a white and mint green striped rug was on the wide-planked oak floor on the right side of the bed. Wyatt was willing to bet that was the side of the bed where Annie slept. It didn't go unnoticed that his favorite side of the bed was the left.

A variety of pictures in mint green frames covered the walls, all filled with black and white pictures of Annie, her granny, her friends, and the animals on the farm. The room was simple and no-nonsense with a hint of feminine charm, totally different from the rest of the house that had Sophie written all over it. But this room...this room looked like Annie.

"Are you ready to go?" Annie came out of the bathroom with the bag thrown over her shoulder. He could see the ties of her bikini he threw in the bag around her neck, her Sandlot t-shirt she was wearing covering the rest. She had donned a pair of jean shorts over the bathing suit bottom and a pair of flip flops on her feet.

"This is about as good as I could do seeing as you didn't tell me *anything* about where we're going," she huffed.

"Well, I should probably tell you I'm taking you to that fancy restaurant in Lakeview," he said. "I wanted it to be a surprise but I don't want you to be embarrassed. It's why I threw the black and white dress in there. I figured you'd get the hint."

"You also threw a *cashmere* sweater in there!" she shrieked.

Wyatt laughed. "Damn, woman. You sure are moody."

"I'm *not* moody. I just hate—"

"Surprises. I know, I know. But you're dressed perfectly. Promise."

"Are we going to a waterpark?"

"Nope."

"The river?"

"Nope."

"Parker Lake."

Wyatt grinned. "Maybe."

"Good. Because I'm not wearing any makeup."

"Like I said. Perfect."

"Before we go we have to feed the animals."

"I thought you would already have that finished."

"Are you kidding? That's what I'm paying you for. There's no such thing as a free ride on this farm, Holloway."

"Well, then. Lead the way, Boss."

CHAPTER 15

*A*nnie tried not to smile as Wyatt whistled what she thought was *Bear Necessities* from the Disney movie, *The Jungle Book*. He had rolled the windows down on the truck, the warm air filtering through the cab, causing strands of her hair that had come loose from the bun on her head to blow in her face. She had her hand out the window, riding the waves the wind was making.

Wyatt turned to look at her. "This is nice, huh, Disney?"

"It might be a little nice."

"I'll take that as I did good."

"You can't do good until I know where we're going."

"I think you've figured it out. We're going to Parker Lake."

Annie grinned. "I did figure it out."

"But what you *haven't* figured out is I'm taking you to my favorite spot on the lake."

"Oh, yeah? What makes it your favorite?"

"The fact that it's a place not everyone knows about, especially the people who visit our lake from out of town. It's strictly for the people born and bred in Parker. More specifically, Griff and me. It's a small island back behind some of the big cliffs on the south side. It looks like the cove dead ends at a bunch of downed trees falling across the water, but what people don't know is that it doesn't. It curves around the cliffs and *bam!* There's a beach. You should feel privileged. I haven't ever gone back here with anyone other than Griffin."

"How'd you two find it?"

"We were fishing in the cove and saw a big crane fly out of the trees. We decided to check it out and saw it through the trees. We felt like Lewis and Clark."

Annie laughed. "I bet."

"We were covered in scratches trying to get through all the limbs. The next day, we went back out with a tree limb trimmer to cut enough away to get through in our boat without getting cut up but not enough that other people could see it."

"You can't tell me you didn't take Jersey back there for a few make out sessions."

"I never took Jersey back there."

"Seriously?"

"Seriously. She would make out with me anywhere at the drop of a hat. I didn't need the island to make that happen," he said with a waggle of his eyebrows.

Annie threw a water bottle cap at him that was next to her on the bench seat. "Braggart."

Wyatt chuckled and turned down the road leading to Griff's Bar.

"Where are we going? This isn't the way to the lake."

"Do you see a boat behind the truck? I have to go get Griffin's boat."

Wyatt pulled behind the bar and backed into the drive until he was close enough to Griff's garage. He grinned and waved at his friend, who was sitting on the deck above the bar that led to his apartment upstairs.

"What brings you to the bar this early in the morning?" Griff called, holding up a cup of coffee as a greeting.

"The better question is why are *you* up when your bar closes in the wee hours of the morning? I thought you'd still be in bed."

"Couldn't sleep. Too much on my mind. I'm guessing you're wanting to borrow the boat?"

"Yep."

"As long as you're taking that pretty lady in the passenger seat with you. I don't loan my boat to lonely, single men."

"I'm taking her to our place," Wyatt called out his window.

Griff whistled. "That's pretty serious, man. Does your momma know? If she does, she's probably planning your wedding. Annabelle, does Beverly Mae Holloway know this news?"

Wyatt looked over to Annie, who had her head in her hands. After a second, she leaned out the window and yelled, "Definitely not serious, Griff. Just two friends going to enjoy a day on the lake. He didn't even tell me where we were going until we were on the way."

"Yeah, yeah. That's what every girl under Holloway's spell says."

Wyatt could see Annie's face turning red. "Definitely not under any spell," she called out.

Griff chuckled. "Okie dokie, Disney."

If looks could kill, Wyatt would be dead meat.

"You told him my *nickname?*" she shrieked.

Wyatt shrugged his shoulders. "It might have slipped out."

"Wonderful," she muttered.

He ignored her. "Let me get out and hook the boat up, then we'll be on our way."

Annie crossed her arms and put her bare feet on the dash and was fascinated when he physically cringed.

"Does that bother you?" she said with an ornery grin, giving her feet a few taps. "My feet on your new dash?"

"Nope. Not at all," he said with a pained expression.

"Then I can type all I want with them?"

With every tap, Wyatt's face grimaced even more. "Tap away," he said, painfully.

Annie laughed. "I guess I'll take pity on you," she said, dropping her feet and shaking her head. Men and their toys.

"Thanks," he said, letting out a deep breath. "That was killing me."

"I never would've guessed."

Wyatt ran around the truck and lifted Griff's garage door. He hopped back in the cab and backed his truck up until he was close enough to hook up the bass boat to the hitch. After a minute, he was ready to go.

"You ready?" he asked, jumping back behind the driver's seat.

"I am if you brought sunscreen," she replied.

"That I did."

"Then let's go."

"You two kids have fun," Griff called, holding his mug up in salute. "Don't do anything I wouldn't do! And don't let anyone follow you to our spot. We catch some damn good fish back there."

"Will do, Griff."

Wyatt waved his arm out the window, pulled out from behind the bar, and pointed his truck toward the lake. Annie felt herself grinning when Wyatt began whistling another Disney classic. This time, she was pretty sure it was the song the Genie sang in *Aladdin*.

"Do you always whistle?" she asked.

Wyatt grinned, his eyes crinkling in the corners. "My grandad whistled, my dad whistled. I'm a third generation whistler. My grandad whistled *The Andy Griffith Show* theme song like a beast. My dad was a master at anything by Elvis."

"Well then, let me correct myself. Do you always whistle *Disney* songs?"

"Only when I'm with certain company."

"Just myself?"

"And my niece."

"Is this the niece whose face you wipe with your shirt?"

Wyatt chuckled. "That's the one. I still can't believe I did that to you."

"I still can't believe it, either."

"So you have a close family?" Annie didn't know much about his family other than who they were. His sister was a couple of years younger than Annie and they hadn't had any classes together, which was ironic in a town as small as Parker. Usually, classes combined with upper and lower classmen was the norm.

Wyatt grinned. "I do. My grandad and meemaw eloped when she was just sixteen. Her father was a preacher and almost disowned her because she ran off with "the heathen" in town," Wyatt finger-quoted.

"My mom and dad have been married for almost fifty years and my sister got married right out of high school to Jacob Perry. They were high school sweethearts, too. I'm the only one who didn't get married young. I married the army instead. And then…then there's Hattie."

"The one who loves Disney?"

"That's the one. She's the only grandchild, and when I say she's horribly spoiled, that's a total understatement."

Annie laughed. "I bet."

"She's five years old and a sucker for all things Disney. Every time it was dress up day at pre-k this year, she would head to her closet for a Disney costume. I think this year she has been Captain Hook, Rapunzel, Nemo, the rat in Ratatouille, Cruella DeVille and...maybe Mulan? I'd have to ask my sister."

"You can find all of those costumes in stores?"

"Most were special order in Beverly Mae's Costume Shop."

"I guess I don't know that place."

"That's because Beverly Mae is my mom."

"Ah! Beverly Mae Holloway. I don't know why I didn't get that."

Wyatt laughed. "Don't worry. I wouldn't have put two and two together, either. But my mom sews. And when your only grandchild asks you to make a costume, what kind of grammy would you be if you didn't deliver?"

"A crappy one."

"A crappy one," Wyatt mimicked her response and nodded his head. "Exactly."

"I kinda like that your niece doesn't do the froo-froo princesses for everything."

"Oh, no. Not Hattie Mae. She only wanted to be Rapunzel because her hair is super long and blonde. Hattie's hair is curly and black. She said she wanted to know what it felt like to have long, blonde hair for a day."

"She's named after your mom?"

"She is. After my sister was in labor for twenty-seven hours, she said she had a new appreciation for what my mom went through delivering two children without an epidural. She said giving Hattie our mom's middle name was the least she could do."

"That makes sense."

"Hattie says she's glad her mom decided to name her Hattie Mae instead of Hattie Beverly because that sounded really stupid."

"I think I would like this niece of yours," Annie said with a smile.

In fact, Wyatt's entire family sounded amazing. Before her granny, her home had just been a dysfunctional, violent place with her parents. Then, it was just her and Sophie. She never had a niece or a sister. Or even parents, really. They may have provided her DNA, but she never considered the people who birthed her as parents, anyway.

"Well, I think she would like you *and* all the animals on your farm."

Annie grinned. "Then you should bring her with you one day. What grade is she in? Kindergarten?"

"Yep."

"Will your sister let her skip one day?"

"I don't know. It's the beginning of the school year and my sister is pretty strict. Hattie and her dad have to sneak chocolate chip pancakes at Sadie's because my sister doesn't want her having too much sugar."

"I doubt she'll lose her scholarship to Harvard this young."

Wyatt chuckled. "I might be able to swing it."

"Tell your sister it's educational. Biological education, in fact. Or zoology. That sounds smarter. She'll be insisting Hattie comes with you."

"That's a good idea. Did you pull any over on Sophie like that?"

"Are you kidding me? I could never pull anything over on Sophie. She knew every trick in the book."

"I believe it. She was a stinker, your granny."

"That she was."

"I wish she hadn't hated me."

"Why do you think she hated you?"

"She thought I bashed in her mailbox and painted a hot pink warning on it to discourage further bashing. I'm sure she wasn't my biggest fan."

"I don't think she hated you. I just think she had fun

messing with you with all her voodoo mumbo jumbo. She liked scaring big, manly men with all her make-believe."

"I was a big, manly man?"

"Nope. But Principal Hammond was."

Annie laughed at the look on Wyatt's face. "That wasn't nice," he pouted.

"But it was funny."

"It was *sorta* funny."

Wyatt pulled his truck to a stop. Annie looked out the window and noticed they were parked in the lot right by one of the lake's boat ramps. "Well, we're here. Ready to go catch some fish?"

"I was born ready. These fish are no match for me."

Wyatt raised one eyebrow. "Have you ever gone fishing before?"

"Do you think my granny was the type of person who would support me putting a worm on a hook?"

"So…I'm guessing that's a no."

"Nope."

Wyatt laughed. "Then I guess I'm in for a treat."

"Good thing I'm a quick learner."

WYATT BACKED the boat's trailer onto the boat ramp. When he had backed in the water far enough, he put his truck in park and looked at Annie. "Think you can get the boat off the trailer?"

Annie's eyes went wide. "Um…no. That's a negative, Ghost Rider. Hard pass. You don't want me backing anything up, much less a boat."

"Are you saying you're not a good backer upper?"

"I once backed into a parked car in a parking lot."

"Oh-kaaaay. No backing up for you."

"Then what are we supposed to do?"

"I'll get out, back the boat in the water, drive it to the dock and tie it off. Then, you'll get out of the truck and get in the boat. I'll park the truck, grab the stuff out of the back and get in the boat. Done."

"What stuff?"

"Oh, no. You're not playing that game."

"What game am I trying to play?"

"The game of ruining the surprise. You already figured out where we were going. I'm not going to let you sneak peeks through everything I've brought."

"Who said I would sneak peeks?"

Wyatt leveled her with a look. "Are you kidding me?"

"As your boss, I *demand* you let me look in the bags."

Wyatt laughed. "I haven't accepted one cent from you so technically, I'm just a Good Samaritan helping you out of the kindness of my heart."

Annie huffed at him. "Fine. No looking."

"You're damn right no looking. I'm making sure of it."

Wyatt took all the bags out of the back of his truck and walked down to the boat.

"What are you doing?!" Annie grumped.

"I'm taking all the bags to the boat so you can't look in them. Then, I'm taking them back to the truck with me, park the truck, and then come back to the boat so I can monitor them at all times."

"I already said I wouldn't look!"

"You also said you're a woman who hates surprises. I'm not trusting you."

"You're no fun."

"Annabelle Cleaver, I'm the definition of fun. Just you wait."

Before she could reply, Wyatt climbed into the boat and backed into the water. Every time he heard the hum of a boat motor, a thrill ran through him. The lake was his happy place. Lots of people said that about the beach, but there were too many things lurking in the water that could hurt a man. Jellyfish, big ass sharks. Plus, Wyatt had never seen the ocean calm. There were always waves. Nothing was more peaceful than a lake in the early hours of the morning, when the water was so still and clear a person could see their reflection like they were looking in a mirror.

Tying the boat to the dock, Wyatt watched Annie walk toward him. She didn't have a spot of makeup on, her hair was a wind-blown mess since they had driven to the lake with the windows down, and her t-shirt and shorts had the worn, faded look of something she had probably had since high school. Even so, she was the prettiest woman he had ever seen. She reminded Wyatt of everything he wanted in his life. Peace. Comfort. Home. He had no clue why he ever thought a woman like Jersey would make him happy. Now, he couldn't picture any woman in his life unless it was one with mint color-tipped hair walking toward him.

"Why are you looking at me like that, Holloway?"

"Cuz I think you're pretty, Disney."

Wyatt grinned at the blush creeping up Annie's cheeks. He loved making her smile.

"Are we going fishing or are you going to keep standing there, staring at me like a creeper?"

"Fishing. Definitely fishing. I want to see what you can do." Wyatt jumped out of the boat and onto the dock. "Have a seat. I'll only be a minute."

"Are you *seriously* going to take all of *that* with you to park the truck?" Annie asked, motioning to the bags and ice chests Wyatt had lugged out of the boat.

"Absolutely."

"You might hurt your back taking all that with you. Better let me keep it safe and sound."

Wyatt kissed her on a cheek. "Not a chance."

He jogged to the truck and pulled it out of the lake before parking it in the lot. He headed back down the dock and hopped in the boat with the bags and ice chest. "Ready to get this show on the road?"

"I was born ready," she said with a grin.

"Then let's go." Wyatt and Annie sat in companionable silence as they trolled across the lake. Not many boats were out on the water at this time of day, even if it was the weekend. When school started, the tourists and summer lake-goers usually dwindled down to holiday weekends only. Wyatt made sure to avoid the lake last weekend, which was Labor Day. It was usually the last hoorah before children returned to school and their parents used up all their vacation time. But today, it was quiet.

"I see why you like it out here," Annie said. "It's peaceful."

"You've lived by the lake your entire life. Don't you ever come out here?"

"Not really. My granny had a cousin who drowned in the lake. They were just sixteen. They went out together but my granny couldn't save her."

"God, that sucks."

"Yeah, it does. So she never really wanted me out here on the water. She was fine with me being *by* the water. *In* the water...not so much."

"That makes sense. I might do the same thing if that had happened to someone I knew."

"You really love it out here, don't you?" she said with a smile.

"I do," he agreed.

"I can tell."

"How?"

"I don't know. There's just a peace about you. I know you

told me how much you love the lake and how it *does* bring you peace, but to see you actually *out here*...I get it."

Wyatt smiled. "I'm glad."

"Why?"

"Because now...you get me."

"I get you."

Wyatt pointed ahead of them. "See those trees up there?"

Annie shielded her eyes with her hand. "I think so."

"That's the spot. We'll be there in a couple of minutes."

Annie rubbed her hands together in anticipation. "I can't wait. Hey, Wyatt?"

"Yeah?"

"Now that we're actually here, can I look in the bags?"

"Nope."

"Fine," Annie grumped, crossing her arms over her chest. "Party pooper."

"Patience is a virtue, Disney. Good things come to those who wait."

"Enough with generic words of wisdom I can find on the back of a fortune cookie," she said. "I just wanna know!"

"Well, I guess it's good we're here, then."

Wyatt pulled around the cliffs and turned off the motor. "See back there? Those are the trees."

"Really? Those?" Annie asked, pointing in the direction of his and Griff's secret island.

"Yep."

"Pull up closer," she said. "I want to see it."

"I can do that. But I'll have to paddle us in. Don't want the motor getting tangled in anything under the water we can't see. It'd make going back to the dock *much* harder than the drive over." Wyatt paddled the boat to the trees. "See? It's there. I promise I wasn't lying."

Wyatt watched Annie's face and grinned when she finally

found the island through the trees. Her eyes widened in shock and a smile split her face from ear to ear.

"It's there! It's really there!" she said excitedly.

"Well, Disney, did you think I was lying?"

Annie shrugged her shoulders. "Maybe a little."

"*Really?*"

"What? I thought it was cute you wanted to impress me."

"Well? Did I?"

Annie took another look through the trees and back to Wyatt, a big smile still plastered on her face. "Yeah. You really did."

CHAPTER 16

*A*nnie could not believe her eyes. There really *was* a little island on the other side of the trees. She had honestly thought Wyatt was feeding her a load of bullshit when he said there was a friggin' island that no one else knew about. But she was mistaken. And it didn't go unnoticed that Wyatt and Griffin were the *only ones* who had ever been here. She didn't know if she should freak out or if she should be flattered at the implication of her being the *third* person to see it. Ever.

"It's amazing," she said, turning to Wyatt. "Thanks so much for bringing me here."

He pulled her close, the boat rocking gently in the water at the motion. "Like I said before, I've never brought anyone else out here. It's a special place. I wanted to show it to a special person."

"Are you telling me I'm special to you, Wyatt Holloway?"

"Haven't you figured it out by now, Annie? Ever since I started working for you, I haven't had near as many dreams. The sounds of gunshots and people hurting haven't gone away, but they've gotten better. At first, I contributed it to my therapy and the Oklahoma sun and earth, which has always been synonymous with home. But I quit going to therapy and the peace remained. It was then I realized something."

"What's that?"

"The peace I feel is because of you. You're the calm in my storm, Disney. And I haven't felt calm since God knows when."

Annie's heart started beating a frantic rhythm in her chest. At his words. At her feelings. At that daunting statement that left her all kinds of scared. She couldn't be anyone's peace. Not when she hadn't experienced a moment of peace of her own since her granny died.

"How can I be your peace? I'm a mess myself."

"I don't know, Annabelle. All I know is I don't ever want to let it go."

At his words, Wyatt pulled her even closer and placed his lips on hers. It was even better than she remembered. She tasted the mint on his tongue from the Tic Tacs he kept pulling out of his pocket and popping in his mouth while they were trolling across the lake. She felt the hard planes of his body as her breasts brushed his chest and his hand tangled in her hair. His tongue ran across her lower lip as he deepened the kiss. Annie opened her mouth even wider, wanting the feel of his tongue dancing with hers.

Wyatt breathlessly pulled away from her and stared into her eyes. "I used to be a cinnamon man. Now, because of you, mint is my favorite flavor."

The boat had been drifting closer to the trees the longer they stayed in it, which Annie hadn't noticed until it ran into a large log with a loud thunk. She felt a tug on her hair and reached up, realizing her bun had gotten tangled in a low-hanging branch.

"I think we're stuck in the sticks and my hair is caught in a branch," she said with a grin.

"It's my fault for not throwing out the anchor. I got carried away in the moment. You're a little distracting," he replied, planting a kiss on her forehead. "Get your hair untangled. I'll go get the anchor and push us off with the oar and get us to shore. Then, I'll drop the anchor. We can fish after we eat. I made you a picnic."

"How do you know what I like to eat? I'm pretty picky."

"A little birdy at the café told me."

"Was the little birdy named Sadie?"

"My lips are sealed," he said, pretending to lock his lips and throw away the key.

Annie rolled her eyes and tried to stand, but her hair was still tangled in the branches. "I'm still stuck," she called out to Wyatt, who was at the front of the boat getting the anchor. She gave her hair another tug, trying to the bun on top of her head to pull free from the stubborn ass branch. With one last tug, she felt her hair break free. Unfortunately, the last tug left her unbalanced and she felt herself falling. And she wasn't falling *into* the boat. She was headed directly for the water.

"Wyatt!" she called. "I'm fall—"

Wyatt took a diving leap to where she was. He was quick enough to grab her arm, but he wasn't quick enough to pull her back in. Her momentum carried both of them over the edge of the boat directly into the water.

Annie came up sputtering, treading water to keep herself afloat. "Wyatt? Where are you?"

Wyatt popped up out of the water next to her, a shocked look on his face. "You went over."

"I went over," she agreed.

"I tried to save you."

Annie started laughing. "I know you did."

"I wasn't in time."

"Obviously."

At her comment, Wyatt started laughing along with her. "I can't believe that happened."

Annie wiped at the tears of laughter running down her face to mingle with the lake water. "I can't either."

"And here I wanted to impress you with a fancy picnic and woo you with my charm. Now, you're all wet. This was *not* how I pictured our day going."

"Well, it *is* hot. And I *do* have my swimsuit on underneath my clothes."

"Thank god for the hint I gave you," he said.

"Yes. Things would be drastically different if you had me wear the cashmere sweater."

Wyatt, still treading water, pulled her close to him and touched his nose to hers. "I've always wanted to try something."

"Oh, really? What's that?" Annie asked breathlessly. She tried to tell herself it was the exertion of treading water while fully clothed. But she knew when to call bullshit on herself. Annie was breathless because she knew Wyatt was going to kiss her again. And she wanted him to more than she'd like to admit.

"Kiss you while treading water. I've always wondered if it is as easy as the movies make it look."

Wyatt ran his finger down her face and over her lips before lifting her chin to place his lips on hers. Their fingers intertwined on the surface of the water while their treading feet played footsies below. He kissed her gently before pulling away.

"This is too much work, isn't it?" he asked, looking down at Annie.

She laughed. "A little. I'm pretty bogged down by all this

clothing. And I think I lost my favorite flip flop. And I *might* have bitten my lip when I fell out of the boat."

He splashed a little water her way. "Maybe I should change your nickname to Klutz. Or Punzie."

"What the hell does *that* mean?"

"Slang for Rapunzel. Her hair is so long I'm sure she got it stuck in everything."

"I don't know," she said, splashing him back. "Disney's kinda growing on me."

"Then Disney we shall keep. Think you can get back on the boat? You'll have to hoist yourself on the back."

"I think I can manage."

"You said your clothing was bogging you down. That means I definitely need to give you a boost just to make sure you stay safe."

"How are you going to do that?"

"I'll make a chair with my hands and you can sit in them. Then I can push you up."

"Is this just a reason for you to grab my butt?"

"Maybe."

Annie laughed. "You can touch my butt all you want as long as it gets me back in the boat. I'm tired of treading water."

"If you insist."

True to his word, Wyatt placed both his hands on her derriere and gave Annie enough of a push to haul herself back into the boat. Once she was fully in, she held her arm down toward Wyatt. He took it with a grin and followed her over the boat's stern.

"Well, Disney. That has to be the most memorable way I've ever arrived at this island."

"I'll take that as a compliment."

Wyatt carefully navigated the boat out of the trees and rowed to shore. "Has the sun dried you out yet?"

Annie grinned. "Not even a little."

"Then I'll be sure to find us a spot in the sun for our picnic."

Annie felt the boat glide to shore, so she hopped out and looked around Wyatt's island. She was standing on a sandy beach about fifty feet long, the sand giving way to a small copse of trees and various bushes about fifteen feet from shore. The waves gently lapped at her feet and the sun shone down on the sand, warming the place she was standing.

"I can see why you're at peace here, Wyatt. This place is perfect."

Wyatt smiled, a soft look in his eyes. "I'm glad you think so. I'd also be okay with you taking off all that water-logged clothing. You look like it's making you *very* uncomfortable."

"Does it now?"

Wyatt nodded and held four fingers in the air. "It does. Scout's honor."

Annie shimmied her shorts down her legs, pulled her t-shirt over her head, and tossed them on the boat. "There you go. Successfully de-logged."

Wyatt's eyes went wide as he looked her up and down. Annie could physically feel the desire written all over his face.

"Have I ever told you yellow is my favorite color?"

"You haven't," she said breathlessly. Annie's pulse quickened and a heat built low in her belly and traveled through her body. She felt like she was going to self-combust any second. And it was all from a simple look.

"The first time I saw you at your farm, you were wearing this exact bikini and a pair of cowgirl boots."

"Really? I don't remember."

"I do," he replied. "It was the best sight I had seen in a long time. Maybe ever. I think there is only one thing that could beat it, in fact."

"What's that?"

"You'll have to watch *Varsity Blues* first," he said with a wink. "Then we can talk."

Annie made herself a mental note to rent the movie from the Red Box in front of Swanson's Market as soon as she got home.

"You're all water-logged, too," she said. "Better take some stuff off before you turn into a prune."

Wyatt grinned at her, his eyes lighting with amusement. "As you wish," he replied, pulling his t-shirt over his head and tossing it on the boat with her clothes, his ab muscles rippling at the motion. Annie's mouth watered at the sight.

"Like was you see, Disney?"

Annie most *definitely* liked what she saw. And she wanted nothing more than to run her fingers up and down his stomach, her tongue following close behind. However, her answer was interrupted when her stomach growled loudly.

"Well, it's time to feed the beast," she said. "When it talks, it gets sustenance. I cannot be held responsible for what happens to you if she isn't fed. And you didn't feed me breakfast."

"I had planned on eating what I brought for lunch, but I don't want the responsibility of letting your stomach go hungry. Besides, we have all day here. There's plenty more time for what else I had in mind."

"Did you have fishing in mind?"

"That's one of them," he said with a wink. "If we get around to it, that is."

Annie's eyes went wide, imagining the possibilities running through his head. If they were anything like the thoughts running through *her* head, they would never drop a line in the water.

"Let's get the beast fed so you can find out," he added.

Annie looked at the bags and ice chest Wyatt had hauled to shore. "That's a lot of food."

"I've seen how much you eat. I had to make sure to bring enough for the bottomless pit you call your stomach. Which I now know you refer to as beast."

"Hahaha," she said, sticking her tongue out at him. "Not funny."

"Be nice or I won't feed you."

"Like I said, that was your best joke yet."

Wyatt shot a wink her way. "That's what I thought."

"So, are you going to show me what you brought? I'm dying to see what Sadie thinks are my favorite foods."

Wyatt started pulling the foods out of the ice chest on at a time. "I had to bring this to keep everything cool," he explained. "All your foods are high maintenance and require refrigeration."

Annie felt the smile on her face grow wider the more items he pulled from the ice chest.

"The main course features Sadie's famous smoked salmon sandwich on focaccia bread spread with cilantro chipotle mayo and topped with fresh romaine."

"It's off to a good start," she replied.

"Complementing the sandwich is her fresh strawberry, banana, pineapple and kiwi fruit salad, sweetened with Stevia."

"No subpar fruits like apples and grapes to ruin the best combination known to fruit salads worldwide."

"And finally, the piece de resistance. Sadie's famous..." Wyatt pretended to drumroll on the ice chest's top, "wait for it...coconut cream pie!"

Annie pretended to be the cheers of a crowd. "He shoots...he scores!" she yelled. "Wyatt Holloway for the win!"

Wyatt took a bow and replied, "Aren't you going to ask what we're drinking today?"

"I assumed water to keep hydrated."

"Ah. A fair assumption. But you assumed wrong. Didn't your granny ever teach you what happens when you assume?"

"You make an ass out of you and me," she deadpanned.

"Exactly!" Wyatt pulled two large mason jars out of the ice chest. "I give you—"

"Strawberry limeade!" Annie finished his sentence, recognizing Sadie's most popular drink she always served in a mason jar.

"Don't forget the side of sweet potato fries and cinnamon butter," he added, pulling a Styrofoam box out of a canvas tote. "Sadie made sure I brought them, too."

"It's my dream meal in one perfect picnic," she said with a smile.

"Really?" Wyatt asked.

"Really."

He grinned her way and pulled out plastic silverware and paper plates. Annie loved seeing this side of him. She'd seen obsessive-compulsive, have-to-get-everything-perfect Wyatt, saddened Wyatt, determined Wyatt, haunted Wyatt, joking Wyatt, and serious Wyatt. He was a combination of sadness, fear, and determination to overcome his past all rolled into a complicated man who had wormed his way into her heart. This was the first time, however, she'd seen carefree Wyatt. It was a good look on him. One she wished would show up more often.

Wyatt looked up from the blanket he was spreading on the sand. "What's that look on your face mean?"

"I have a look on my face?"

"It's the face you make when you're in deep thought. So spill."

"How do you know I have a look on my face when I'm deep in thought?"

Wyatt stared at her. "Seriously? You have no poker face whatsoever."

"I do, too!"

"Remember when I gave you the paint samples for the shutters on the house?"

"Yeah."

"Remember telling me you agreed with the color I liked? The dark turquoise that complemented the hot pink door?"

"Yeah again."

"Why do you think I changed my mind and showed you the mint green color instead and told you it was a better fit?"

"Because you realized mint green is my favorite color?"

"Nope. Because I saw the look of horror on your face when I suggested a color outside the realm of your comfort zone."

"Fine. I might not have the best poker face."

"You really don't."

Annie laughed. "I was trying not to hurt your feelings."

"I was trying to get you to branch out and choose another color. What's with the mint green, anyway? Usually adults aren't stuck on one color for life."

"The day I moved in with Granny, I was terrified. I had no clue what to expect. All I had heard were the stories my mom and dad told me about my dad's crazy mother. I expected the worst. But that day, she took me to Sadie's Café and let me pick out a double scoop of any ice cream flavor I wanted. I told her I wanted what she was eating. She chose mint chocolate chip." Annie shrugged her shoulders. "Since then, the color has always been synonymous with the day my life finally turned around."

"That's a pretty cool story, Disney."

"She was a pretty cool lady."

"I'm beginning to agree. Now, are you going to tell me about this look on my face you think I have?"

"I was just thinking I like this look on you."

"What look?"

"You don't have the haunted look in your eyes I have seen since you set foot on my farm. No matter how hard you try or how happy you appear to be, it's always been there. For the first time ever, it's not." Annie walked toward him and softly ran her hand down the scar on his face. "I don't see the scarred Wyatt who's seen too much. I simply see the Wyatt you were in school. Cocky. Proud. Carefree. The only difference is you're even better than I remembered."

Wyatt looked down at her, a raw vulnerability reflected in his eyes. "Didn't you believe me when I told you, Disney? You're my peace. I don't feel those things when I'm with you. I'm not reminded of what this scar represents. When I'm with you, all I can feel is the thoughts of you that consume me day and night."

Wyatt pulled her against him and planted a soft kiss on her lips. Dragging her down on the blanket, he placed both hands on either side of her face, his body inches above hers.

"The day I saw you walk around your barn, wearing my favorite color yellow, your mint-tipped hair up in a messy bun, I knew I would never be the same," he said, kissing her nose. "Now, let's eat."

Several minutes and lots of food later, Wyatt was leaning against the trunk of a tree, Annie between his legs, her back leaning against his chest.

"I'm so full," Annie groaned, rubbing her stomach. "Why'd you feed me all that food?"

"Why'd you eat it all?"

Annie laughed, the echo rumbling against his chest. "Because it's my favorite meal ever!"

"Then no complaining."

"Okay, okay." Annie moved off his chest and turned to

face him. "Now, are you taking me fishing? I'm dying to catch a big one!"

"Since you've never caught a fish before, any one is going to be a big one."

"So? A girl has to start somewhere."

"That is true. However, I wanted to do something else before our hands got all fishy."

"Oh, really? What's that?"

Wyatt took her face in his hands and stared into her eyes. "It involves you, me, and decidedly less clothing than we currently have on."

Annie's eyes widened as she processed what he was saying. "Are you saying you might want to go to third base with me, Wyatt Holloway?"

"I was thinking more along the lines of a homerun."

"If someone had told high school me that adult me would one day be sitting on a magical island, having Wyatt Holloway serving me my favorite foods and kissing me senseless, I would have laughed in their face."

"Do you feel like laughing now?"

"I feel like now is the perfect time to kiss me."

Wyatt apparently agreed because his lips smashed into hers with an urgency she hadn't felt in the first kiss they shared. He laid her gently down on the picnic blanket, his body on top of hers. Annie moaned at the contact. His body perfectly aligned with hers. Her hands roamed his back, feeling the hard planes of muscle rippling under her hands.

Wyatt began trailing kisses down her neck, collar bone and shoulder before stopping right where her bikini top covered her breast.

"You know, I tried to be a gentleman the first time I saw you wearing this bikini, but I'm afraid my eyes might have lowered to catch a glimpse of these perfect breasts a time or two," he whispered against her skin.

Wyatt reached up and untied the top string of her bikini before reaching behind her back to untie the second string. Slowly, he pulled the top off her and threw it to the end of the blanket and stared. "They're even more perfect than I thought they'd be."

Annie gasped as he took her right breast in his mouth, sucking gently. Her eyes rolled back in her head as she marveled in the sensation of his lips on her sensitive skin. His left hand roamed over her body, leaving a trail of fire on her skin. He gently kneaded her other breast and Annie felt like she would melt at the fire he was bringing to life in her body.

"I can never get enough of how you taste," he whispered. "Sunshine and hope. That's what I taste when I put my lips on your body."

He began working his way down her body, unbuttoning her shorts and pulling them down her legs. "I want to kiss every single inch of you before we leave this island. Can I do that, Disney? Will you let me taste you?"

Annie was rendered speechless and couldn't form a coherent thought. All she could do was nod in agreement.

Wyatt woke to a soft hand running down his cheek.

"Wake up, sleepyhead," Annie whispered. "You're going to sleep the day away and you promised you'd teach me how to fish."

Wyatt sat up, leaning back on one elbow. "How long was I asleep?" he asked, rubbing his eyes. It was the most rested he had felt in a long time.

"A couple of hours. At least."

"A couple of hours? I never sleep a couple of hours straight. I usually—" Wyatt trailed off.

"You usually what?"

"I usually wake up from a nightmare. Or can't sleep at all," he said quietly. "Huh. That's different."

"Well, you slept so well you were snoring, so I'm guessing that's a good different," Annie replied. "But I can't wait any longer. I want to go fishing!"

Wyatt chuckled. "You sure are excited for a person who's never baited a hook in her life."

Annie stared at him in horror. "I have to bait a hook? With what? I thought I'd just use those brightly colored rubber things you can find in the fishing aisle at Walmart."

"Those are for amateurs. They don't catch the big ones."

"Then what does?"

"Shad."

"Huh?"

"Shad. It's a fish like a minnow. I caught them last night with a net and put them in the bait tank to keep them alive. The more wiggling they do, the more fish we'll catch."

"So we're using a *live* little fish to catch the big fish?"

"Yep."

Annie's face blanched. "But they'll be alive. And we'll put a hook in them. Won't that hurt?"

"I don't know. I've never asked a shad what they think about being bait."

Annie shook her head. "I don't know if I can do that."

Wyatt mentally sighed. He knew Annie loved animals. He just didn't think a tiny bait fish would fit under her animal umbrella. *Hell,* she ate meat. He'd just have to tread lightly. "You eat salmon all the time. You even ate it for lunch. You know how that salmon got so big and tasty?"

"Nope."

"Eating lots of shad."

"Really?"

Wyatt had no clue. He was probably lying out his ass. But

if it would get her to be okay with baiting a hook with a shad, then he was going to do it. "Absolutely. Shad is their favorite food. Besides, shad don't have feelings like we do. They don't even feel the hook."

Another lie.

"I thought you said you'd never asked them about being bait. How do you know it doesn't hurt?"

Wyatt refrained from sighing. "I just remembered a documentary I watched on the Discovery Channel one time. Fish don't feel things. At all."

Annie looked at him skeptically. She wasn't buying it.

"Besides, if we don't use them, a big fish will eat them anyway. Or they won't and the shad will go nuts overpopulating the lake. We're really doing our town a favor. A lake overrun by shad is not a lake where people like to swim. Then where would all the businesses be? *Out* of business, that's where."

Annie rolled her eyes. "Fine. Teach me how to bait a friggin' hook."

Wyatt grinned and helped her onto the boat. He showed her the bait tank and walked her through the process of grabbing a shad and baiting a line. To her credit, he only caught her wrinkling her nose in disgust one time. Once she had it down, Wyatt pulled up the anchor and headed away from the beach.

"Where are we going?"

"Over here by the cliffs. That's usually where me and Griff catch the big ones. The water is really deep over there."

The boat's motor hummed as they traveled over the water. Annie was facing the front of the boat, her hair a tangled mess on top of her head, wayward strands of mint tickling her face. Her bronze skin glowed in the sun and her hazel eyes sparkled. She was breathtaking.

Looking at the depth finder above the steering wheel,

Wyatt killed the motor. "Twenty-three feet. This is good fishing depth."

"So we're ready? To catch fish?"

"It depends."

"On what?"

"Are you ready to make these fish your bitch?"

Annie grinned, her eyes crinkling in the corners. "These fish don't know what's coming."

Wyatt chuckled. "Listen to you, already talking like a fisherman."

Wyatt walked her through the fishing process again, this time showing her how to cast her line, let the bait drop to the bottom before reeling up just a bit.

"Now, we wait," he said, wrapping his arms around her from behind and showing her how to hold the reel.

"When you feel a tug on your line," he whispered in her ear, smiling when she shivered, "pull up quickly to set the hook and then reel it in."

"Sounds easy enough," she said, a determined look on her face.

"Just wait until that fish starts taking your line. That's when the fun begins." Wyatt cast his line out into the water, sat down beside Annie, and ran his hand over her thigh. "This is nice."

"I'm glad you brought me here, Wyatt."

"Me, too."

Annie's eyes widened in shock as she looked down at her pole. "I think I felt something," she whispered.

"Well, what are you waiting for?" Wyatt laughed. "Give it a tug and reel it in!"

Annie jerked her pole over her head and began reeling frantically. Wyatt watched the rod of her pole bend toward the water.

"You definitely have something!" he said with a grin. "Keep going!"

"Oh, my lord! This thing probably weighs twenty-five pounds!"

"Keep going! You almost have it!"

Wyatt sat his pole down and reached beside his leg for the net. "You got a striper!" he called.

He laughed out loud as he watched Annie's tongue jut out of her mouth in concentration.

"What do I do now?" she shrieked. "It's at the top of the water!"

Wyatt put the net down next to the fish and scooped it out of the water. He grabbed the line close to the fish's mouth and held it up so she could see. "Here you go. Your first ever catch. What do you think?"

Annie's face practically glowed. "That's the biggest fish I've ever seen. Is it going to break a record or something?"

Wyatt willed himself not to laugh. She had no clue how big the fish in their lake could actually get. "Not quite. It's only about three pounds. But it's a great size for your first fish."

Annie wrinkled her nose in disbelief. "It felt like I had a fifty pound fish on my line."

"That's because striper are fighters," he said with a grin. "So whaddya think? You like it?"

"Fishing?"

"Yes. Fishing."

Annie nodded enthusiastically. "I do."

"Wanna get it off the hook and throw it in the tank?"

"The bait tank?"

"No. The tank where we keep what we catch."

"Why would we do that?"

"Because we can cook what we catch."

"You mean we get to eat them?"

"Absolutely. No fish tastes better than the ones you catch yourself."

"Then let's do it!"

Wyatt showed her how to take the fish off the hook and chuckled at her squeal when she held it. "Let me snap a picture of you with your first catch," he said, reaching for his phone. Annie proudly held the fish up to her face and pretended to kiss it as Wyatt clicked the shot.

"How does it look?" she asked.

"Beautiful."

"The fish?"

"No. You."

Wyatt was rewarded with a blush that tinted Annie's cheeks a rosy pink. He didn't think he would ever get tired of looking at her, drinking her in. She was quickly becoming someone he couldn't imagine not seeing on a daily basis, not smelling the soft scent of peaches that always wafted off her skin, not hearing her laugh. She wasn't just his peace. She had become his everything.

They fished for a few hours until the sun was high in the sky. Annie proved herself to be a pretty good fisherman. She had caught several striper, a couple of catfish, and a few drum. Wyatt had to explain that drum were the scum of the fishing world and *not* good to eat, which is why they threw them back in the lake.

After she had yawned several times in a row, Wyatt commented, "You think you're ready to head home?"

Annie smiled sleepily his way. "I think so. I need a nap. Mornings are for the birds."

"But wasn't getting up worth it?"

Annie nodded her agreement. "It was worth it."

"So? Fishing a success?"

"Absolutely."

"Since it was such a success and we caught more than either of us will *ever* eat, wanna do me a favor?"

"What's that?"

"Have a fish fry. With my family." Wyatt had no idea what possessed him to blurt the invitation out of nowhere. But now that it was, he couldn't take it back. And he really didn't want to. The idea of Annie spending time with his family was comforting. And he knew his mom and sister would be jumping for joy and have his parents' entire house decked out like Christmas before he and Annie even set foot on their property.

Annie's eyes widened. "What?"

"Have a fish fry with my family. They don't bite, I promise." Wyatt shrugged his shoulders and tried to remain nonchalant. He didn't want Annie to freak out. Maybe if he appeared calm, she wouldn't notice how his hands and voice were trembling in anticipation of her answer.

"Are you serious?"

Wyatt laughed. "I'm serious. But if you don't want to, I get it."

Annie appeared deep in thought. Wyatt crossed his fingers, hoping she would say yes. Even though the invitation seemed to leap out of his mouth without asking permission, he realized how much he wanted her to officially meet his family.

"No, I can do that," she replied after what felt like forever. Wyatt exhaled the breath he didn't even know he was holding. "You taught me how to fish, after all. I just want to do one thing first."

"What's that?"

She grinned. "Go home and take a shower. Fishing is smelly business."

Wyatt leaned over and pretended to smell her skin before

kissing her on the cheek. "That, Disney, is something we both *definitely* need to do."

"Are you saying I stink?"

"I didn't say you stink. Fishing is smelly business are your words, not mine."

"Then are you asking to shower with me?"

"Are you asking me to ask you to shower with you?"

His breath hitched in his chest at the look in her eyes. "What if I were?"

"Then I would absolutely say yes. But only if you're asking."

"The pipes are old in my house and the water takes forever to heat up."

Wyatt pulled her in for a smoldering kiss, his body coming alive the moment his lips met hers. "Good thing I know another way to heat the water quickly," he said with a grin. "Let's go get that shower. Now that my nose is working again, I have to agree. You really do smell."

CHAPTER 17

*M*uch like the early morning hours before Wyatt had picked her up for a day of fishing, Annie was now standing in front of her closet, a towel wrapped around her body, staring at the clothing on her hangers.

"This is starting to become a habit with you, Disney," Wyatt said.

Annie turned to the sound of his voice. Wyatt was leaning against the doorjamb of her bedroom, a towel wrapped around his waist. After they dropped Griff's boat back at his house, Annie had thrown Wyatt's clothes in her washing machine while they showered. Together. It was the most delicious way Annie had ever showered in her entire life. His breath mingling with the steam, his kisses feathering her skin, his hands roaming her body as the water sluiced down her legs. They had stayed in until the water ran cold. Annie couldn't complain, though. Wyatt had heated her up in a whole other way. And then they took a three hour nap. It was the perfect day.

"I have no clue what to wear," she said.

"I would start with clothing."

Annie stuck her tongue out at him. "I know that, dummy. But *what* clothing?"

Wyatt walked over to closet and took a hanger off the rod. "Here. Wear this."

Annie held the hanger up in her hand and stared. "Seriously? You want me to wear *this?*"

"What's wrong with it?" Wyatt asked around a mouthful of apple. Apparently sometime between the laundry room and her bedroom upstairs, Wyatt had found his way into the kitchen. Annie frowned when she saw Sebastian weaving his body in and out of Wyatt's legs. *Traitor.*

"What's *wrong* is that it's *September* and you grabbed a long-sleeved sweater dress."

"Are you telling me it's too hot for a sweater dress?"

Annie rolled her eyes. "Does your mother still pick out your clothing, Wyatt James? You're ridiculous."

Wyatt leaned down and started rubbing Sebastian's ears, eliciting loud purrs from her traitorous cat. "See, Bass. *This* is how you get out of picking clothing for a lady. You play dumb," he whispered.

Annie stomped her foot. "I'm *serious*, Wyatt! I'm meeting…well, not really meeting, because I kinda sorta already know them. In a town as small as Parker you have to kinda know everyone even if you don't actually know *know* them. But I'm actually officially *knowing* them today and I want it to be perfect."

"Not kinda-sorta but officially knowing who?"

"Your *family!*" she wailed.

"My parents don't care what you wear, Annie," he said softly. "They just want to meet you. The girl who has my heart."

Annie stilled. "I have your heart?"

"You have my heart. And it's at peace now. Because of

you," Wyatt walked toward her and planted a kiss on the tip of her nose. "Now pick something out that makes *you* feel comfortable. I'm going to get my clothes out of the dryer. Hopefully, they'll smell more like your Gain laundry than fish guts."

Annie smiled. At her feelings. At his words. She had Wyatt Holloway's heart. Who'd have ever thought? "Hey, Wyatt?"

"Yeah, Disney?"

"Just so you know, I don't just have *your* heart. You have mine, too."

Wyatt grinned, a smile lighting up his face. "It took you long enough to figure that out. Now, wear the pink dress. The one you wore to your granny's funeral. It's my favorite."

"Finally! A suggestion I can actually take! You don't think it's too fancy?"

"Nope. And it makes your legs and boobs look hot."

"I don't want my boobs to look hot in front of your parents!"

"Then it definitely does *not* make your boobs look hot. Wear it? For me?"

Annie rolled her eyes. "Fine."

Wyatt leaned over to Sebastian and scratched between his ears again. "And *that's* how you do it, Bass. Bat your eyes a little and the ladies will do anything for ya."

Annie picked up the gold sandal that went with her dress and threw it at his head. "Go get your clothes! We're going to be late."

Wyatt grinned his trademark smile that Annie saw more often the longer they were together. The one that caused the butterflies to wake up and flutter in her stomach. "It's my parents' house. If they say five, they really mean five forty-five. That's my family for ya. They won't even expect us."

"Well, they said five, so that's what time *I* expect us to be there."

Wyatt saluted her and walked out of her room. She could hear his feet padding down the stairs and hoped it was toward the laundry room instead of the kitchen for another apple.

"Don't get me wrong, I'm glad you like him," Annie said when Sebastian jumped on the bed next to her where she had sat to put on her shoes. "But it's really bothering me that you seem to like him more than me. What would Granny think of your traitorous nature, huh?"

Sebastian answered by making himself at home in the middle of her lap, curling up in a ball and swishing his tail in her face, his body rumbling in contentment.

"As long as you show me love, too, I guess I can forgive you," she said, rubbing under his chin to elicit more purrs. "After all, he is pretty cuddly, isn't he?"

"Are you talking about me, Disney?" Wyatt had returned from downstairs, his shirt now accompanying the towel still draped around his waist, his swim trunks thrown over his shoulder. "Am I pretty cuddly?"

"No," she replied. "I meant Nemo."

"I haven't seen Nemo lately," he said. "Where has he been?"

"Every so often, Mr. Grant's dog, Clementine, goes into heat. Nemo stays around her, foaming at the mouth, until she gets sick of him and sends him packing."

"Mr. Grant doesn't care?"

"He sells the puppies for fifty bucks a pop, so he tolerates it. Nemo's like a bumblebee. His seed is spread all over the county."

Wyatt chuckled. "What kind of dog is Ms. Clementine?"

"A goofy looking Rottweiler. I have to admit, though. They do make some cute puppies."

"I bet. I foresee a puppy for Hattie's birthday in the near future."

"Won't your sister care?"

"Oh, she'll hate it. But that's what uncles are for. To spoil and not listen to parents who protest too much."

Annie shook her head. "You're such an ass."

Wyatt pulled her in for a kiss. "Maybe. But my niece thinks I'm the most amazing uncle on the planet."

"I see why if you get her gifts like puppies and ponies."

"Who said anything about a pony?"

Annie rolled her eyes. "Tonight, you need to ask your sister if she'll let Hattie skip school one day and come hang out with us at the farm."

"I still don't know if Lucy will let her. Why can't we come over next weekend? I'll even bring George, my horse, like I said I was going to. We can ride and let her hang out with your zoo. It'll be fun."

"I guess that works."

"Why do I sense some hesitation from you?"

"Well, because it's—"

"It's what?"

"You've never been to my house on the weekend before."

"Except for now."

Annie frowned. "You know what I mean. You've never been here except for when we're working."

"Do you not want me here on the weekend?"

"No! It's not that. It's just—"

"Just what?"

"It will just take some getting used to, that's all."

"I'm getting the feeling I'm not wanted."

"That's not true! It's just always been my granny and me here. Sometimes my friends. Having another person in the home is just—"

"Weird?"

"No. Different."

"Good different?"

Annie smiled and nodded. "Good different."

Wyatt leaned over and kissed her shoulder. "Then can I ask my sister if Hattie can spend Saturday with us next weekend? It will make it more likely for her to say yes because Hattie won't miss school."

"Can't lose that full scholarship to OU. I hear they recruit kindergarteners hard nowadays."

He chuckled. "Now you're speaking my sister's language."

"Are you ready to go?"

"Let me put on my swim trunks and I will be. You know, it was kinda pointless of me to wash these."

"Why?"

"Because I have to clean the fish when we get to my house. I'll stink all over again."

"But at least I won't have to smell you on the way."

"Touché." Wyatt laughed. "Doesn't mean I won't rub my fish fingers all over you when I get finished, though."

"Do it and you'll never see me in this dress again," she warned.

Wyatt held his hands up in agreement. "Deal. Because I definitely have plans for you in this dress."

"Oh, you do?"

"Yes, ma'am," Wyatt said, pulling her off the bed and into his arms. "And you'll be wearing it with nothing on underneath."

Annie's breath quickened at the thought. "Is that so?"

"Yep. In fact, we could get in a practice run right now."

"It's ten till five!"

"Remember what I said before?" Wyatt asked, trailing kisses down her neck. "When my parents say be there at five, they aren't expecting anyone until five forty-five."

"Even the person who's responsible for cooking the fish?"

she asked breathlessly when he ran his tongue down the sensitive spot behind her ear.

"Absolutely. In fact, they almost expect it. Can't cook the fish before everyone else gets there. Then it'd be a soggy mess."

"But what about—"

Annie was interrupted when Wyatt placed his lips on hers and opened her mouth with his tongue, exploring and inter-twining his tongue with hers. All of a sudden, being at his parents' home at five didn't seem that necessary. Almost overkill, in fact.

When he felt her body relax in his arms, Wyatt grinned and placed her gently on the bed. Never breaking eye contact, Wyatt placed his hands under her dress and slowly pulled her panties down her legs. "Now, let's get that practice in, shall we?"

As Wyatt ran his hands up her legs and under her dress again, Annie let out a moan and nodded. All of a sudden, showing up at five didn't seem that important at all.

WYATT PULLED his truck into the driveway at his parent's house and put it in park. Annie was twisting her hands in her lap, a frantic look on her face.

"Wyatt, what if they don't like me?" she said, chewing on her lip.

He grinned her way. "Disney, my parents already love you."

"They don't really even know me."

"But they know *of* you. They've heard how amazing you are and have seen how hard you work. Everyone in town has nothing but good things to say about you. You'll be fine. I promise."

Annie looked at him, a nervous smile on her face. "You think so?"

"I *know* so."

Wyatt watched the rise and fall of her chest as she took a deep breath. "Okay," she said. "Let's do this."

He hopped out of the truck and ran over to her side before she could open the door. "You look real pretty, Disney," he whispered in her ear. "Hot pink is quickly becoming my favorite color."

Annie grinned and took his hand. "Thanks, Wyatt."

Wyatt intertwined her fingers with his and walked up the stairs to the front porch of his family home. Last week, his mom had bought two large, red ceramic pots on clearance at Nailed It. They had been empty when Wyatt left that morning. Apparently, after he called her about a last minute fish fry, she had made a quick trip to town to buy some flowers at Nailed It, too, because huge white geraniums and light green sweet potato vines filled both pots.

"If this isn't confirmation they like you," Wyatt said, pointing to the pot by the front door and the other one sitting between his parents' rocking chairs, "I don't know what is."

Annie looked at him blankly. "What?"

"My mom bought these two pots on clearance at Nailed It last week but refused to buy any plants. She said she wasn't going to pay Max Wilson three times what the plants were worth this late in the summer and if he thought he was going to get that *clearance* price for them he was out of his mind."

"So?"

"So, I was in Nailed It yesterday. The flowers were the exact same price she was complaining about last week." Wyatt winked at her. "See? My mom is willing to get scammed on clearance plants so she can impress you with a pretty front porch. You're already in."

Wyatt opened the front door and was assaulted by a head of black curls dressed in a Wonder Woman costume. "Uncle Wy! Uncle Wy! Are you gonna cook me some of my favorite fish?"

Wyatt let go of Annie's hand and swooped his niece up in his arms. "I was going to cook my *niece* some fish, but I'm not sure about you, Wonder Woman. Do you even like fish?"

Hattie giggled and bopped him on the head with the plastic bat she was holding. "I'm not Wonder Woman, silly. I'm *Hattie!*"

"Well, I'm sorry! I didn't recognize you. You look *just like* Wonder Woman! But I don't remember Wonder Woman having a bat. Didn't she have a lasso?"

Hattie rolled her eyes. "She did. But Poppy won't let me borrow one of his *real* lassos because he says they're too 'spensive. So I gotta play with this dumb plastic bat. It don't even hit a plastic ball a foot!"

"Doesn't, Hattie. It *doesn't* hit the ball a foot. And you know better than to ask Poppy to use one of his lassos. They aren't supposed to be played with. You know that." Lucy walked up to Wyatt and tapped her daughter on the nose. "Don't be rude."

Hattie blew a curly strand of hair out of her eyes. "I know! But Poppy has such *cool* lassos! Wonder Woman just ain't…*isn't*…as awesome with a green bat!"

Annie leaned over Wyatt and tapped Hattie on her shoulder. "I bet your uncle has some gold spray paint somewhere. If you ask nicely, he'll probably spray the bat to look shiny just like Wonder Woman's lasso. And it's a lot easier for you to hit bad guys with a bat than a lasso, anyway."

Hattie placed her finger on her cheek, contemplating this new potential weapon. "Uncle Wy? Will you do it?"

"Paint the bat?"

Hattie bopped him again on the head. "Yes! What else would I be asking about, huh?"

Wyatt grinned. "I will. It will just have to be after I cook the fish."

Hattie returned his smile. "Deal. You can put me down now. By the way," she whisper-shouted in his ear, "Your girl-friend is real pretty!"

Hattie jumped out of his arms and held out her hand to Annie. "Are you Annie?"

Annie smiled and shook Hattie's hand. "I am."

"Nice to meet ya. I'm Hattie, Uncle Wy's most favoritest niece in the whole world. *And* your granny's most favoritest student!"

"You're my only niece, Hattie Mae," he said and then laughed when his niece held her hand up to silence him.

"I *love* your dress," Hattie continued talking to Annie. "Pink is my favorite color. Did your granny tell you that?"

"She didn't," Annie said, hiding her smile.

"Well, it *is*. And when I grow up, I'm gonna have hair just like yours. "Cuz mint chocolate chip ice cream is my favorite ice cream and they *match!*" Hattie held her hands up in the air and shrugged her shoulders. "We *have* to be friends."

Annie laughed. "I agree."

"Okay! Now, I gotta go find my poppy. I bet he can find me some paint and help me paint the bat and I won't even have to wait on Uncle Wy!"

"Sounds like a plan, Hattie."

"Hey!" Wyatt yelled as Hattie ran down the hall. "I thought I was going to paint it for you!"

"But you gotta clean all the fish and I don't wanna wait!"

Wyatt grinned and turned to Annie. "*Annnd*…that's my niece."

"She wouldn't act like that if you and our parents didn't give her everything she wants!" Lucy held her hand out toward Annie. "I know we know who each other are, but it's nice to officially meet you. I'm Lucy, Wyatt's smarter, younger sister."

Annie took his sister's hand. "It's nice to officially meet you, too. I'm Annie. Of course, you know that already."

Wyatt pulled Annie to his side. "Don't listen to Lucy. I'm obviously the smarter one. She's just jealous. Where's your better half, sis?"

Lucy rolled her eyes. "He got called out to the Callahan's. They had a pipe burst under their house."

"Yikes."

"Yep. I'm a plumber's widow most days." She shrugged her shoulders. "What's a girl to do?"

"You could bust your own pipes. You know, to keep him occupied."

Lucy punched him on the shoulder. "That would be dumb."

Wyatt rubbed his arm. "Jeez! Forget about ever suggesting things to you again."

"I didn't ask for your opinion. Come on, Annie. My mom is dying to finally meet you. *Officially.*"

Annie gave Wyatt a finger wave and walked off with his sister. As soon as the women walked out of sight, his dad came up beside him and put his arm around Wyatt's shoulders.

"Hattie is looking for you, Dad."

"She is? What does she want? I hope it's not another piggyback ride. I carried her around so much last Friday I couldn't get out of bed all day Saturday."

"She didn't want a piggyback ride. She wanted you to paint a plastic bat since you won't let her play with your lasso."

"I never said she couldn't play with my lasso!"

"No, but Mom did."

"Well, better not usurp the authority around here. Almost fifty years together, I'm pretty sure we all know who rules the roost."

"I love you, Dad, but there's never been a question."

His dad chuckled. "I can't disagree. She sure is pretty, Wyatt."

"Who? Hattie or Mom? Because I think they're both pretty beautiful. Even Lucy. Just don't tell her I admitted it. I've always claimed to be the pretty one."

"I'm talking about Miss Annie."

Wyatt was pretty sure the grin split his face. "I know."

"Is she as pretty on the inside like everyone in town says?"

"She is."

"Not saying more than two words in response to every question when I start talking about the girl. I guess it's safe to say you've passed the boss-employee relationship."

Wyatt grinned and clapped his dad on the back. "We never actually had the boss-employee relationship. I've never accepted a penny from her."

His dad chuckled. "Why the hell not?"

"Because I didn't want to give it all back if she ever decided to give me the time of day. The first day I walked onto her property and she walked out from behind the barn wearing a yellow bikini and Daisy Dukes, her being my boss was the last thing on my mind."

"Well, it looks like you're taking a step in the right direction if the way she looks at you is any indication."

"How does she look at me?"

"Like you invented chocolate. It's a good look. Trust me." His dad winked at him. "I got lucky the first time I saw that look on your mom's face."

"*Dad!* Too. Much. Information!"

His dad clapped him on the back and headed to back of the house.

"Where are you going?"

"I'm going to start cleaning and fileting those fish you caught today. We all know I am way better than you!"

"That's a lie and I'm going to come prove it!" Wyatt followed his dad into the kitchen where his mom and sister had Annie sitting on a stool at the island. Annie turned to him, a big smile on her face.

"Wyatt James! I was just telling Annie it was about time you brought her around to meet us. I knew her granny Sophie, but I never had the pleasure of knowing her grand-daughter. She's a *delight!*" His mom pulled him in for a hug. "Now I know why you've been keeping her from us."

"No one is keeping anyone from you, Mom," he said with an eye roll. "We've just been busy. Working. On her farm. You know this."

"Doesn't mean you couldn't take a break every now and then."

"Which we did today. It's also why we're having a fish fry. We caught so many we couldn't eat them ourselves."

"She's quite the fisherwoman, is she?"

"I am!" Annie piped up. "In fact, I caught the most!"

"Really? That's impressive."

"It's also very debatable," Wyatt added. "I'm pretty sure I caught more."

"You did not!"

"Do I need to name everything I caught and then every-thing *you* caught? Because I totally can do that."

Annie rolled her eyes. "Fine. You might have caught a *couple* more."

"Well, since it was her first ever time fishing and you only caught a couple more, I think that means she wins!" Lucy called from her perch on the other bar stool.

"*What?* That's totally not how it works!" Wyatt argued.

"Oh, I *totally* think that's how it works," Lucy stated.

"I agree," his mom said with a head nod.

"Me, too!" Annie added.

Wyatt threw his hands in the air. "Jeez! You women are all alike. Twisting the rules so you're always right."

His mom grinned and pointed to the bright red apron she had on over her clothes. "Well, you *did* buy me an apron professing this to everyone who walks into my kitchen. Should you expect any less?"

Wyatt let out a bark of laughter when he read the apron. *I'm the boss. End of story* was emblazoned on the front in large, fancy white letters. "I like this one a lot better than the one Lucy got you."

"What does the one Lucy got you say?" Annie asked.

"It says, *Dear Mom, Thanks for putting up with a bratty, spoiled, ungrateful, messy child like my sibling. Love, your favorite*," Lucy said with a grin. "Very fitting, I thought."

Annie giggled. "That's funny."

Wyatt pulled her into his chest and rubbed his knuckles on top of her head. "It's *not* funny! Besides, everyone knows *I'm* the favorite. Isn't that right, Mom?"

His mom held her hands in the air. "It depends on the day. When you were sneaking girls in your room through the window as a teenager, your sister was."

Lucy stuck her tongue out at Wyatt.

"*But,*" his mom continued. "When your sister went through the stage where she wanted to wear all the black clothing, goth makeup, dye her hair gray, and paint her nails black, *you* were my favorite."

"It was for a month!" Lucy said with a huff.

"That was a month too long," his mom replied. "Sadie asked me if someone in our family from out of town died. Everyone thought you were in a perpetual state of mourning!"

"You snuck girls in your room?" Annie asked.

"Oh, yeah, he did," Lucy said. "Jersey even made herself a whipped cream bik—"

Wyatt covered his sister's mouth with his hand. "You can't know that story until you watch *Varsity Blues*, Disney. Now, are you ready to see how to clean some fish?"

"Sure."

"It's a messy, stinky business," Lucy said. "Good luck with that."

Annie wrinkled her nose. "Do I actually have to do anything? Or can I just watch?"

"You can just watch. If you ask nicely, that is."

Annie playfully punched him on the arm. "Let me watch."

"Ow! Okay, okay. No asking nicely."

Lucy high-fived Annie. "*That's* how it's done, Annie. Got him trained already."

Wyatt resorted to childish behavior like his sister did earlier and stuck his tongue out at her. "I'm *not* trained. I'm being respectful."

"Whatever you say."

Wyatt started to reply back, but then thought better of it. Because when it came down to it, he didn't really care what anyone thought. Trained or not trained—Annie just made him happy.

CHAPTER 18

"I think that was the best fish I've ever eaten." Annie pushed her chair back from the table Wyatt's parents had on the back deck of their house and groaned. "I don't think I'll be able to eat anything for an entire week."

"It is pretty tasty," his mom replied. "I think it's the air fryer. It makes it so crispy and delicious."

"I'm still amazed at how that thing works," Wyatt said. "Are you sure there's no oil or anything in it?"

"Nope."

"It's just air?"

Lucy yelled. *"Yes!* Get it through that thick skull of yours already."

Wyatt shook his head. "That's mind boggling."

Annie laughed. "The fish wasn't the only thing good. Everything was so delicious. Thanks so much for inviting me."

"You're so welcome," he mom said, patting Annie on the hand. "We'd be happy to have you any time you want to come over."

"I expect you to come over more than once," his dad chimed in. "We've enjoyed having you. And the smile on my son's face is something I haven't seen in a while, so *I* should be thanking *you* for that."

Annie grinned when she saw the blush creep up Wyatt's neck and cheeks. "I don't know about that. He's a pretty happy guy."

All of Wyatt's family smiled softly. "He was before," Lucy said softly. "Not so much for a long time now."

"Enough talk about me already," Wyatt said, pushing back from the table. "It's time to do the dishes."

"I'll even help," his dad said. "Your momma cooked a great meal. I might as well pitch in."

"Don't do that!" Annie said, jumping up from her seat. "You guys invited me and I didn't have to do anything. I need to contribute."

"Absolutely not!" his mom said. "You're our guest and guests don't clean in this house."

"Come on, Mom," Wyatt cajoled. "I need to get the details on what she really thinks about y'all."

"Only if you tell me everything she says."

Now it was Annie's turn to blush. She could feel the burn of her face at Wyatt's mom's comment. "It will all be good, I promise."

"Deets, Wyatt James! I want the deets!" his mom called out.

"Dad, have you been letting her look up stuff on Urban Dictionary again?"

His dad shrugged his shoulders. "I don't even know what that is."

"Mom! No more Urban Dictionary! You'll read some stuff you don't want to read about, trust me."

"I just want to be up-to-date on all the hip lingo," she said. "That's the go-to spot."

"It's the *go-to* spot for finding weird words for disgusting sexual fetishes," he said, finger-quoting *go-to*. "Please. Just don't. If you want hip lingo, watch *Parks and Recreation*. Tom Haverford has it all. In fact, he calls details the tails instead of the deets. Another way of being innovative."

Annie stared at him, mouth open. "How have we worked together for over three months and I not know you like *Parks and Recreation*?"

"*You* like *Parks and Recreation*?"

Annie nodded. "I do."

Wyatt grinned at her. "I do, too."

"Chris Pratt was so cute and chubby. I like him as dumb Andy Dwyer way better than hot, muscly Owen from *Jurassic Park* or Star Lord from *Guardians of the Galaxy*."

"A woman after my brother's heart!" Lucy said with a grin. "*Parks and Recreation* is his all-time favorite television show. I even sent him the series DVDs when he was overseas."

"Oh, is that the show with the man that has the huge mustache? And the Indian kid who's a big nerd but thinks he's cool?" his mom asked.

"That's the one," Lucy agreed.

"Tom Haverford, Mom. Check him out," Wyatt said. "He's way better than Urban Dictionary."

"Huh. I never knew that was the name of the show you liked."

"Apparently, it's the name of the show *Annie* likes, too," Lucy said with a waggle of her eyebrows.

Wyatt rolled his eyes. "Come on, Annie. Let's go to the dishes."

They walked toward the kitchen, their hands loaded with plates. "So, *Parks and Recreation*, huh?"

Wyatt was rewarded with the uninhibited smile he loved so much. "Yep."

"Who knew?"

"Yes. Who knew? We should have a marathon one week-end. It's on Netflix. We could do nothing but sit around and watch episode after episode and eat nothing but popcorn and Junior Mints and drink beer."

"So you think our relationship has advanced to the point of you staying the weekend at my house?"

"I don't want you staying over at my parents' house, that's for damn sure."

Annie laughed. "That would be awkward."

"So awkward. So, what do you say? Wanna have a sleepover?"

Annie was up to her elbows in soapy water in his moth-er's huge farmhouse sink. Wyatt loved the sight.

"I think that would be okay," she said with a smile.

Wyatt blew out the breath she was holding. "Thank the lord. For a minute there I thought you were going to say no."

"I thought about it. But then I thought that would be unnecessarily mean."

Wyatt planted a kiss on her cheek. "Thank you. Not just for that. For being your wonderful self. My family loves you. I can tell. I had no doubt that would be the case, but still. So what do you think of them?"

"I like them. I really do. I was scared shitless when we first got here, wondering what in the hell I was doing. It was just me and my granny forever and I had no clue how to act. I was afraid they would hate me. But they made me feel so welcome. It's nice."

"You have no idea how happy that makes me."

He and Annie kept washing the dishes in companionable silence, her washing and Wyatt drying.

"Popcorn and Junior Mints?" she asked with a wrinkle of her nose.

Wyatt laughed. "You're just now realizing I said that?"

"No. I'm just taking it in."

"So what do you think?"

"I think it sounds disgusting."

Wyatt bumped her with his hip. "Don't knock it until you try it, Disney."

She felt the smile splitting her face. Wyatt did that to her. He had a way of always making her smile. "I guess I can give it a chance."

They had just finished washing the dishes and were putting them away in the correct cabinet when Hattie came barreling into the kitchen.

"*Look* what Poppy did for me!" she squealed, holding a shiny, gold bat in her hands. "He found gold spray paint in the garage and sprayed it right there! And *now* I have a bat that's even better than a lasso!"

Wyatt picked Hattie up and hoisted her on his shoulders. "That's great, Hattie Mae! And I agree. Bats are *way* better than lassos. Now, you can bop bad guys on the head instead of trying to rope them with a lasso. Just don't bop me."

"I would never bop you, Uncle Wy. You're one of the good guys."

"Well, that makes me happy, Hattie Mae."

"Uncle Wy, why do you always call me by my first and middle name? You can just call me Hattie."

"I know. But I like the way Hattie Mae sounds."

Annie grinned when Wyatt's niece wrapped her arms around his neck and squeezed. "Then I like the way it sounds, too."

She tapped him on the cheek with her chubby hand. "And Uncle Wy?"

"Yes, Hattie Mae?"

"I like this scar on your face. It makes you look like a superhero. Cuz you were. You fight-ed all the bad guys far away. That's what my mommy told me. Did you win?"

Annie teared up at the sad look on Wyatt's face. "Not all the time, kid. But I got the meanest ones."

Hattie grinned. "I believe it. You're the bravest army man I know."

Wyatt kissed her on the forehead. "Then that's all that matters."

Hattie hopped out of her uncle's arms and, to Annie's surprise, grabbed onto Annie's leg and pulled on her skirt. "Annie, help me up. I need to talk to you."

Annie grinned and hoisted the little girl in her arms. "Yes, Hattie Mae."

"My uncle is my favoritest uncle in the whole wide world. I love him a lot. Do you love him, too?"

Annie froze at Hattie's words. What the hell was she supposed to say to that? "Um..." she stammered. "Well, it's complica—"

Wyatt patted his niece on the head. "I sure hope she loves me, Hattie Mae. Because you wanna know a secret?"

Hattie's eyes went wide. "I do love secrets!" she said, leaning over so he could whisper in her ear.

"I really love her."

Hattie squealed and started clapping her hands. "I *knew* it! I bet I'm gonna lover her, too, Uncle Wy!"

"She's pretty lovable," Wyatt said, locking eyes with Annie. She felt her breath hitch in her chest. Wyatt loved her? That was...that was...amazing, she realized. Because she loved him, too.

"So, Annie? Do you love my Uncle Wy?"

"Yeah, Annie. Do you love me?"

Annie grinned and looked the adorable girl in the eyes. "Yeah, kiddo. I think I do."

"So are you gonna get married?"

Wyatt nearly choked on the water he was drinking. "Nope. Not getting married right now."

Annie giggled. The look on his face was priceless.

"Why not? My mommy and daddy love each other and *they* got married."

"It's just something we need to talk about first."

"Okie dokie," Hattie replied. "You can put me down now, Annie. I wanna go tell my mommy you love each other."

Before Annie could reply, Hattie had wiggled out of her arms and ran toward the dining room.

"Hattie!" Wyatt called. "That should be our sec—"

He stopped before finishing his sentence and shrugged. "It doesn't matter what I say. She's my sister's kid. She can't keep a secret for nothing."

"Then why'd you tell her?"

"Because I wanted to be honest. And I figured letting you know through my niece was pretty creative. Did I impress you?"

Annie leaned in and kissed him softly on the lips. "Pretty impressive move."

Wyatt wrapped her in a bear hug and Annie breathed in the scent that was Wyatt, the smell of the breeze off the ocean on a beautiful day. It reminded Annie of the time her granny had taken her to Gulf Shores, Alabama, for summer vacation shortly after she moved into the farmhouse. Annie had loved the feel of the ocean salt on her skin and the sand between her toes when she wiggled them as deep as they could go. She hadn't wanted to come back to Oklahoma. That's how she felt when she was in Wyatt's arms. Like she never wanted to leave.

WYATT COULDN'T BELIEVE what had just happened. He had told Annie he loved her. Even better, she told him she loved him back. He took a deep breath and let it out slowly. His heart was beating a rapid rhythm in his chest and his hands were shaking.

It wasn't that he just *loved* Annie. In just a short time, she had become his world. When he felt like he couldn't breathe, when he couldn't get the sounds of guns and screaming children out of his head, he thought about the sound of her voice. When his brain wouldn't stop scrolling through images of dead soldiers and civilians, he remembered what she looked like the first time she came around her barn, her skin as golden as the sunset reflection on the lake, her mint-tipped hair falling out of its bun and curling around her face. As long as he could see her face, hear her voice, smell her skin, he was okay. He was *alive.* He was at peace.

"What's going on in that handsome head of yours?" she asked.

Wyatt pulled her to his chest and breathed in the smell of peaches that always wafted off her hair. "Just wondering if we could start this weekend sleepover tonight."

"Tonight?" she squeaked.

He chuckled. "Yes, tonight. I have to take you home, anyway."

"What would your parents say?"

"I'd say I'm a twenty-nine-year-old man who doesn't have to tell his parents where I'm going."

"But what would *they* say?"

"I'm thinking my dad will probably say, *Atta boy.* And my mom will probably tell me to be a gentleman."

Annie took a deep breath. He could see the wheels turning. "Okay, fine. You can come over."

"Don't sound too excited."

He grabbed her hand and walked back outside on the deck. "The dishes are all finished. I think Annie and I are going to head out."

"All right, you two. Annie, again, we're so glad you could make it."

"Me, too. Thanks for the invitation."

Hattie ran up and hugged both their legs. "Bye, guys! Annie, come back soon! Oh, and I didn't tell my mommy and Grammy and Poppy. Cuz I can keep a *secret* really good."

"What secret can you keep?" his sister asked.

Hattie pretended to zip her lips and throw away the key. "What secret? I don't know about a secret."

Wyatt high-fived his niece. "Atta, kid. Don't let her break you."

"I'm going to go to the bathroom before we leave. Is it okay if I use your bathroom?" Annie asked his mom.

"Absolutely. There's a half bath right under the stairs."

His mom turned to him after Annie had gone back inside. "Just so you know, your father and I don't plan on waiting up for you to get back from taking Annie home. We're both pretty pooped. Isn't that right, Kent?" she said, elbowing his dad.

"Hmm?" his dad said, looking up from his phone.

His mom shot daggers his way. "I was just *saying*, we aren't going to wait up for Wyatt to come back from taking Annie home."

His dad shrugged his shoulders. "He's a grown ass man, Beverly. I haven't waited up for him since he graduated high school."

His mom smiled. "See?"

"Subtlety was never your strong suit, Mom."

She laughed and kissed him on the cheek. "I wasn't trying to be."

"Bye, guys." Wyatt waved to his family and headed back inside the house to pack a bag. He turned the corner and ran right into Annie.

"Oh, hey," she said breathlessly. "Are you ready?"

"I have to go pack a bag first."

"I thought we were going to lie around in our underwear all weekend."

Wyatt grinned. "Oh, we definitely are. But I have to pack different underwear because I plan on getting very sweaty. And Disney?"

"Yeah?"

Wyatt winked. "I don't plan on getting sweaty by going outside."

CHAPTER 19

*A*nnie and Breckin were sitting in massage chairs in CC's shop, their feet soaking in tubs of hot water attached to the chair. Janette's Curls and More had just been a place for a person to get a haircut and the latest gossip just two short years ago. Then, CC's mom had surgery on her back to repair a herniated disc and decided she didn't want to own a beauty salon anymore. CC had purchased the shop from her mom for practically nothing and had slowly started changing it to suit her more vivacious, hip personality.

The shop that was once drab and featured green linoleum flooring and beige walls was now painted a soft turquoise accented with black doors and frames. CC had ripped up the old floor and installed black and white checkered tiles and a surround sound to play music throughout the shop. True to her personality, she hung brightly colored quotes and pictures on the wall and even installed a hip sitting area and coffee bar for people who came in early for their appointments.

The best part of the shop's overhaul, however, was the fact that CC had decided Parker needed more than a place to get a haircut. She had installed two pedicure chairs, a tanning bed, spray tan booth, and manicurist's table. CC had even leased the empty building next door to the salon and was in the process of turning it into a workout facility. Now the good citizens of Parker could get their daily dose of gossip in style. The only thing her friend had left alone was the name. She stated it was the name of the shop when it was first opened in 1952 and the old ladies in town might hang her high if she tried to change it.

"I really love what you've done with the place. It looks so good," Annie told her friend, looking around the space. She also grinned at CC's hair choice for the week. A couple of weeks ago, CC's hair had been the purple-streaked lilac color Wyatt had seen. Today, it was platinum blonde dyed fire engine red at the tips. "And your hair looks good, too. Did you take a play from my playbook? I thought *I* was the only cool one who thought of colored tips."

"I'm the one who gave you the colored tips," CC said. "As to your other statement, thank you. I like it. Lord knows it's taken long enough to get it all finished. Why couldn't hottie army man come to *my* rescue when *I* needed him, huh? I had to hire Max's son, Walter, to help me on the construction stuff. I think I saw his ass crack more than I saw his actual face."

Breckin cackled with laughter. "At least Max gave you a discount at Nailed It for hiring his son. There's always a bright side."

"Yeah, I saw his *bright side* way more than I wanted," CC muttered. "His bright side needed a lot more coverage from his tighty whities."

She began rubbing vigorously on Annie's foot she had taken out of the hot water.

"Ow, Cees! Tone it down a bit. I'd like to have some skin left on my foot when you're finished." Annie squealed.

Her friend let go of her foot. "Sorry. I still get angry when I think about his large, white, nasty ass."

Annie grinned. "It really looks amazing."

CC grinned. "It really does, huh?"

"When do you think you're going to be able to open the gym next door?" Breckin asked. "I need to work out before my butt gets any bigger than it already is. School cafeteria food is wreaking havoc on my metabolism."

Annie and CC both glared at their friend. "Oh, please," CC said, rolling her eyes. "You probably weigh one hundred pounds soaking wet."

"One twelve," Breckin replied. "But for me, that's the equivalent of weighing two hundred pounds."

Annie threw the towel CC had placed on her lap at Breckin's head. "I'm with CC. Shut. Up."

Breckin shrugged her shoulders. "I can't help it I'm a shrimp. I'm like a kid-sized Happy Meal when all I want to be is a supersized number one."

"Number one?" Annie asked.

"A Big Mac meal. From McDonald's."

"I guess that's why God made you such a hard ass. Otherwise, you wouldn't be able to handle all those high schoolers the way you do. You're a Big Mac meal in a Happy Meal package," CC said with an ornery grin.

Breckin stuck her tongue out at her friends. "Whatever."

"Hey! You're the one who said it, not us."

"Ow!" Annie yelled again. "What are you doing?"

"I'm cleaning underneath your toenails. There's a lot of dead skin."

"I thought pedicures were supposed to feel good, not feel like you're getting interrogated by the Nazi regime!"

"It will. Right after I get out all this dead skin."

Annie braced herself as CC ran the torture device under her big toenail one last time.

"All finished," CC said, tapping Annie's calf. Now I'll just rub your calves down and wrap 'em. Then you can pick out your color."

Annie held up a hot pink nail polish. "Already did."

"You get that color all the time. Venture outside your nail polish box. I'm going to pick for you."

Annie rolled her eyes. "Just don't paint them black."

"Deal."

CC scooted in her chair across the floor on its wheels and got a pair of towels out of a drawer. She then scooted back to Annie, soaked them in the hot water, wrung them out, and wrapped Annie's legs. "That should feel better."

Annie sighed in contentment. "This feels so good. These chairs were such a good idea," she added, increasing the kneading feature of the chair. "I've been working so hard at the farm my muscles need this."

"How is it going on the farm?" Breckin asked, moaning as CC wrapped her legs. "Has he taken off any more clothing while he's working?"

Annie felt her face turn red. "Not really."

Her friends stared at her. "Your face is turning red," CC said.

"So?"

"So your face only turns red when you're hiding something. What happened?"

"I'll tell you what happened," Breckin said. "Wyatt stuck his tongue down her throat. That's what happened."

"*What?*" CC yelled. "How do I not know this?"

"I haven't seen you to tell you."

"I have texting on my phone like every other American. Why does Breck know?"

"She came to my office right after it happened and spilled the beans," Breckin said.

"Now my feelings are hurt," CC added with a pout.

"Don't be! I didn't leave you out intentionally!"

"Fine," CC huffed. "I forgive you."

Breckin continued to stare at her. "You're not telling us the whole story."

"What? Yes, I am."

"No, you're not. I can tell by the look on your face."

"What look?"

"You've had the same look of guilt on your face since you were twelve years old. You have a horrible poker face."

Annie sighed. She might as well spill the beans. Her friends wouldn't quit until they found out. "Fine! Wyatt and I have done more than...well, more than *kissing.*"

Her friends squealed. "You slept with him, didn't you?" CC asked.

Annie could feel her face flaming. She was surprised she hadn't burst into flames. "Yes," she whispered.

"What?" Breckin said, holding her hand to her ear. "We couldn't hear you."

"Yes, all right? We slept together. More than once." Annie couldn't keep the smile off her face.

"I *knew* it! Was he as good in the sack as I imagine him to be?" CC asked. "Please tell me yes."

Annie nodded her head. "*So* much better."

Both her friends let out a sigh. "That's so great. So, what's next? Is it just a fling or something more?"

"Well, Friday night I went to his parents' house for a cookout. He took me fishing and we ate the fish we cooked."

"You fished?"

"Yes. And I'm actually pretty good at it."

Her friends looked at her skeptically. "Whatever you say."

Annie stuck her tongue out. "I *am*!" she said indignantly.

"You met his parents?" CC asked. "That *is* serious."

"He also spent the weekend with me."

Breckin took one of the towels wrapped around her leg

off and threw it at Annie's head. "You little slutty McSlut face!"

"You guys are the ones who told me to sleep with him!"

Breckin grinned. "I'm kidding. I'm just jealous."

"And he might have told me he loves me."

It was CC's turn to throw a towel at Annie, this one wrapped around Annie's leg. "So? Do you love him, too?"

"I do."

Both her friends sighed. "I'm so happy for you," Breckin said softly. "You really deserve this."

CC nodded her agreement. "Ditto. And Wyatt does, too."

"What's the next step? Are you going to move in together?"

"What? No. We're nowhere near that. He's looking for his own place. He actually found a place he really likes, actually. But he won't buy it."

"Why not?"

"He says it is out of his price range. But it would be so perfect for him. At least I think so by the way he describes it." Annie felt a lightbulb go off in her head. "I think I might have a way to help him get it."

"What's that?"

Annie began explaining to her friends how much money her granny left her and the fact she was a millionaire. When she finished, they both looked at her in disbelief.

"No. Way," Breckin breathed.

"Yes way. I didn't believe it at first. But Harry told me when he read me her will and then I checked her account at the bank. It's true."

"Why in the hell wouldn't she *tell* you?" CC asked. "You could have done so much with it when you were growing up. Your house is practically falling down. You *definitely* could have gotten a better car then the clunker you painted."

"I don't think she wanted me to have it. I think she

wanted to make sure I was set up when I was an adult, so I didn't have to worry about anything. She did enough to get us by when I was a teenager. If she saved, I would have more when she passed away. When I think about it, it really makes sense. I never even saw a medical bill for when she was in the hospital. I should have been suspicious."

"So what are you going to do with the money?"

"I don't really know. I thought about setting up an anonymous college fund for the senior students at the high school," she said, looking at Breckin. "You can tell me the kids who could benefit from it most and I could give it to them if you made sure they applied. Then I was going to invest some of it, just so it wouldn't run out in case oil ever tanks again."

"That would be so amazing," Breckin said softly. "I can think of a lot of kids off the top of my head that would be so deserving."

"And what if I paid off the loans for your shop and helped you open the gym?" she asked CC.

"I couldn't ask you to do that!"

"Why not? I want to. You deserve it. I insist."

CC shrugged her shoulders. "I'm not going to turn away a helping hand. Will you let me pay you back?"

"Absolutely not."

"Seriously?"

"Seriously."

CC huffed. "Fine."

"I want a lifetime free membership."

Her friend smiled. "Deal."

"Hey! I want one, too!" Breckin said.

"I'll pay for one for Breck, too."

"Double deal."

"So what was your bright idea earlier?" Breckin asked.

"I thought about buying Wyatt his house."

CC raised her eyebrows. "I don't know if that's a good idea, Annie."

"Why not?"

"He might see it as charity."

"I don't think so."

"Maybe not. But I think you should ask him first."

Annie shrugged her shoulders. "I'll think about it. But I for sure want to see the house before I do anything. Breck, what do you think?"

"I'm with CC on this one. He might see it as charity. You definitely need to ask him."

"We'll see," she replied. She knew her friends meant well, but they didn't know Wyatt like she did. Wyatt needed this house and she wanted him to have it.

"So what color have you chosen for me?" she asked her friend, changing the subject. "You said you were picking the color."

CC held up a bottle of dark gray nail polish.

"Cees! I said not black!"

"It's not black. It's gray. And I'm going to paint some pretty pink flowers on your big toe so you get your normal color, too. Deal?"

Annie sighed. Her friend was going to paint them that color anyway. "Fine."

CC grinned. "You're gonna love 'em. Promise."

"Like you love *Wyatt*," Breckin sing-songed.

Annie laughed. "You're such a nerd."

"But you love me."

"I do."

"As much as you love Wyatt?"

"Always."

∽

"ARE YOU READY, HATTIE MAE?" Wyatt called, opening his sister's front door. "It's Annie's farm day!"

He had called his sister after the cookout to see if Hattie could spend the day at Annie's farm with the two of them and his sister had agreed, as long as it was a Saturday. After asking Annie, he agreed and told his sister he would pick his niece up bright and early the following Saturday morning.

Since he and Annie had utter those three little words, they had settled into an easy, familiar routine. He spent most of his nights at her farmhouse and had even transferred his clothes and toiletries little by little until the majority of them were at her house. His parents hadn't said anything about it; they had just smiled knowingly.

Hattie walked into the living room, her hair in a wild, curly mane around her face, rubbing her sleepy eyes. He grinned at her pajamas. She had paired a minion from *Despicable Me* holding a banana top with T-Rex bottoms that looked two sizes too small.

"Uncle Wy, why did you pick me up so *early*?" she said. "I like to sleep in on Saturdays. School makes my brain tired. Saturdays help it recharge."

Wyatt chuckled. "It's nine o'clock. It's not *that* early."

"It's early for your niece," his sister said, walking around the corner, holding a glass of milk in one hand and a chocolate chip waffle in the other. "She is never even up for Saturday morning cartoons on the weekend."

His sister held out breakfast to her daughter. "You don't have to go. You can go back to bed if you want," she said. "But I hear Annie has lots of animals on her farm, including chickens."

His niece's eyes widened. "Chickens are my most favoritest animal!"

"I know. That's why I thought I would tell you. But if you're too tired…"

Hattie turned around and ran around the corner as fast as her little legs would carry her. "I'm gonna go get dressed, Uncle Wy! I'll be right back! Don't leave me!"

Wyatt plopped down on his sister's couch and put his feet on her coffee table. "You sure know how to get her up and moving."

"I had to learn how. Otherwise, she'd sleep until noon. She definitely didn't inherit her dad's early bird personality."

"If I remember correctly, you were as bad as her about getting up in the mornings as a kid."

"That's why I don't give her a hard time. And have figured out things that work. I thank Mom for all her methods. So far, they work on my daughter, too. Now, why don't you tell me about the secret you swore Hattie to keep last weekend?"

"I don't know what you're talking about." Wyatt played dumb and hoped his sister dropped it. He wasn't ready to let his family know how he felt about Annie. It was something he wanted to keep between them.

"Just so you know, your niece spilled the beans on Sunday night. All I had to do was bribe her with chocolate cake and strawberry icing."

Wyatt groaned. "The little traitor!"

"I don't know why you're afraid to tell me. I think it's great, Wyatt. I haven't seen you this happy since before you left for your first tour. Don't think I haven't noticed how much you've changed. I can't imagine what you saw over there. It would change anybody. But I know how big of a heart you have. It couldn't be easy."

"It wasn't."

"You're different with Annie. She's good for you."

Wyatt smiled. "She is. I can't even explain what it is about her. I just know I want her in my life. For always."

His sister hugged him. "That's so great."

His niece came barreling around the corner wearing a

Russell Westbrook jersey from the Oklahoma City Thunder and a pair of pink polka-dotted shorts. Her feet were clad in her favorite pair of cowgirl boots and a Parker High baseball cap two sizes too big was on her head.

"I'm all ready to go, Uncle Wy! Let's go see some chickens."

Wyatt turned to his sister. "Are you going to let her wear that?"

"On the weekends, I let her choose her outfit. It's the only way I can choose normal clothing during the week. I have to choose my battles."

Wyatt chuckled. "I have the coolest niece ever."

"Uncle Wyatt? I *said* I'm ready to go!"

"She used my full name. She means business." Wyatt turned to the door and barked out a laugh. Hattie had pulled a Captain America umbrella out of the umbrella stand by the front door.

"Why are you taking an umbrella, silly girl? There's not a cloud in the sky."

"It's Oklahoma. You never know when it's gonna rain."

"That's the truest statement I've heard in a long time. Who am I to argue with the girl who's getting to dress herself today?" Wyatt took his niece's hand and walked out the door.

"What time will you be home?" his sister called.

"I don't know. When Hattie Mae gets tired."

"She never gets tired!"

"Then I guess I'll call you."

His sister shook her head. "She'll wear you out."

"I wouldn't expect anything else."

Wyatt made sure to drive extra slow since his niece was in the front seat because the International didn't have a back-seat. He had brought her super fancy, super complicated car seat his sister insisted he take with him. It felt like it had taken an hour to install.

Hattie was tapping her hands on her knees to the beat of the song, *Body Like a Backroad* by Sam Hunt, playing on the radio. When it ended, she turned and looked at him. "I like your music, Uncle Wy. All my mom likes to listen to is Britney Spears and Lady Gaga." She rolled her eyes.

"I take it you don't like them?"

"Not really. All they talk about is boys. I'd like them better if they talked about superheroes."

"Makes sense."

So, do you still love Annie?"

He chuckled. "I do."

Hattie grinned. "Good. Cuz I do, too. And I really love that she lives on a farm with animals. Do you think she'll let me come over more than once?"

"I think she'll let you come over whenever you want."

"Then I *double* love her."

The duo drove in companionable silence the rest of the way to the farm, Hattie trying to sing the lyrics of songs on the radio she didn't know. It was adorable. He hoped if he ever had kids they were as cool as his niece. Finally, Wyatt turned right and headed down the dirt road to Annie's house, Hattie staring out the window.

"Wow!" she said breathlessly when the house came into view. "Her house is *huge*!"

"It is. And just wait until you meet all the animals. They're named after Disney characters."

"*What*? This is the coolest place in the whole wide world!"

Wyatt chuckled. "Be sure to tell Annie that. I'm sure she'll love hearing it."

"I *will*!" she yelled, unbuckling herself from her car seat before throwing open the truck's door, running up the porch, and pounding on the front door of Annie's house.

"Hey, Annie!" she yelled. "Open up! I'm ready to see all your animals!"

Annie opened the door, a smile on her face. "Well, hello there, Hattie Mae. I'm so happy you're getting to visit me today."

Hattie threw her arms around Annie's waist. "*I'm* so glad I'm getting to visit you, too! And Uncle Wy says I can visit any time I want!"

"Now, Hattie, I didn't—" Wyatt walked up the front step.

"He's exactly right," Annie said, ignoring Wyatt's protests. "You can come over anytime."

"Woohoo!" Hattie jumped up and down in celebration. "This is the best day ever!"

Wyatt walked up to Annie and wrapped her in a hug. "Good morning, beautiful."

"Good morning," she replied, laughing into his chest. "Even though I just saw you an hour ago when you left to pick up Hattie."

Wyatt chuckled. "But it felt like so long."

"You're such a dork."

Wyatt kissed her on the top of the head. "Maybe. Do you have an exciting day planned? Miss Hattie is expecting big things."

"I sure do." Annie leaned down so she was eye level with his niece. "First things first. You, my dear, are looking awesome in your outfit."

Hattie bowed. "Well, thanks. On Saturdays and Sundays I get to pick my own clothes."

"I can tell. You have excellent taste."

Wyatt grinned. Annie had his niece eating out of the palm of his hand.

"If you get to pick out your own clothes, do you want to pick out what you want to do first?"

"I don't know if I can choose! Uncle Wy says there's so many fun things to do here!"

Annie grinned. "Then how about this? Big animals or little animals first?"

Hattie started jumping up and down. "Big animals! No! Little animals! No! All of them!"

Wyatt and Annie started laughing. "How about we just start with what's in the barn?" Annie asked.

The three of them walked toward the barn, Hattie between Annie and Wyatt, her hands in theirs. "Can you swing me?" she asked.

"Sure," Wyatt said. "On the count of three."

"One," Hattie giggled as they began swinging her arms back and forth. "Two...three!"

Peals of little girl laughter echoed through the trees as Hattie went flying through the air. She landed on her feet and immediately shouted, "Again! Again!"

Annie and Wyatt continued swinging her in the air until they reached the barn. Before she could open the doors, Hattie ran around the corner of the barn toward the back of Annie's land.

"Where is she going?" Wyatt asked.

Annie sighed and began jogging after Hattie. "She saw Animal Land."

"Animal what?"

"The place where we kept all the stray animals. You know! Animal Land!"

"I didn't know that was what you called it!" he yelled back, but Annie and his niece were already gone. Wyatt couldn't do anything but follow.

He never realized it had an actual name, but Animal Land was one of the first places he and Annie had worked on in the beginning after he had tackled the gutters of the farmhouse. Annie's granny had created a haven for stray animals of all shapes and sizes. She had built pens for dogs with concrete doggie pools, dog runs, and dig pits. On the cat side, she had created cat trees twelve feet high and an old clothesline with probably every feathery, stringy cat toy sold at all the pet stores within a hundred mile radius. Sophie had even created a place for birds, guinea pigs, ferrets, rabbits, and hamsters. It had probably taken a good chunk of her oil royalty change to keep it running. He had always known Sophie took in strays. He just hadn't known she had put them up at the animal version of The Ritz.

Animal Land was brilliant and amazing...and also in a great state of disrepair. He and Annie had basically cleaned it up and put a big bandage on a wound that needed several stitches. When he asked Annie what her plan was, she looked at him sadly and said she didn't know. He knew Animal Land was something Sophie loved by the way Annie talked about helping her granny with the animals who were dumped on their land. She never said it, but Wyatt thought visiting it and remembering what it once was when her granny was healthy and could take in the strays made Annie sad.

"This is...*was*...a placed called Animal Land."

Wyatt had caught up to Annie and Hattie, who were standing in front of the fence that separated Animal Land from the rest of the farm. Annie's hand was on Hattie's shoulder and Hattie had her head on Annie's thigh. He wished he had his phone in his pocket. He would've loved to have a picture of it.

"Well, you remember my Granny Sophie?"

"Yep. She was my favorite."

Annie laughed softly. "Mine, too, Hattie. Well, she really loved animals. So she made this place for animals who didn't have a home."

"If it's called Animal Land, then how come there aren't any animals who live here?" Hattie asked, wrinkling her nose in confusion. "Right now, it should probably be called Dump Land, cuz it *kinda* looks like a dump."

"Hattie!" Wyatt said with a frown. "That's rude."

Annie shushed him with her hand. "It does kind of look like a dump right now," she told Hattie. "But you should've seen it when I was a kid. There were animals of *all* shapes and sizes. One time, we even had a zebra."

"No. Way!"

"Yes way. It came from a rescue shelter that couldn't stay open. They knew my granny had a license to take all kinds of animals. When we go back to the house, I'll find some pictures of what it was like when I was a kid."

"Why isn't it like that anymore?"

"Well, because my granny got sick and then it was too hard for her to take care of all of them. And I had to take care of her so it was really hard for me to take care of them, too."

"Where did they all go then?"

"I made sure to find them all homes or sent them to other rescues who could take care of them."

Hattie leaned against the fence and stared inside. "I bet the cats really liked climbing those cat trees, huh?"

Annie grinned. "They did. You know who the best climber was?"

"No. Who?"

"A cat with three legs."

Nuh-uh!"

"Yep. He could leap higher than any of the rest of the cats because all his other legs got so strong to make up for missing the fourth one."

"That's so awesome!"

"It was."

"So why don't you open it up again?" Hattie asked. "I bet there's lots more animals that need a home."

Annie didn't answer, choosing to change the subject instead. "I thought you were here to see the *actual* animals, not talk about them, silly! Let's go to the barn!"

Hattie giggled and took off running. "I'll beat ya!"

Wyatt pulled Annie in for a hug before she could chase after his niece. "You okay?"

She took a deep breath. "I will be. One day."

He kissed her on the forehead. "I love you."

"I love you, too. Now, let's go. I've got a kid I need to impress."

Annie walked up to the barn where Hattie was jumping up and down in excitement and pulled open the doors. "Welcome to the barn, Hattie," Annie said. "I'd like to introduce you to Cinderella, Drizella, Anastasia, and Fairy Godmother. I just finished milking them before you got here. They're ready to go out to the field now."

Hattie looked at Annie, eyes wide and mouth agape. "You *milk* them?"

"Yep. If your lazy uncle had picked you up earlier, you could've helped me."

Hattie glared at him.

"Hey! Don't look at me, kid! You're the one I had to practically *pull* out of bed by the toes!"

"Well, if I knew I was gonna get to milk a *cow*, I woulda been nicer!" Hattie turned to Annie. "Can I move in with you?"

Wyatt chuckled. "I don't think your parents would go for that, kid."

Hattie frowned. "Dang it."

Annie picked up a small bucket of cake feed and handed it to his niece. "Here you go, Hattie. Just shake that bucket and all the girls will follow you to the field. Perdita is probably out there. I bet Timon, Pumba, and Nala are out there, too."

"You have all these animals and they're all named after *Disney movies?*" she shrieked. "This just keeps getting better and better!"

Wyatt took Annie's hand in his as they followed the

spoiled cows, who followed his excited-beyond-words niece out the barn doors. "Thanks for doing this for her," he said, kissing the top of her hand. "It's something she'll always remember."

"Why are you acting like this is just going to be a one-time thing? I plan on her coming out here way more often. In fact, I might even give her a job when she's a teenager."

"Are you two comin', already? I wanna meet all the other animals!"

Wyatt and Annie took Hattie around the farm, introducing her to every single animal. She rode bareback on Perdita *and* Nemo, fed Cheerios to Timon, Pumba, and Nala, and bread to Lilo and Stitch, and chased Sebastian under the front porch of the house. Annie had been saving the best, and Hattie's favorite, animals for last.

"All right, Hattie. Are you ready to go? You've seen them all," Annie said.

Wyatt's niece frowned. "But I thought you had chickens."

"Who told you I had chickens?"

"Uncle Wyatt."

"Well, do you think I have chickens?"

Hattie stared at Annie and Wyatt could see her wheels turning. "I *want* you to have chickens. They're my most favoritest animals in the whole, wide world."

"Even more than dolphins? I thought everyone loved dolphins the most."

"Uh-huh."

"That's a weird animal to have as a favorite. Why chickens?"

Hattie grinned. "My mommy showed me a video on Facebook of a chicken giving a kid a *hug!* How awesome is *that?* It just runned up and put its head right on the kid's shoulder. I wanna get a chicken to do that to *me!* That would be the best thing *ever!*"

Wyatt didn't know if it were possible, but he hoped like hell one of Annie's chickens would miraculously decide to hug his niece. Since his sister had Hattie, he totally understood the idea of people doing anything for their kids. *Hell,* Hattie Mae wasn't even his kid and he felt that way. He couldn't even imagine how he would feel if it were a baby he made.

Immediately, thoughts of a little girl with hazel eyes and blonde hair tinted mint green at the tips ran through his head. When he came home from overseas, he never thought he'd have a normal life, or a normal relationship for that matter, ever again. He thought he was too damaged. Slowly but surely, Annabelle Cleaver had repaired his wounded heart, soothed his mind, and rebuilt his image to, not the man he once was, but an even better version of himself.

"Well, I don't know if they'll hug you, but they sure are friendly," Annie said to his niece, pulling his thoughts back to the present. "Wanna go see them?"

"Yes! Yes! Yes!" Hattie yelled, jumping up and down.

"Then follow me."

The trio walked around the barn to the shaded area of trees where the chicken coop had been built to keep its inhabitants shaded and cool. Annie opened a small door to a cupboard attached to the coop and pulled out a bag of dried meal worms.

"This is their favorite snack," she said, sprinkling some in her hand.

Hattie wrinkled her nose. "Worms? I don't wanna hold worms!"

"They're not alive, Hattie Mae," Wyatt added. "It's like holding confetti in your hand."

His niece didn't look like she believed him but held out her hand, anyway. She must really love her chickens.

"Now, we just go in here and call them. They'll come out of their coop when they hear me," Annie told her.

She opened the gate to the outside part of the pen and he and Hattie followed her inside. "Girls!" she called. "Come get a treat!"

Wyatt heard some bocking inside the coop and then, one at a time, the three chickens came out of their tiny door and hopped out in the grass.

"Now, just crouch down and hold out your hand," Annie told Hattie, demonstrating by bending down and following her own rule. "Then, just be really still and they'll come eat them right out of your hand. Don't be wild or you'll scare them."

Hattie mimicked Annie and bent down, carefully holding out both her hands full of worms. Merida, the biggest chicken covered in rust red feathers, walked up to Hattie and began pecking the worms out of her hand. His niece giggled.

"That tickles," she whispered.

Annie grinned. "It kinda does, huh?"

Annie carefully poured the rest of her worms into Hattie's hands and stood up. Without Annie's hands there, the other two chickens, Pocahontas, the petite black chicken, and Rapunzel, the blonde chicken, ran over to Hattie's hands and began eating with Merida.

Hattie's eyes grew large and Wyatt didn't think she was breathing. Her grin stretched from ear to ear. "This is the best. Day. Ever," she breathed.

Wyatt grinned at his niece. She didn't get a hug from a chicken, but by the look on her face, this was just as good. His grin grew even bigger when he looked at Annie. Her eyes were just as large as his niece's and her grin was just as wide. It was a moment he would always remember.

CHAPTER 20

*G*uns firing. Soldiers screaming. Pain. Heat. Death.
Wyatt jerked awake with a scream and sat up in bed, his hands curled into fists. Eyes wide, breathing heavily, he looked around, not recognizing the room he was in. All of a sudden, it registered. He was in Annie's bedroom. Turning in bed, his eyes locked with hers, which were frozen in fear. She was by the headboard, curled into herself, almost as if she were trying to make herself as small as possible.

"Annie?" he asked, horror in his voice. "Oh, God. Did I hurt you?"

She shook her head. "No," she whispered softly. "You didn't hurt me."

"Did I touch you?"

"No—" her voice wavered.

"Annie," he said, trying to keep his voice level despite the rapid beating of his heart. "Did I *hurt* you?"

"I tried to wake you up and you shoved me but—"

"Son of a *bitch!*" he yelled, jumping out of bed.

Annie grabbed his arm before he could get very far. Her

voice wavered and cracked on a sob. "You didn't hurt me. I just couldn't get you to wake up. I'm fine. Really."

Wyatt began pulling on his shorts and threw his shirt over his head. He had to get out of her house before he did something to her. Before he *hurt* her. How he thought he could do this was beyond him. "I can't stay, Annie. If I had hurt you—"

Annie ran past him and blocked the door with her body. The moonlight shining through the window shone on the tears running down her face. "I *said* you didn't hurt me. You had a nightmare. I get it. I'm surprised this is the first one you've have since you started staying the night. Aren't they getting better?"

"They are," Wyatt said softly, sitting on the edge of the bed. The adrenaline that had been coursing through his system a few short minutes ago had drained his body, leaving nothing but sadness and helplessness in its wake.

Seeing he wasn't going to leave, Annie walked over to the bed and sat down beside him. She put her hand on his face and ran it gently down his scar. He loved it when she did that. It didn't just soothe his mind. It soothed his soul. She was so good. So incredibly good.

"But I *wouldn't* be fine if you left," she said, making him look her in the eyes. "Wyatt, I don't want you to go. Please believe me. You aren't the only one in this relationship who needs the other person. I *need* you here. Without you, all I can hear is the emptiness that reminds me my granny is never coming back."

Wyatt stilled at the sound of fear in her voice. Not fear of him. Fear of him leaving. "How is it possible?"

"How is what possible?"

"How is it possible I got so lucky for you to fall in love with me? I don't deserve you. I don't deserve anything. Not after everything I've done."

"What is it exactly you think you've done?"

Wyatt took a deep breath. "It wasn't what I *did*. It's what I *didn't* do."

Annie waited patiently for him to explain himself. He knew she wouldn't push him, but it was something she deserved to know.

"Before I got this scar," he said, covering her hand which was still gently caressing his face, "I was a sniper. Well, I guess I was always a sniper. I'd always been good with guns, even as a little kid. My dad bought me a BB gun when I was like four or five. My mom kept saying I would shoot my eye out like that kid on *A Christmas Story* but I never did."

"I've seen you shoot," she said with a small smile. "The skeet competition at school your senior year, remember? You won it. Smoked everyone's ass."

Wyatt laughed. "I'd forgotten all about that."

"Yeah, you were pretty much the best at everything you ever did."

"Not everything."

"What does that mean?"

"I never talked to you."

Annie smiled. "You don't have to tell me if you don't want to, Wyatt. I'm fine not knowing."

He shook his head. He hadn't told anyone this story. Not even his parents. It was something he wanted her to know. The *only* one he wanted to know. "I was on a roof with another sniper. Our platoon was clearing a building. All of a sudden, this little kid comes out from behind a pile of rubble in the street, with a bomb attached to his chest."

Wyatt heard Annie gasp but she didn't say a word, so he continued. "We tried radioing them, but something was wrong and we couldn't get through. I had the better shot, so the other sniper kept telling me to take it. But I couldn't. I just kept staring at that kid with the bomb strapped to his chest, walking toward the building where all my friends were. He probably wasn't even more than eight years old. He should've been playing outside with his friends, not walking to his own death, you know? And there were tears running down his face. Like he knew what was happening. Of course he did. His dad probably strapped it to him. And of course he couldn't play outside. His town was a battleground. A walking cemetery."

Wyatt knew he was rambling but he couldn't seem to stop the words from coming out of his mouth. Silent tears began streaming down Annie's face. She looked so sad, but he knew if he didn't finish the story, he never would. It was part of who he was; a part of him that would never go away. And he had to tell her.

"All of a sudden, a bunch of my guys ran out of the building. The kid started running toward them, his thumb on a trigger he held in his hand. And there I was. Just sitting there. Frozen. Listening to Tom yelling at me to take the shot. But I couldn't. And then I saw the kid drop to the ground. Saw a pool of blood seep out from under his head. Tom had taken the shot. And he'd saved all of our buddies. He'd done what I couldn't."

"Did they send you home?"

"No."

Why not?"

"I begged Tom not to say anything. I told him I was fine. We all had days like that over there. We were each other's family. We always had each other's backs. He said he wouldn't say anything unless it happened again."

"Where's Tom now?"

"Buried in Alabama. Three weeks later we were driving to another town and ran over a mine. It exploded and Tom was one of the ones thrown from the truck. Broke his neck on impact. His wife was pregnant with their third kid."

"Damn."

"It should've been me. I didn't have anyone. He had a family. He's the one who took the shot that saved our platoon. He should've been the one who lived."

"Wyatt, no."

Annie pulled him back down on the bed and into her arms. He let her. He was too tired to fight.

"Don't ever say that again. What happened was horrible and I can't imagine what his family went through. But don't wish your death because you didn't take one shot and he was married with children. Do you not think your parents would have mourned your loss just as much? Your sister? Your *niece?* You don't get to play God, Wyatt James, and you don't get to place more value on another man's life just because he had a wife and kids."

Annie leaned back on the pillows and pulled him to her chest. He was surprisingly unashamed to feel tears fall out of his eyes and trickle down his cheeks. The speech she just gave him was something Dr. Wilkerson had told him numerous times in countless therapy sessions, but for the first time, it actually made sense. He never really believed Dr. Wilkerson. He felt like it was something his therapist had to say to lead him down the road to recovery. But with Annie, the words held meaning. Merit. He knew she wasn't saying them because she needed to be validated as part of her profession. She meant them because she loved *this* version of him and all the scars that came with him, both the visible and invisible.

"I need you, Wyatt, so don't you *dare* say you don't deserve to be alive," she whispered into his hair. He felt tears she was shedding fall onto his shoulders. "You hear me?"

"I hear you," he whispered hoarsely. Now it was time to lighten the mood. "But would you quit crying already? Jeez, woman!"

"Rude," she complained. "Notice I didn't say anything about *you* crying on my boobs!"

Wyatt scoffed. "I wasn't *crying*. Did you think I was crying? I woke up with bad allergies."

"You woke up with a nightmare."

Wyatt kissed her forehead. "Good thing you made it all better. Now, let's go eat breakfast. I'm starving. I'll make you some of my famous scrambled eggs."

ANNIE SMILED across the kitchen table at Wyatt. He was right. He made some killer scrambled eggs. "These eggs are really good, Wyatt."

"Told you. I don't lie about my knack for making breakfast food. It's my favorite meal of the day."

"And the most important."

"That it is."

"If you're so good at making breakfast food in general, why did you only make me scrambled eggs?"

Annie laughed when Wyatt quirked his eyebrows at her. "Did you seriously just ask me that? What do you want me to do? Ask the bacon or sausage fairy to magically deliver some to your fridge? You have some live bacon and sausage out in your backyard."

Annie threw a piece of toast at him. "Not funny! Those are *pets*, not food!"

"You sound like the sharks on *Finding Nemo*. Fish are friends, not food."

Annie laughed. "How can you quote *Finding Nemo?*"

"Have you not met my niece? Try telling her no when she wants to watch a movie and see where it gets you."

"That's fair."

"You know what's not fair?"

"What?"

"She'll *quiz* you after the movie, just to make sure you watched it. You can't even play on your phone!"

"She's one smart girl, that niece of yours."

"You can say that again."

"Pretty, too. You can tell she'll be a stunner when she's a teenager. Her daddy will have his hands full scaring all the horny teenage boys away."

Wyatt shot a glare her way. "Don't even joke about that."

Annie grinned. "It's inevitable."

"You know what's inevitable?"

"What?"

"Me throwing you over my shoulders and tickling you until you wet your pants if you say that about my niece again."

"She'll be gorgeous," Annie shouted and then took off running, Wyatt following close behind.

"You'll pay for that, ACDC!" he yelled.

Annie stopped mid-run. "You did *not* just call me by my initials. I *specifically* remember telling you to *never* do that!"

"That was when I was groveling for a job. Now that I'm your boyfriend, I figure I have the privilege of calling you anything I want."

Annie stilled. "You're my boyfriend?"

"I'm your boyfriend."

"That makes me your girlfriend."

"Yes. It does. What do you think about that?"

Annie pretended to think about it. "I think I like it."

"Me, too. Too bad you're not going to like the tickling I'm about to unleash on you!"

True to his word, Wyatt threw her over his shoulders and took the stairs two at a time. "Wyatt James! Put me down!"

"Pulling out the middle name, too, ACDC? Too bad mine isn't after a band who sang what I'm pretty sure was the background music when a lot of women became baby mommas. Yours included."

"Ew! Don't remind me!" Annie wanted to complain again about him carrying her like a sack of potatoes, but if she were being honest with herself, all thoughts of complaining flew out the window as soon as she realized how great the view of his ass was as she got up close and personal with it.

When they got to her room, Wyatt threw her on the bed. Before she could run away, he pounced on her and began tickling her. Everywhere. Her stomach. Her ribs. The junction of her hips and leg. Her inner thigh. Nothing was off limits. And it was the worst kind of torture. She began laughing uncontrollably.

"Wyatt! Get off me!" she screamed between laughs.

"Not a chance. I'm a man of my word."

"Wyatt, please!"

"Begging won't help."

"I'll do anything! Wyatt! Please! Just stop!"

"Anything?"

"Anything!" she laughed breathlessly. If he didn't stop soon she was seriously going to wet her pants.

"Marry me."

The tickling stopped. "Wh…wh…what?" she stuttered.

"Stop freaking out. I don't want to get married tomorrow. Or even six months from now. I just want to know you're going to be mine forever." He ran his fingers down her face. "I *need* you to say yes. You're the air I breathe. The beat of my heart. My soul. My everything. Marry me, Annabelle Cleaver. I promise not to give our children big hair band initials."

Annie grinned and could feel the tears running down her face. "You're turning me into a crying baby, Wyatt Holloway. I haven't cried this much in my entire life. Granny always told me Cleaver women don't cry."

"I take it that means yes. Or are you crying because you're about to break my heart? Please don't break my heart."

"If I broke your heart, I'd be breaking mine, too. Yes, Wyatt. I'll marry you. Someday. I'll be yours forever."

Wyatt smiled and kissed her gently. In his kiss, Annie could feel the promise of forever.

CHAPTER 21

"**A**re you sure you want to do this?" Annie, Breckin, and CC were standing in the middle of the house Wyatt had told her about. He was right. It was perfect. And after they had decided to spend forever together just a few days ago, Annie knew it would be the best present she could ever give him.

"I'm positive. He'll love it."

CC looked at her skeptically. "And you really didn't ask him if he was okay with it?"

Annie sighed. "For the thousandth time, I don't *need* to ask him. I know he won't care. His drill sergeant even dropped the price way down once he found out Wyatt was the one buying it."

"But Wyatt *isn't* the one buying it," Breckin said. "You are."

"But I'm buying it for him. It's practically the same thing. Guys, stop trying to talk me out of it. I'm doing it. With or without your approval."

Her friends sighed. "Whatever you think," Breckin finally said. "He's your boyfriend. You know him better than we do."

"That's what I've been trying to tell you!"

Annie was feeling triumphant. This was one of the best ways she was spending her granny's money. Well, she guessed she should consider it her money now. She walked outside where the realtor from Lakeview was waiting. Annie was going to go through Wyatt's aunt but didn't trust her not to ruin the surprise. She'd just anonymously donate the commission his aunt would have made.

"I'll take it," she told the realtor.

"That's wonderful!" he said. "I'll write up the contract as soon as I get back to the office. We'll need some earnest money up front, just so the seller knows you're serious about buying."

"How about if I not pay any earnest money and just pay for the entire house in cash?"

Annie thought the realtor's eyes were going to bulge out of his head. "What did you say?"

"I want to pay for the house. In cash. I don't need to finance it. I have the money."

Well, that sure will make everything much easier," he said, clearing his throat. Annie smiled as she pictured the celebratory cartwheels he was turning in his head. "When do you want to do it?"

"How about today?"

He gulped. "I'll have to check with the seller, but I don't think he'll have a problem with that. I know he wants to sell it as soon as possible."

"Then just give me a call!"

The realtor was already on the phone, Annie assumed with the seller. She headed back in the house, a smile on her face. "Guess who will be a homeowner by this afternoon?"

"You? Or Wyatt?" CC asked. It was impossible not to detect the trace of snark in her voice.

"Yeah, how does that even work exactly? Can you even put the house in his name if he isn't the one signing for it?"

"I'm paying for it in *cash.* I'm pretty sure I can do what-ever I want."

She did not like the looks on her friends' faces. "You guys are not being very supportive. I thought you were going to be supportive." She suppressed the urge to stomp her foot. CC and Breckin pulled her in for a hug.

"Honey," Breckin said, "You know we love you. We just don't want Wyatt to feel like he's your charity case."

"He won't think that."

"Then buy away," CC added.

The realtor came back into the room. "Good news! The seller is actually in town and said he would be happy to sign today. You don't even have to drive to Lakeview. All you have to do is pick up a check from your bank."

Annie clapped her hands in excitement. "I'll let you know what he says when I tell him," she called to her friends as she headed to her car. She had a house she had to buy.

WYATT WAS GETTING REALLY WEIRDED out the longer they drove. As soon as Annie had gotten back from wherever she had been for the morning, she had been totally giggly and bubbly and...*girly.* It was odd and unnerving. He didn't know what to expect. And *then* when she told him he had to put on the *blindfold*...well...suffice it to say he was a little freaked.

"Annabelle, I'm getting a little freaked out."

She laughed. "That's the fourth time you've said that since we've been driving."

"That's because you have me *blindfolded!*"

"Relax! I'm not taking you out to the woods to kill you and bury your body where no one will ever find it."

Wyatt rolled his eyes, which he realized was completely

pointless right after he did it. "I know you're not going to do that."

"And it's not a kinky sex fetish or anything. Just trust me."

Wyatt couldn't lie. He was a little disappointed it wasn't a kinky sex fetish. "Fine."

"We're almost there."

"Where's there?"

"Wouldn't you like to know?"

"Yeah. Yeah, I would."

"Well, you'll know in about five minutes."

Wyatt leaned back in the seat of Annie's truck and sighed. "Since I can't see anything, could you at least turn up the radio so I don't have to listen to myself breathing? I'm a loud breather."

Annie laughed. "You sure are a whiny ass when you can't see."

Wyatt grinned when his favorite new song by Eric Church began playing. He sang along to the beginning lines of *Round Here Buzz*.

"I like this song, too," Annie said. "It reminds me of you."

"Why? You catch me drinking in the high school football parking lot a bunch?"

"No," she replied, laughing. "It just reminds me of you... and Jersey."

"Because she left?"

"Yeah...I guess." Her voice changed in tone, from laughter to uncertainty.

Wyatt didn't like not being able to see her face but he wasn't going to break his pinky swear and take off the blind-fold. Instead, he fumbled around with his hand until he felt hers on the console between them. He pulled it to his lips and kissed her knuckles one at a time.

"Trust me, Annabelle. I haven't cried one time since she

left. And I sure haven't drank in any parking lot to drown my sorrows. I just like the song. Eric Church is kick ass."

"He does. And he's pretty sexy."

"Hey, now. Let's not go crazy."

Wyatt felt the truck lurch to a stop and grinned. "Can I take the blindfold off now?"

"Yes," she breathed.

Wyatt took off the blindfold and looked around in confusion. "This is the house I wanted."

"It is."

"The one way out of my price range."

"Yep."

"Why did you bring me here? And why did you blindfold me to do it? I would have showed it to you if you wanted me to. But I really didn't want to come back here, especially when I realized I couldn't buy it."

"You don't have to worry about that now!" Annie said, a huge smile on her face.

Wyatt frowned. He had a bad feeling in his gut that he wasn't going to like what she was about to say next. "What do you mean, I don't have to worry about that? Did the price magically drop drastically to one I could afford?"

"No."

"Then Annie, *why* did you bring me here?"

The smile fell from her face. "Well, because...because...I kinda sorta bought it. For you."

"You bought this house. For me."

She nodded. "Yes?"

Wyatt started shaking his head. "Annie, that was really thoughtful, but I can't accept this house."

"Why not?"

"Because you can't just go around buying people houses!" He was really trying to keep calm but the fact that she decided to buy him a house without even asking him was infuriating.

"Again, why not? I love you. You love this house. I thought you would *love* my gesture!"

"Did it not even cross your mind to ask me about this? What if I changed my mind and decided it was something I really didn't want?"

"That wouldn't happen. You said this place was perfect."

"That's not the *point!*" he yelled.

"Then what is the point?" she yelled back.

"The *point* is you didn't even take into consideration how this would make me feel! How I would feel liked I owe you something now."

"Says the person who wouldn't take a penny of payment from me the entire time you were working at my farm."

"You aren't listening to a thing I'm saying."

"I'm listening to *everything* you're saying. It's just everything you're saying doesn't make *any* sense!"

"How would you feel if the shoe was on the other foot and I was the millionaire and decided to buy you a house?"

"I would be ecstatic," she said after a long pause.

"I call bullshit."

Annie rolled her eyes. "Fine. I might be a *little* upset. But then I'd be super happy about the amazing gesture of love."

"That's what you don't get. I didn't need this house to know you love me. I have you and that's totally enough. But I guess you don't get that."

"I *do* get that! I just thought—" Annie trailed off. "I don't know what I thought."

"Exactly. You didn't think. Just take me to Griff's, Annie. I need time to think."

"Are you serious?"

"I'm serious."

"You don't want to even go inside?"

"What's the point? I already know what it looks like."

She sighed but put her truck into drive. They had never even gotten out of the truck. The ride to Griff's Bar was made in silence. Before he got out, he leaned over and planted a kiss on her cheek. "I love you, Annie. That hasn't changed. I'm just a little disappointed right now. And confused. Just give me a bit to cool off, yeah?"

"Yeah," she said softly. "I love you, too." As she backed out of the bar's parking lot, he tried to pretend like he didn't see the tears running down her face.

CHAPTER 22

"*S*he bought you a *house?*"

As soon as Annie's truck had driven out of sight, Wyatt had headed straight to the bar and ordered two shots of fireball whiskey from the cute bartender who most *definitely* wasn't Griff. He wondered when Griff had hired someone new but then his shots had come and he'd downed them quickly, which made him think about Sophie's funeral, which made him think about Annie. He *then* ordered two shots of Jack, which was not connected in any way with Annabelle Cleaver. Even so, she'd still remained in his head.

He was currently nursing a third Blue Moon with an orange slice Griffin had brought him whenever he'd seen Wyatt chugging shots like they had done when they were sneaking liquor at seventeen.

"She bought me a house."

"How?"

"With the money her granny left her when she died."

"Her granny must've left her a hefty sum of cash if she was able to buy you a house."

"She did. She actually left Annie over a million dollars. Over two, actually."

Griff literally spit out lemonade he was drinking. "Two million *dollars?*" he choked out on a cough. "Where in the hell did that old lady get that kind of cash?"

"Apparently from oil and mineral rights to some land," Wyatt explained. "Annie had no clue about any of it until Harry read her the will. Don't say anything to anyone about it. I think I'm the only person who knows other than her friends."

"Who am I going to say anything to, huh? I'm the bartender in town. It's my job to keep town secrets."

Wyatt shrugged. "Still."

Griff began wiping the lemonade he shot out his mouth off the bar top. "Wow. She's probably the richest person in town."

"Probably."

"Did she tell you why she bought it?"

"Said she thought I would be happy because she knew I couldn't afford it but knew I really wanted it."

"That was a nice thought," Griff said, shrugging his shoulders.

Wyatt stared at his friend.

"What? It was."

"Would *you* have been happy?"

"Well, I don't know—" Griff said.

"Okay, so she wanted to buy me a house because she loves me and wants to see me happy. I get that. But to not even *ask* me how I felt? Not even try to drop it into everyday conversation? 'Oh, hey, Wyatt. I was thinking. Since I have all this money now, how about we, oh, I don't know, buy that house you really want?' If she had done *that,* I would have been a lot more understanding about it. But the fact that she didn't even *ask*…I just don't know what to think. Is that how it's always going to be? She has this money so anytime I want something...*poof!* My money fairy named Annie gets it for me? I'd feel like she's my keeper."

"To be fair, I don't think she meant it that way at all," Griff replied.

"I don't, either. But the fact that she didn't even think to *ask* me about it really upset me. I just don't know what to do. And she acted like she didn't know why I was upset. Like I was the one being unreasonable."

"Just give it a few days, man. You'll cool off, she'll have time to think about it, and then you can talk it out."

"I guess."

"So are you going to take it?"

"The house?"

"No, the new donkey she bought you." Griff rolled his eyes. "Yes, dumbass. The house."

"Oh. I don't know. How the hell do I decide? I take it, I look stupid because I threw a fit because she bought it. I *don't* take it, I look like an ass. What do I *do?*"

"You're asking the *wrong* person, man. I live in the apartment above my bar that hasn't been renovated since my uncle lived in it in the seventies. I'm still expecting a disco ball to pop down from the ceiling one of these days. But it's free, so you don't hear me complaining."

"Well, this place was most definitely *not* free."

"How much were they asking for it?"

"Well, the seller wanted three hundred sixty thousand for it when I was looking."

"Good lord!"

"Yeah. With the lake access and the acreage and the way it was constructed, it really is a good deal. But it's a good deal for someone who can afford it. See why I'm upset?"

"That's like a lot of her money out the window."

"No shit."

"Maybe they knocked the price way down. Hasn't it been on the market a while?"

"I don't know. All I know is that is way too much for her to just buy it for me. That's ridiculous."

"She must really love you, dude."

"If she really loved me, she'd know that's not something that would make me happy. Being with *her* makes me happy."

"Like I said, give yourself a few days to cool down and then go talk to her. You may be surprised what a little perspective will show you once you've thought about it and can be rational."

"I'm not being rational?"

"I think you're pissed off and you're looking for anything to make it seem like she had an ulterior motive for doing it when she might've just really been doing it out of the kindness of her heart. So take some time to think." Griff knocked his knuckles on the bar top and threw the towel over his shoulder.

"I guess you're right," Wyatt sighed. "Can I crash with you? I really don't feel like going back to my parents'. I've been staying at Annie's place almost all the time now, and if I go home I know I'm going to get the third degree."

"I was going to suggest that, anyway," Griff said as Wyatt got off the barstool and swayed on his feet. "There's no way I'm letting you drive after you took four shots of whiskey and drank three beers."

"Two and a half," Wyatt said, plopping down on the barstool again. All of a sudden, the room starting spinning and he began to feel the alcohol streaming through his system. "I haven't even finished this one."

"Whatever, man. I still remember you're a lightweight when it comes to drinking. I was going to take your keys no matter what."

"Too bad I don't have any keys," he replied. "I rode with Annie. I'm homeless and truckless."

"I can take you to get your truck at her place whenever you want."

"Let's sneak through town to see if we see her truck first. I don't want to go home and see her. All my willpower will go away if I see her sad face again and I'll forget to be upset."

"You really do have it bad, don't you?"

"I love her, man. I just don't like her very much right now."

Griff chuckled. "Welcome to a relationship, Wyatt Holloway. That is a sentence both of you will become very familiar with."

ANNIE BANGED her head on the table at their favorite booth in Sadie's Café. After the utter failure of showing Wyatt the house she had purchased for him, she had called her best friends and begged them for an emergency sundae date and they had come immediately. It wasn't even a Wednesday, so they had known things were serious.

Annie had eaten not just her part of the triple decker sundae, but had eaten another sundae all by herself. She could currently feel the contents roiling around in her stomach, threatening upheaval all over the table. She willed them back down. No way was she going to make herself sick over damn Wyatt Holloway.

"I thought for sure he would be *happy*!" she said, whimpering as her stomach continued its churning. "Why wasn't he happy?"

Breckin continued scratching Annie's back in soft circles. "Cees and I were afraid this was going to happen," she said sympathetically. "Men have egos, Ann. Even good men like Wyatt."

"It was a nice gesture! Why didn't he like it? I don't get it," she muttered, wincing as she banged her head again on the table.

CC reached across the table and put her hand under Annie's head before she could bang it again. "Okay, girl, I'm going to need you to quit doing that before you give yourself a concussion. Like Breck said, men have egos and you just bruised his big-time."

Annie leaned back and slumped down in the booth. "How?"

"Because you spent a a lot of money on a house for him without even asking if he wanted it."

"Or if he would be okay with you buying it for him," Breckin added. "Even I would have a hard time with that and I *know* you would do it without expecting anything in return."

"You would?" Annie asked. "Why?"

"Because that's a huge sum of money to spend on *anyone.* Especially when they didn't even get a say so in the matter. If you had talked to him about it, explained your reasoning, I bet he would've been more understanding."

"Or maybe you could've even given him a loan or something so he wouldn't have had to pay interest to a bank. And given him a discount for all the work he did for free on the farm," CC said. "I bet that would've been way better for him. That way, he wouldn't have felt like charity and he could've felt like he was just being *helped.*"

"Why didn't you guys give me these suggestions before I went and bought it?" Annie groaned.

Her friends stared at her. "Would you have even listened?" Breckin asked skeptically. "We kept trying to tell you we didn't think it was a good idea and you basically told us to butt out."

"Probably not," Annie said with a sigh. "I really screwed up, didn't I?"

Her friends nodded. "You did," they agreed simultaneously.

"The good thing, though," CC added, "Is that he obviously loves you. Just give him a couple of days to cool off and then you can talk to him about it. Maybe approach him with the ideas we just told you about. Better late than never."

Annie nodded. "I think you're right."

Sadie chose that moment to walk up to their table. "How's that sundae treating you, Miss Annie?"

"Don't ask," she mumbled. "It's a definite possibility I might not make it home before I puke the contents up on the side of the road."

Sadie scooted CC over in the booth and threw her order pad on the table. "Feels good to sit down," she sighed. "We've been hopping today. All these people trying to get their last boat rides on the lake before it gets too cold. So, what has you all fired up enough to get you to try and take on that triple sundae by yourself? Man troubles?"

Annie sighed and nodded. No sense lying. Sadie could always see right through them.

"I knew it! So, what happened?"

Annie told her, including the part about the money her granny left her. Otherwise, Sadie would just ask how Annie came up with the funds to purchase the house.

"Well, I *never*!" Sadie said. "Your granny, a millionaire! I shouldn't be surprised, though."

"What does that mean?"

"A few years back, we had some trouble with the café. Thought we were going to lose it, in fact. A lot of stuff broke in the kitchen and had to be replaced and then the fire marshal from Lakeview told us that all of our wiring wasn't compliant with city code and we had to replace it all. We thought we were going to go under. I had confided in your granny. A few days later, a private investor had donated enough money to cover all the costs and added a cushion to get us back on our feet." Sadie wiped her eyes, which were tearing up behind her glasses. "I don't know why I didn't think about your granny being the investor. I guess I was just so thankful for the money I didn't care where it came from."

Annie wiped her eyes, too. "That was my granny. Always looking out for other people."

"So, what are you going to do, honey?"

"I guess I'm going to give him a few days to cool off and then try to talk to him. Maybe come up with a plan that gives him a way to partly pay for the house, too." Annie explained her friends' ideas to Sadie.

"I think that's a wonderful idea!" Sadie agreed. "I know when my Clyde and I were young and we got into a fight, I'd always try to get him to talk it out right in the middle of it. It always made it worse."

"The longer we were together, the more I realized he just needed time away from me to think. He still loved me. He just didn't like me very much. I felt the same way." Sadie chuckled. "Now, I just make a lot of pies and he goes out and plays some horrible rounds of golf and cusses and throws a lot of clubs. Then we feel better and can talk it out. And makeup sex is the best!"

Annie held up her hand. "Too much information, Sadie. I don't want those pictures in my head."

"I'm just saying, girl. Keep that in mind. Sometimes a fight is a good thing, just so you can make up. Since this is your first fight, it will probably be some *good* making up. Well, I better quit dilly-dallying. These orders aren't going to take care of themselves. Do you feel better?"

Annie took a deep breath and let it out slowly. "I do."

Sadie nodded. "Good. Too bad your stomach doesn't."

Breckin and CC smiled at her. "He'll be fine, Annie," CC said. "Just give him time."

Annie stood up from the booth and stretched her arms over her head. "Okay. Advice taken. I'm not going to make the same mistake twice and ignore my best friends."

Breckin and CC stood up and wrapped her in a hug. "We love you."

"Love you, too. You really are the best."

Breckin tapped her on the butt. "Don't you forget it."

Annie hopped in her truck and headed home. She let out a big sigh when she noticed Wyatt's truck missing from the driveway. He must've come and gotten it while she was at Sadie's. Annie trudged up the porch steps and headed to her bedroom, dreading what she'd find. If all his clothes were gone, she didn't know what she'd do. She breathed a sigh of relief when she noticed the majority of his clothes were still in the closet and dresser drawers she had given him. Just a few things were missing, which she assumed he had taken to Griff's. She didn't think he could go home to his parents'. They'd have too many questions.

She held back the tears when she walked into her bathroom and found his toothbrush, cologne and deodorant missing from the shelves. Just those few items' absence made her bathroom seem completely empty. Funny how she had so quickly gotten used to them being there.

Annie crawled into bed and hugged her favorite pillow to her chest. "I'm not going to cry," she whispered to herself. "He'll be back once he's cooled down. Then I can explain to him and everything will be fine."

Annie smiled when she heard Nemo barreling around the corner. He ran into the door frame and shook his head. "You goofball," Annie laughed. The day before Hattie visited, he had come back from his vacation at Mr. Grant's. Annie had found him sprawled out on the front porch after she had finished feeding the other animals.

Nemo jumped on the bed and plopped down by her head, trying to cover her face with kisses. "Nemo, no! You know I don't like your slobber all over me."

With a snort, he attempted one last lick before Annie pointed to the foot of the bed. "You know the rules. If you stay in here with me you have to give me my space."

He moved to the foot of the bed and turned in a circle before curling his paws under his head and plopping down with a huff.

"Yeah, yeah. I'm a big meanie," she said with a smile.

All of a sudden, Sebastian walked around the corner, too, his tail swishing. He hopped up on the bed and plopped down in the middle of her chest, kneading her t-shirt and purring.

"Well, hello, Bass," she said softly. "I guess you guys knew I needed some loving today, huh?"

Sebastian meowed softly and rubbed his head under her chin. "I love you, too, but you can't stay on my chest. You swish you tail and your hair gets in my mouth."

Annie turned on her side and he curled up next to her stomach. With her dog at her feet and her cat where her legs were curled up by her stomach, Annie decided it was a great time for a nap. Her pets weren't Wyatt, but they ran a close second. And if she couldn't have him, she'd take the next best thing.

CHAPTER 23

*A*nnie was sitting in a chair in Breckin's office, her feet propped up on her friend's desk. "Do you know how many times I wanted to do this when I was a kid?" she asked.

"Quite a lot, probably."

"Yep."

"Too bad Mr. Marks was a total creep and no one wanted to go to his office."

Breckin sighed. "Not much has changed in that aspect. Being summoned to the school counselor is a lot like being called to the principal's office. *Not cool.*"

"I don't know about that. You're cool, Breck."

"Not to high school teenagers. They don't think anyone over the age of twenty-one is cool. So, why are you here, exactly? Haven't heard from Wyatt yet?"

"No! I don't know what to do! Tell me what to do! Shouldn't he have tried to call or come to the house by now?"

It had been four days since she and Wyatt had fought in front of the house she bought for him. Since then, nothing. She had typed out a million text messages that ran the gamut of emotions. Some of them were sappy apologies. Some of them were angry diatribes arguing how she was right and he was wrong. Others simply read *I miss you.* She had erased them all before hitting send. She was doing what her friends said. She was letting him cool off. And it totally sucked.

Breckin grabbed a bag of beef jerky out of a drawer in her desk and popped a piece in her mouth. She dipped the bag toward Annie, asking if she wanted some. Annie curled her nose and shook her head no.

"I don't see how you eat that stuff, Breck. Sodium must run through your veins."

Breckin shrugged. "It keeps me from starving. I hardly have time throughout the day to eat. This is my sustenance."

"You know you could bring your lunch. Or an apple."

"But what's the fun in that? This is protein. Protein is good."

"You sound like Ron Swanson on *Parks and Recreation.* All he eats is meat and breakfast food."

"A man after my own heart. Too bad he's a fictional character."

"Seriously, Breck. What am I going to *do?* This is killing me!"

"How long has it been? Four days?"

Annie groaned. "*Yeeeeessss!*"

"Then be proactive. It's the twenty-first century. Call him. He's had plenty of time to cool off. Maybe he feels like he hasn't called in so long it's awkward."

Annie stared at her friend. "Or maybe he decided he doesn't want me."

"Oh, honey," Breckin said softly. "If he did, he's all kinds of a fool and you're better off without him. But that's not going to happen."

"How do you know?"

"Because I saw the way he first looked at you before you even went out on your first date."

"Looked at me how?"

"Like you were a piece of Sadie's famous cheesecake she only makes twice a year."

Annie's eyes went wide. Sadie's bi-annual cheesecake was a *big deal.* People waited in line overnight outside the café when they knew she was making it to be sure they got a piece before she sold out. It was that good.

"No! Really?"

"Yep. And I think he'd even give his piece to *you.* He loves you, Ann. Everyone can see it. So talk to him."

Annie stood up and gave her friend a grin. "I can see why you do this counselor thing, Breck. You're really good at it."

"I'm not *that* kind of counselor. I'd be making a lot more money if I were, trust me."

"I'd pay for you to give me advice. As long as you let me lay down on a comfortable couch. A counselor isn't a counselor without a comfy couch to lie down on and share your sorrows."

Breckin smiled. "I'll keep that in mind."

Annie walked out of her friend's office with determined steps. She was going to call Wyatt. Before she did, though, she was going to consult her other best friend. If she knew she had the backing of *both* her best friends, it would give her the boost of confidence she needed to hear whatever it was he had to say to her, good or bad.

It was the second week in October and the trees were finally starting to change colors. It had even cooled down by Oklahoma's standards. Annie had on a pair of jeans and didn't feel like she was going to melt when she exited the school building. This morning, when she went to feed, it felt like fall. The dew on the ground was frosted over and the sun was shining. She knew it was going to be a beautiful day.

Fall was Annie's favorite season. Hoodies, football games, and evenings roasting marshmallows by the fire pit. Sure, it was cliché, but she loved it. Feeling invigorated, she decided to walk the half mile or so to the town's center to CC's shop. She could leave her truck in the school's parking lot and get it after she finished in town. Within a few minutes, the crispness in the air had tinted her cheeks a rosy pink and quickened her breath.

With a grin, she opened the door to her friend's shop, the bell jingling her arrival.

"I'll be with you in a minute," CC called from the back of the shop before quickly rounding the corner. "Well, if I had known it was you, I wouldn't have rushed. I would have taken my sweet time. Next time, announce yourself."

Annie laughed. "Nice to see you, too, friend of mine."

"You know I always like seeing you. We need to plan a girl's night soon. I need some Breckin and Annie time."

"Sounds good to me."

"So what brings you here? Need some more advice about your man?"

"How'd you guess?"

"Because I haven't gotten a text from you saying the issue has been resolved. I'm assuming that means you haven't heard from him yet."

Annie sighed and plopped down on the bright purple couch by the front door. "I haven't. And it's driving me crazy! Breckin told me it was the twenty-first century and it had been four days so I should just call him. Do you agree?"

"You asked Breck first? Traitor!"

"I pass the school first on my way into town!"

"Yeah, yeah. Likely excuse."

"Next time I'll detour to your shop first. Deal?"

"Deal."

CC began sweeping the hair off the floor that surrounded

her stylist's chair. "I agree with Breckin. I think you should call him. Maybe he doesn't know what to say so he's been putting it off."

"She said that, too."

"Boy, for us being lonely, old women with no relationship prospects, we sure act like we know what we're doing when it comes to the opposite sex."

Annie laughed. "If you guys are old, then that makes *me* old because we're the same age. Actually, it makes me even older because my birthday is first." The three of them had always celebrated their birthdays together because their birthdays had even fallen in the same month, completely solidifying their friendship. "Besides, we aren't even in our thirties yet. We still have three good years left. Well, two and a fourth, if we're being honest."

"Each year the birthdays come faster and faster. Before you know it, we'll be the old ladies in the nursing home pinching the hot male nurses on the ass."

"At least we'll be the *cool* old ladies."

"Oh, yeah. We'll be kick ass."

Annie pulled her friend in for a hug. "They'll have to make sure we have rooms next to each other or else it's a no go. I'll save some money to make sure of it. We'll be living in style."

"That's some money I can take."

With a wave, Annie walked out of her friend's shop and headed back to her truck. She always felt better after talking to her friends. On her way, she decided to stop in at Sadie's and grab a peach tea for the road. She rounded the corner and looked in the big picture window of the café. The second after she did, she wished to God she hadn't, because what she saw broke her heart into a million pieces.

❦

WYATT WAS MEETING Griff for burgers at Sadie's for lunch. Sadie had six dollar burgers every Thursday and always had a specialty burger not regularly featured on the menu. Today's was a chipotle, jalapeno, and avocado cream sauce burger with a side of sweet potato fries and chipotle ketchup. A spicy burger was right up Wyatt's alley and you couldn't beat six dollars for a half pound burger.

He had just perched on a stool at the longer counter by the cash register when Sadie walked his way with a menu in hand. "No need for a menu, Sade," he said. "I already know what I want and it's written on the chalkboard sign outside by the window. Hit me with the special."

To his surprise, Sadie walked up to him and hit him on top of the head with the menu she was holding. "Sadie! What was that for?"

"Oh, you *know* what that is for, young man," she said with a scowl. "Like you didn't think I would eavesdrop on Annie's conversation with her friends and how you blew up on her for no reason."

"Then you heard the wrong conversation, because I didn't blow up for no reason," he muttered. "You shouldn't pass judgment until you hear both sides of the story."

Sadie's face softened. "She feels real bad about doing that to you, Wyatt. You should talk to her."

"I know," he sighed. "I just don't want it to be weird. And I don't really know what to say. It's been almost a week and I haven't even tried to call. I miss her."

"We all told her to give you time but I think you should put the poor girl out of her misery and call her. She deserves to know where you stand."

"You're right, Sadie. She does. I'll call her today, but not until you cook me my burger. I can smell them cooking in the kitchen."

Sadie grinned. "Just wait till you taste the ketchup for the fries. I wanted to lick it off the spoon when I was making it this morning."

"I can't wait."

"Is it just you eating?"

"Nope. Griffin should be here any minute."

"Okay. I'll get your drink and your burger started. Want a Coke like usual?"

"Yes, ma'am."

"Alrighty."

Wyatt began scrolling the latest updates on his Sports Center app when he heard a voice he never thought he would hear ever again.

"Well, Wyatt James Holloway, aren't you looking fine as ever."

Trying not to grimace, he turned in his seat at the bar. "Never thought I'd see you here again, Jersey," he said with as little emotion in his voice as he could muster.

"I never thought I'd say it, but I missed this place," she replied, sitting on the barstool next to him and crossing her legs. The California sun had tanned her skin and she had done something fancy to her hair, its natural dark auburn color streaked with light copper strands. She was wearing three inch, spiked gold heels, a ton of gold bracelets on both wrists, and a white dress so tight it left nothing to the imagination. It also barely covered her ass. She looked like money and everything fake Hollywood represented. She couldn't hold a candle to Annie's down-to-earth, simple, natural beauty. He couldn't believe he had ever thought he wanted to spend his life with the woman sitting beside him.

"How did you know I was here?"

"Easy. I just drove around town and saw that new pickup that looked like the hunk of junk your grandfather gave you and you always said you were going to fix up. I'll admit, you did a good job. I never thought it would look as good as it does."

Wyatt rolled his eyes. "Whatever, Jersey."

Jersey put her hand on his leg and rubbed her hand up and down his thigh. "That's not quite the welcome I imagined. I thought you'd be happy to see me."

"With the way you jetted out of here as soon as I got back? Why in the hell would you think that?" he asked, pushing her hand off his leg.

Jersey drew her lips into a pout. "Maybe I missed you and realized the mistake I made."

Wyatt snorted. "Not hardly. There's always an agenda with you, Jersey. Might as well tell me what it is."

"Fine," she huffed. "Hollywood didn't exactly turn out the way I wanted."

"What is that supposed to mean?"

"It was a lot harder than I thought it would be. Nothing went my way. I mean, look at me. You'd think producers would be *begging* me to be in their films. The only thing I could get was some stupid commercial about acne medicine," she huffed.

"Did you ever stop to think they might be looking for talent instead of just a pretty face? Maybe you suck at acting."

Jersey pretended to be hurt. "That hurts my feelings, Wyatt," she said, reaching up and scratching her fingers on his hair at the nape of his neck. "I can't believe you think I wouldn't be good. That's not nice."

"Well, Jersey, you weren't exactly nice to me when you left. Why should I be nice to you now?"

"I've been thinking. You told me you wanted to spend the rest of your life with me. I still love you, Wyatt. Hollywood life is not for me. I just needed to go out there and realize that. But now I'm ready to settle down and I want to do it with you. How about we get married and move to the city?

I'm sure you could find a job doing something and I could make a house our home. There's no way I want to stay in *this* town."

Wyatt looked at her incredulously. "You can't be serious."

"What do you mean? Of course I'm serious."

Wyatt laughed. "You are unbelievable, Jersey. I don't know why I should be surprised, though. You're just as shallow as you were in high school. I'm just stupid and didn't realize it then."

Jersey's eyes went wide. "You can't be serious!"

"Oh, I'm dead serious. I have no desire to ever do anything with you ever again, Jersey, much less marry you and move to the city. I'm happy with my life here. I have a woman I love and a life that never includes you in it."

"A woman? What woman?"

"Annabelle Cleaver. And she's good and caring and the complete opposite of you."

Jersey wrinkled her nose. "You mean that weird loser with the green hair from high school with the crazy grandma? You've really started to slum it, Wyatt."

Wyatt saw red. "Let me tell you something, Jersey. She is the best thing that has ever happened to me. I think I even loved her in high school, I just didn't have the balls to admit it back then. But she's way better than you will ever be."

She stood up and to his surprise, slapped him on the face. "Screw you, Wyatt Holloway. I always knew you were a dumbass, redneck hick who would never leave this stupid town. I can't believe I wasted all my time on you. It's your loss. Don't come crawling back to me when you realize what you gave up."

Wyatt rolled his eyes. "Trust me, Jersey, that will not be a problem."

"Whatever, Wyatt," she said, echoing his words from earlier. "See you never."

"Thank God."

The diner erupted in cheers when she sashayed out the doors. "I never thought I'd see the likes of her back in town when she hightailed it out of here," Marty Samson, the checker player, yelled from his booth across the diner. "Good riddance, I say. She looked like a fancy hooker in that garb she was wearing."

"Your burger's on me, Wyatt," Burt Gallagher added. He and Marty were sharing the same booth. Apparently, their rivalry only existed around a game of checkers. "I've always thought she was a hussy."

Sadie walked over to him, his burger in tow. "Never thought she'd be ballsy enough to show her face in town again," she said. "She's a piece of work."

"No joke," Wyatt replied. "I can't believe it, either."

"I can't believe you didn't come unglued when she slapped you. If I could've reached her in time I would've done it myself."

Wyatt took a big bite of his burger and moaned. It was burger heaven melting in his mouth. "She's not worth it, Sadie. But thanks for wanting to come to my rescue."

"So when are you going to talk to Annie?"

"As soon as I finish this burger."

"All right," she said with a grin. "Proud of you, son."

"Thanks, Sadie."

Wyatt heard the bell above the door jingle and groaned. He prayed to God it wasn't Jersey coming back for more. He let out a sigh when Griff sat down on the barstool beside him and slapped him on the back.

"Please tell me it wasn't Jersey I saw getting in the gold Mercedes and peeling down the street."

Wyatt nodded. "Oh, it was."

"What the hell did *she* want?"

"Apparently, me. She told me she failed in Hollywood and

wanted me back. Expected me to move to the city with her, buy a house, and get married."

Griff's eyes widened. "You have to be kidding."

"Afraid not."

"She's evil."

Wyatt laughed. "I agree one hundred percent."

"What did you tell her?"

"That she probably failed in Hollywood because she sucked as an actress and there was no way I wanted to be with her. Oh, I also told her I loved Annie and that she was way better than Jersey would ever be."

"I bet she took that well."

"She slapped me and called me a redneck hick that would regret ever letting her go."

Griffin guffawed. "Wow. I can't believe I missed it."

"Yep. It was definitely the best entertainment we've had for a while. I got a standing ovation from everyone in here after she left. Apparently, everyone has always thought she was a bitch."

"Here, here!" Marty and Burt called, lifting their coffee mugs in salute. They might be old coots and pushing one hundred, but there was nothing wrong with their hearing.

Wyatt threw his napkin down on his empty plate and stood. "I hate to leave you to eat alone, man, but I gotta go see about a girl."

Griff grinned. "Decided to quit being a dumbass?"

"Yep."

"Took you long enough."

"I know. Hopefully, she'll still want something to do with me."

CHAPTER 24

As soon as Annie saw Jersey's hand rubbing up and down Wyatt's leg and his body turned toward hers on the barstool, she felt her heart stop beating. Her limbs went numb and she couldn't catch her breath. Maybe she should've stomped in and confronted him. Instead, she held back a sob and ran back to her truck as fast and she could and sped home.

She was currently curled in the fetal position on her bed, tears flowing down her cheeks. As soon as her hands had stopped shaking, she had texted her friends and told them to bring Ben and Jerry's and any liquor they could find. She wanted to drink herself into a coma.

How could she have been so dumb? She couldn't ever compare to the glamor of Jersey. She was stupid to believe he would ever want her more than a woman like her, no matter what he said.

"Annie?" She heard her screen door slam and her friends come inside. "Where are you?"

"In my room," she called, sitting up and wiping the snot

dripping out of her nose on her t-shirt sleeve. She didn't even care. That's how pathetic she was.

Her friends entered her room and their eyes widened in shock. They both ran to the bed and sat down on either side of her. "What is *wrong?*" Breckin asked, putting Annie's head on her shoulder.

Annie could feel the tears falling harder. "Wyatt," she sobbed.

"What about Wyatt?" CC asked, a frown on her face. "Did he call? Was he a dick?"

Annie shook her head. "No. Even worse. I saw him. With…with—" Annie couldn't even manage to say her name.

"With who?" Breckin asked.

"With *Jersey,*" Annie replied, her body racked with sobs. "He was with *Jersey.*"

"What? I didn't even know she was back in town!" CC said incredulously.

"I didn't either."

"Are you sure it was Wyatt with her? And more importantly, are you *sure* he wanted her there?" Breckin asked softly. "I'm not saying you're lying, but maybe you didn't see what you thought you saw. Maybe there's more to the story."

"She was rubbing her hand up and down his leg," Annie replied. "And as far as I could see, he wasn't trying to stop her."

"That little shit," CC said, malice in her voice. "I'll kill him. I swear I will."

She jumped out of the bed and headed to the door. Annie grabbed her friend before she could go far. "Cees, no! I'm already mortified. I appreciate the gesture, really I do. But it would just make it worse. Please. I just want you guys here with me."

CC sighed and plopped back on the bed. "Whatever you

want, Ann. Wanna get drunk and make yourself sick on ice cream?"

Annie nodded her head.

"I'm not trying to defend him, Ann," Breckin said. "But did you even go in and try to talk to him?"

"With Jersey sitting right there? Absolutely not. I saw what I saw and there was no sense asking about it."

"Okay," Breckin said softly, pushing Annie's hair back from her forehead. "I'm so, so sorry."

"Me, too," Annie whispered.

CC took the lid off Annie's favorite ice cream from Ben and Jerry's, Chunky Monkey, grabbed Annie's empty water glass off her bedside table, and poured a significant amount of coconut rum in the glass. "We even brought plastic spoons," she said, pulling them out of the plastic bag and holding them up triumphantly. "Now it's time to get all thoughts of Wyatt Holloway out of your mind."

Annie tipped back the glass and downed its contents in one swallow.

"Damn, killer," Breckin said. "That's one way to forget him quickly."

Annie could already feel the numbing effects of the alcohol as it hit her system. She had always been a light-weight when it came to drinking. The liquor might make her forget about Wyatt tonight, but she knew he was the first thing she was going to think about in the morning. In fact, she didn't know if she would ever wake up and not think of Wyatt Holloway.

WYATT PULLED into Annie's driveway, a smile on his face. He hadn't gotten to talk to her yesterday like he wanted to after he left the diner. His dad had called him and asked for his help working on the tractor that had broken down in the field. He had worked on it until late in the evening.

When he had gone inside his parents' house to clean up, Lucy and Hattie were visiting since school was out the next day for parent-teacher conferences. Hattie had fallen asleep in his lap around eleven-thirty and he hadn't wanted to move, loving the feel the soft curls of her hair and whistles of breath on his chest. He had actually fallen asleep in his dad's recliner, holding his niece. He hadn't even felt his sister take her off his chest until he had woken up around three a.m. and the house was dark.

Knowing how much she loved her sleep and how grumpy she tended to be if she were woken up, Wyatt had waited as long as he could to head to Annie's house. He had even texted her to see if she was up but she hadn't replied. Finally, when nine-thirty rolled around, he couldn't take it any longer. He had gotten in his truck and headed to her house.

Getting out of his truck, he noticed CC's car parked by the barn. *They must've had a girl's night and stayed up late,* he thought. It was probably why she wasn't answering his texts. He was guessing they were still asleep.

Whistling, he hopped up the porch steps and tried opening the front door, but it was surprisingly locked. Annie never locked her door. With a sigh and a cross of his fingers that he wouldn't be waking the devil, he knocked. And waited. Then waited. And waited some more. Impatiently, he knocked again, louder this time.

"Annie?" he called. "Your door is locked and I can't get in. We need to talk."

All of a sudden, the door was jerked open by a wild-eyed, angry Colleen Chandler holding a Louisville Slugger.

"Whoa!" Wyatt yelled. "Watch where you're swinging that thing, CC! You almost hit me in the head."

"I *was* watching where I was swinging that thing, you asshole," she replied. "I'm just sorry I missed."

"What the hell?" he asked. "Where's Annie? I need to talk to her."

He tried to pass CC and head into the house, but Annie's friend blocked his entrance with the bat she held in her hands. "Nope. Sorry, buster. Not happening."

"Seriously, Colleen? Stop it! I need to talk to Annie." Wyatt rolled his eyes. "Annie!" he yelled around her friend. "Would you come get your crazy friend so I can come in?"

Breckin walked around the corner, a sad look on her face. "Let him in, Cees," she said.

"*Thank* you," he replied, trying not to make eye contact with the woman holding the bat.

"Why are you here, Wyatt?" she asked.

"Because I need to talk to Annie," he replied, feeling something bad in the pit of his stomach. "Why? What's wrong? It's not Annie, is it? Oh, God. Did something happen?"

"Yeah, something happened, you moron," CC said. If looks could kill, his family would be planning his funeral. "*You*. You happened."

Wyatt turned to Breckin, who seemed to be the only woman in the room who wasn't completely insane. "What is *wrong* with her, Breckin?" he asked. "You'd think I'd gone and killed all the newborn kittens around the world. All I want to do is see Annie. I want to tell her something."

"Oh, we *know* what you want to tell her," CC said.

"She doesn't want to talk to you, Wyatt," Breckin added.

Wyatt shot a confused look her way. "What? Why? Is it about the house? That's what I want to talk to her about. I realize I was being—"

Colleen wouldn't even let him finish his sentence. "Can you believe this piece of work?" she smirked. "He had the *audacity* to come here and talk to her about the *house* after what she *saw*?"

"Could you please clue me in on what Crazy over there is talking about?" Wyatt asked Breckin, pointing to CC, who was now standing guard at the foot of the stairs in the living room, still holding her baseball bat. "She isn't making any sense!"

"She saw you, Wyatt," Breckin said sadly.

"She saw me what?"

"She saw you. At Sadie's. With Jersey."

"I wasn't at the café with Jersey."

"Oh, really? Because that's not what Annie told us. In fact, she told us all about how she saw Jersey with her hand running up and down your leg, your barstool turned toward her as you were engaged in conversation. Are you calling her a liar?" CC yelled at him.

Wyatt felt all the blood drain from his face. "What? Oh, hell. No! That wasn't what happened. Jersey just showed up and said all this crazy shit...Breckin, you have to believe me! I would *never* do something like that to Annie. Where is she? Just let me talk to her. I promise I can explain everything."

"Well, too bad. She doesn't want to talk to you," CC said vehemently. "In fact, she told us if you were brave enough to come out here, we were to kick you out and tell you she never wants to see you ever again."

Wyatt looked at Breckin, heartbreak in his eyes. "Is that true?"

"I think it's best if you just go, Wyatt," she said, walking him to the front door. He heard what he thought was, *Good riddance, you asshole*, come from CC's mouth, but he couldn't be sure.

Breckin held open the screen door and ushered him outside. "I'm sorry, but she just doesn't want you here. You heard, Colleen," she said loud enough for her friend to hear.

However, before going back inside, she quickly whispered behind her hand, "She's in the barn feeding the animals. Don't tell her I sent you."

As soon as she slammed the screen door and he heard the front door slam right after, he jumped off the porch and ran as fast as he could to the barn. Just as her friend said, Annie was in the barn with her animals. Currently, she was brushing Perdita's coat, making the black and white hair shine. Nemo was at her feet and Sebastian was weaving in between her legs, his tail swishing back and forth.

Annie's hair was pulled on top of her head in a messy bun and she was wearing the same Gulf Shores t-shirt he had seen her in the first time he had visited the farm. Her gorgeous legs were covered in a pair of worn jeans, but they did nothing to detract from her beauty. She was breathtaking. But his breath hitched in his chest when she raised her eyes to meet his. They were red and swollen and so full of heartbreak he couldn't move.

"Hey, Disney," he said softly. "It's been a while."

She didn't say anything, just kept staring at him with the same sad eyes. It was breaking his heart. "I've missed you."

Still nothing. Of course, after what she thought she saw, he couldn't blame her. Sebastian sauntered over to where Wyatt was standing and began weaving himself between Wyatt's legs. He finally picked up the cat and held him in his arms, smiling softly when Sebastian began purring when Wyatt scratched him under the chin.

"Heard you saw something yesterday in the café window that could've looked like something it totally wasn't," he said gently. "Can I explain?"

Annie gave a slight nod of her head but still didn't speak. He hated seeing her this way. Hopefully, once she heard what he had to say it would erase the haunted look in her eyes.

"Well, I was going to eat lunch with Griff because it was

Burger Thursday but I had beaten him there. I was sitting at the counter, minding my own business, when I heard Jersey's horrible voice say my name."

Wyatt saw Annie's lips tilt in a small smile. That was progress. He took a step closer. "She then had the audacity to plop herself down on the stool beside me and tell me how she failed in Hollywood and decided she still loved me. She also said we needed to move to the city so I could get a job and she could be a homemaker. *And* she had the balls to rub her hand up and down my leg as if she hadn't lost permission to do that long ago. I *think* that might have been the most unfortunate time for you to peek that pretty head of yours in the window. I can only imagine how it looked."

Annie finally made eye contact with him, hope reflected in her eyes. Still she said nothing. Wyatt placed Sebastian on the ground, walked toward Annie, and held her face in his hands. "She didn't like it much when I told her to piss off and that she failed in Hollywood because she sucked as an actress and I never wanted to be with her because I had fallen in love with a woman who was the complete and total opposite of everything she had ever been or would ever be. You should've seen the look on her face when I told her it was you."

Annie's finally spoke. "What did she say?"

"Well, she slapped me in the face." He chuckled.

Her eyes widened. "No way."

"Yes way." Wyatt pulled her into his chest, inhaling the scent of her peach shampoo. "Baby, why didn't you come in and say something?"

He could feel Annie's tears soaking into his shirt. "I thought you had chosen her. How can I ever compete with how she looks?"

Wyatt pulled her off his chest and looked at her incredulously. "How can you even think that? You are *everything* I want. I've loved you since high school, Annabelle Clara Diane Cleaver. I just didn't know it. You have my heart. Always have, always will."

"Right back at ya, Wyatt James Holloway." When Annie caressed the scar on his face and smiled up at him, he felt like his heart was going to beat out of his chest. He leaned down and pressed his lips to hers, sealing their promises to each other. She was his and he was hers. Always and forever.

EPILOGUE

Six Months Later

"*A*re you ready for this, girl?" Breckin was standing at the foot of the stairs in Annie's living room, holding two bouquets of pink stargazer lilies she had picked from her own yard in her hands. Annie took a deep breath and one last look at herself in the mirror hanging on the upstairs hallway. Her hair was twisted in a loose, multilayered braid, soft strands falling around her face, pale pink cherry blossoms woven throughout.

When Annie had told the workers at the wedding shop in Lakeview she wanted a pink wedding dress, they laughed at her. They quickly tried to turn their laughter into coughing when they realized she was serious and had gotten to work looking for the perfect dress. Apparently, finding a simple, unassuming pink wedding dress wasn't an easy task. Annie had finally found a bridesmaid dress in a catalog and ordered it as her wedding dress. She was pretty sure the owner of the shop had swallowed her false teeth. But the dress was perfect.

The bodice was a strapless, fitted pale pink satin. A dusty rose strip of satin wrapped around her waist and the same color satin flared softly to her knees, a pale pink lace overlay on top of it. The only thing she was wearing that was *not* pink were the brown leather and mint green cowgirl boots Wyatt had surprised her with. "You have to wear *something* that has your favorite color on it, and your hair doesn't count," he had said, jokingly pulling on a strand.

Her friends were draped in the same pink colors, Breckin opting to wear a floor-length, simple light pink satin gown, CC choosing the dusty rose. As flower girl, Hattie had chosen a miniature version of Annie's dress, the only difference being the straps and the big pink satin bow on the back. All of the girls had also chosen some form of mint green shoes. Wyatt had even gotten on the pink and mint green bandwagon, choosing to pair pale pink shirt with a mint green tie and pale gray suit, his groomsmen matching.

Annie took one last look at herself before walking down the stairs. "I'm ready," she said, taking her bouquet from Breckin.

"Wow, you sure look pretty, Annie," Hattie said breathlessly.

"Well, that means you look pretty, too, Hattie Mae, because we match. We even have the same flowers in our hair," Annie replied, gently patting the little girl's curls.

"I think your granny would like your pink wedding," Hattie said with a smile. "It *was* her favorite color."

"That it was, kiddo. I think she would be happy, too. I just wish she could be here to see us in our matching dresses."

Hattie motioned to Annie to lean down. When she did, Hattie hid her mouth behind her hand and whispered in Annie's ear. "Don't ya know, Annie? Miss Sophie's watchin' from heaven. I bet she even made *Jesus* wear pink. God, too.

And *all* the angels. I bet it's nothin' but pink up there. God even probably colored the *clouds* pink!"

Annie grinned at Hattie's enthusiasm. "You're probably right. Now, are you ready to throw those flowers?"

Hattie held up the basket that was filled with pink rose petals from the rose bushes in Annie's flower bed. That was one reason Annie insisted on waiting until spring to get married. Everything would be blooming and she could use all the flowers her granny had lovingly planted as part of the wedding. That way, it was like having a part of her granny with her on the best day of her life.

"I can't believe I'm walking you down the aisle to this song," Clyde, Sadie's husband, grumbled under his breath as Annie, Hattie, Breckin, and CC walked onto the front porch. "It's ridiculous."

When they were choosing songs, Wyatt didn't even have to look through Annie's list. "Let me choose these, Annabelle," he begged. "Please. They will even go with your pink theme."

He then showed her what he had in mind. She had sighed, rolled her eyes, and pretended to be perturbed, but she secretly hid a smile behind her hand. His song choices were actually pretty perfect.

The opening line to *Sink the Pink* by ACDC began to play on the speakers set up in her yard as the wedding guests stood to usher the bride to her groom. "You have to admit, it's a great song choice, albeit an unorthodox one," she replied to Clyde. "It's about pink, my granny's favorite color, and it's by ACDC, the band with my initials. Just admit it, Clyde."

He rolled his eyes but his lips drew up in a smile. "Unorthodox, my ass. Crazy is what it is. But you're right. Your granny would've loved it."

Annie watched as Hattie threw her rose petals perfectly and then chuckled along with the guests as she took an unplanned bow at the end. Griff walked in with CC, and an army buddy of Wyatt's linked arms with Breckin. As soon as the final chords of *Sink the Pink* ended, *Pink Cashmere* by Prince began to play.

Clyde chuckled. "Pretty perfect, Annabelle."

Annie grinned. Her wedding was absolutely perfect. At that moment, her eyes locked with Wyatt's and she forgot to breathe. He stood under her granny's magnolia tree, light shining from his eyes. He took her hands from Clyde, who kissed her softly on the cheek before sitting in the front row with Sadie. Prince sang the final notes and Anthony Peters, the preacher at Parker Baptist Church, told the guests they may be seated.

"We are gathered here today to join Annabelle Cleaver and Wyatt Holloway in holy matrimony," he began. "I was told the couple has written their own vows. Is that correct?"

Wyatt nodded.

"Then you may begin," he continued. "Ladies first."

Annie looked into Wyatt's eyes and expelled the breath she was holding. "When you first stepped foot on my farm, I knew you'd be trouble," she began. "You waltzed right up to my front door with your sexy army muscles and I knew I wouldn't be able to resist you."

The crowd chuckled. "I'd always had a thing for you in high school, but I never thought you'd give me the time of day. I was the strange girl with the even stranger grandma. No way someone like you would want to be with a girl like me. But then, as I began working with you day in and day out, and started seeing the real you, I began to realize you were nothing like the all-star, high school icon I had remembered you to be." She smiled at Wyatt.

"You were a man who was so amazing, so *good*, so loving,

I couldn't help but fall in love with you. Even though you had scars of your own, you opened up and let me see them. I realized you weren't your high school self. You were even better. I love you, Wyatt James Holloway. I loved you from afar in high school but today, I love you close to my heart. And I always will until my last breath."

Wyatt took a shaky breath and gripped her hand. "I've always loved you, Annabelle. Loved your spirit, loved how you stood up for those who needed it, loved how you didn't conform the way every other high schooler did just so they could fit in. You were your own person and completely comfortable in your skin. I was so envious of that because even though I seemed like I had it all together, I was terrified of being one of the outcasts." He squeezed her hand.

"When I came home from overseas, I was broken. I had seen too much hurt, experienced too much anger, woken up from too many nightmares. I didn't think I would ever be whole again. But little by little, you began to fix me. Made me believe I wasn't the sum of what I had seen and done. Understand I wasn't what the scar on my face represented. I'm whole because of you. And I'll never stop loving you. The girl who you were and the beautiful woman you've become."

With those final words, Griff handed Wyatt the ring he had picked out especially for her. It was a square pink diamond surrounded by small regular diamonds and a fourteen karat gold band with tiny pink diamonds circling the entire band. When he had picked it out, Annie had gasped at its price tag. Wyatt had told her if he was going to accept the house she bought for him, he was going to spend part of the money he would've spent on a house to buy her whatever damn ring he wanted. And he wanted her to have a pink diamond. Annie could do nothing but agree. It was a fair trade.

After the nuptials, the guests headed to the backyard

where an outdoor tent was set up for the reception. Of course there was a mint green and pink wedding cake, fireball whiskey, and her granny's favorite cookies. And she and Wyatt danced to *Pink* by Aerosmith and even *Witchy Woman* by the Eagles. After all the guests had gone home and it was just Annie and her husband, they walked hand in hand to the back of the property and Animal Land.

"So we're really going to do this? Redo the whole thing and expand into your acreage to make an even bigger rescue for animals of all shapes and sizes?" Wyatt asked.

"Yep," Annie agreed. "It would be what my granny would want."

Wyatt kissed her temple. "I think it's a great idea, Disney. You still planning on hiring a vet and some staff and letting them live in the farmhouse?"

"Absolutely. I want the animals that come here to have the best care possible. And I want to visit my granny's farm whenever I want. This way, I get it all."

"So do I, baby. And I wouldn't want it any other way."

"Maybe we'll get an unwanted ostrich. Or llama! Wouldn't that be fun?"

"Aren't ostriches mean? And don't llamas spit?"

"Sure. But we can tame them."

"Whatever you say."

"I'll even name them Pinky and Minty."

Wyatt chuckled. "I thought you didn't like those nicknames."

"For me, no. For animals, they're fine."

"Whatever you say, ACDC."

Annie grinned and kissed her husband. "That doesn't work anymore, mister. It's ACD*H* now."

"I guess if giving up your awesome initials makes you mine, that's something I can handle."

Annie bumped him with her hip. "You can still call me ACDC if you want."

Wyatt grinned. "You really do love me."

"Always and forever."

BEFORE YOU GO...

If you enjoyed my book please take a second to leave a short review. These reviews help me as an author be found by other amazing readers like you.

Thank you so much! :)